JACK MOODY

CROOKED
SMILE

(e-book) ASIN: B09QQJXVVY

(print) ISBN-13: 978-1-7379829-2-0

For Roxanne

Author's Note

With the full understanding that I never could have written this novel—let alone get it published—without the works of authors who came before me opening up the way forward, I'll begin with two disclaimers.

As written in Charles Bukowski's 1978 novel, *Women*, I feel the need to state the same: This book is a work of fiction and no character is intended to portray any person or combination of persons living or dead.

And in the spirit of Augusten Burroughs, in the aftermath of his 2002 memoir, *Running With Scissors*: Given the fickle and fleeting nature of memory, fictional or otherwise, some dates, details, and occurrences have been changed and/or rearranged for the sake of narrative. And legality.

Lastly, "July, 2018," and "April-May, 2019," were originally published by *Horror Sleaze Trash* under the titles "With Feet at the Edge of the Abyss" and "A Series of Poor Decisions." Thank you to *HST* for publishing stories that no one else has the balls or stomach to touch. Additionally, "March, 2019," originally appeared as "Monster" in *Expat Press*.

— Jack

I.
DEPARTURE

FEBRUARY, 2018

"Neonatal cerebral infarction," I said.

"*Gesundheit.*"

"No, that's what it's called."

The man lifted his glass over the bar and stared at my right hand. "That sounds like something you made up. Hey, kid, if you can't open a beer bottle with a lighter, you can't. You don't need to make up stuff. Hell, I can't whistle. We all got shit."

Mississippi Fred McDowell howled over his acoustic guitar from the corner jukebox. The man swayed and nodded to the music on his barstool, one eye now closed in concentration. The other watched me through the white cloud of cataracts. It reminded me of the marbles I collected as a child. I would pick my favorite few and arrange them around each other on the floor, imagining that they were big, bright gas giants all in orbit around the biggest and prettiest sun marble.

I tasted the cheap whiskey on my tongue, letting it sit and seep into my bloodstream. "Wish I made it up, but I didn't. Just a fancy term for a stroke at birth. Can't use the right side of my body so well. That's all. Here, look—" I shot him a big grin. "See, I can't smile on that side. The nerves are paralyzed. It's gotten better over time. Or at least I'd like to think so."

The man leaned in, studying the drooping right side of my mouth. The milky, blind marble maintained eye contact as if operating on a mind of its own, looking past me, through me. "Nah, that's no stroke, kid. That's a malady of the soul." His voice was a hoarse growl, drenched in bourbon and rubbed raw with cigarette smoke.

I laughed. "How's that?"

"That's your body trying to show you what your mind's been telling you. But you haven't been listening. You think you're happy, but deep down in there... in *there*,"—he pressed on the center of my chest with a cracked and calloused finger, the nail brittle from vitamin deficiency—"you know you aren't.

You better change your ways, kid. It's not doing you the good you think it is."

I watched the mist swirl in his dead eye like an approaching hurricane and flashed another lopsided smile. "Who knows."

"You do, kid, that's what I'm telling you. Open your ears to that little voice that's been trying to talk to you. It won't always be there. That's when you know you're good and lost. Then there's no coming back."

I ordered two shots of whiskey and slid one in front of him. "Alright, old man. Thanks for the advice."

He picked up the drink. "Don't mention it. If it is that, *ah*, neo—"

"Neonatal cerebral infarction," I said.

"Yeah. If it is that though, you sure you should be drinking?"

"Should anyone?"

The old man snorted, showing his teeth, yellow and worn like eroded rock. "You got me there, kid. What're we drinking to?"

I held up the glass, staring at that marble eye. "To luck and happenstance."

"Well, alright then," he said.

We drank.

II.
THE CALL

MARCH, 2018

The hospital opens up and swallows me behind the automatic doors. I clutch at a copy of *One Flew over the Cuckoo's Nest* because I don't know how long I'll end up being here, and at the least, it may get a chuckle out of one of the nurses. My hair is wild and frayed like an old lion's mane after a skirmish for a mate. My flannel is buttoned incorrectly, with one button hanging at an awkward angle towards the bottom, and a patch of pink-white skin showing through a gap over the middle of the abdomen. I wear slippers with the laces missing, a memento from my arrest at eighteen.

I walk to the portly woman behind the desk, a sea cucumber of a woman—all torso and no limbs—and tell her I'm here to check myself in. A man in a wheelchair screams from the corner of the emergency room. He is alone but I suspect his handler is outside, gathering something up for him or considering escape. This man, the sea cucumber in a light blue uniform, and I are the only people in here. His screams carry well. The acoustics in an empty hospital are better than you'd imagine.

The cucumber asks me what I'm checking myself in for. I tell her.

Her eyes are a stark gray, like a newly paved sidewalk in the sunlight. They hold life in them so I trust her and support my decision to tell her the truth.

I comply when she tells me to hold out my arm to clasp a pink, plastic bracelet around my wrist. I look down at it:

GALLAGHER, HENRY
#0074527
GOOD SAMARITAN
ADULT PSYCHIATRIC

They spelled my name right. I appreciate this and decide to show it by grinning at the sea cucumber, but realize she won't understand, so I stop and vomit the words, "My name is my name."

This means nothing to her and she responds, "Sit down over there and you'll be brought in to see the on-call psychiatrist shortly."

I nod and sit in the corner opposite the screaming paraplegic.

His handler returns and hands him something small enough to fit inside his palm.

His fingers curl around it and squeeze. This calms him, deescalating the screams to lulled moans like an infant drifting to sleep. I don't know what this object is, but am glad he has it. His handler, whom it has become apparent is his father, approaches the sea cucumber to explain the situation. I catch the buzzwords. I hear voices hearing voices. I hear Xanax. I hear alcohol. I hear mental illness, undiagnosed mental illness. The paraplegic moans softly in the corner.

I soon grow tired of my invalid neighbor's subdued wails, and the cucumber is no good to look at, and for some reason, I'm unable to decipher the words in the book, so I leave to find cigarettes. The hospital doors allow me to leave and for this I'm thankful. It's difficult to remember if there are consequences to this, how far I've gone.

But no alarm sounds and the moans of the paraplegic are strangled by the mechanical whir as I'm ushered into a much darker, much less sterile environment. My skin glows red beneath the ER's signifying lights—a sinister red, a clinical red. There is the welcoming neon red of bar lights—a red that you bathe in, that you fade into like the notes of a siren's song—but these are not the same. You feel that immediately. This red is death. This red is fear. The hollow, pale white of the hospital's interior soaks through the glass and settles at the bottom of my stomach as a dull nausea.

I set off in a direction that feels right. This faux sense of instinct is the most I can go off of. The night is always dark but tonight, a visor has wrapped itself across my eyes, and even the half-full moon cowers behind a thick, dim blue film. I wander down empty suburban streets, scanning for a main road, for civilization. I'm among the professionally undead, the 9-to-5 middle-class elite—the last remnants of the American

Nuclear Family Dream. I don't remember how I got here. Was I escorted?

The vague, ghostly form of a woman approaches. Her hair hangs down around her shoulders. This is all I can identify besides the air of femininity that's filled the space between us now. She feels fear. Or I do, but either way, it's there and it exists, compressed tighter and tighter like a volatile chemical as the gap shrinks. I release the tension and make contact once the full shape of her outline becomes visible: "Hey," I shout.

Her head darts up from resting against the pocket of her sternum. Words fail her.

"Hey," I repeat, "do you know where a 7-Eleven is? Or something like that?"

The terror stabs her throat and she sputters around the hole it creates: "I—I don't know what you want! Just stay away!" She trots across the street, lifts into a light jog, tears past me like a wild mouse, turns the corner behind me, and sprints away into the tinted blue-black cloud obscuring my vision.

I am left alone in the darkness. I am a monster, deformed. Not the prettiest person in the tri-city area but undeserving of this kind of treatment. Is my appearance that altered? I grope at the curves and contours of my face for open wounds or pustules. Instead, my fingers brush cold plastic, which falls off the bridge of my nose and scrapes against the concrete like a dulled knife. Everything has changed. The moon's glare sings through the current of the wind, a static and pregnant yellow. The specters lingering behind the streetlight's shadows withdraw into the manicured lawns closing in on me. The visor has been lifted. I look down at what burden I've shed: a pair of cheap sunglasses rests at my feet. I've been wearing sunglasses and haven't realized it. This explains a lot.

I smoke half a cigarette before giving up and walking back into the sterile, pale light. The paraplegic is gone, as is his handler. The sea cucumber remains, an impassive fixture like the centerpiece of some postmodern Gothic painting. I am happy to see her. I wave and the pink bracelet slides down to the center of my forearm.

She doesn't acknowledge this. Her hands are occupied by an out-of-date iPhone and her gray eyes are hidden from me.

I return to the book and find that the words have become decipherable. I feel as if I've overcome a great obstacle. I remember I'm reading from the Indian's perspective when a nurse in a gray uniform enters from the end of the hollow room. Her eyes are blue and I feel the kindness in the worry lines impressed deep into her forehead.

She introduces herself with a name that dissolves once it reaches my ears, and I'm led into a small room alive with the beeps and buzzes of equipment worth more than the organs from the bodies they save. My vitals are taken and questions are asked about my general wellbeing. Most of my responses are lies. I am growing paranoid, and the diluted logic that the words I use can, if uttered incorrectly, result in my lobotomization and confinement begins to overtake me. I am McMurphy, and this realization is deeply unsettling.

To overcut the piercing terror, I interrupt the nurse's line of inquiry and blurt out the first thing that comes to mind: "Can you not walk cows upstairs or downstairs? I can't remember which."

Without missing a beat, she removes the pulse monitor from my index finger and answers, "Downstairs. You can't walk them downstairs. They'll tumble over. Your pulse is 120, are you anxious?"

I'm brought into a room farther into the bowels of the hospital and instructed to sit in the chair against the wall. The on-call psychiatrist sits rigid behind a wraparound desk at his computer. He is balding and indifferent and laughs with the nurse next to him about the season finale of a show I'm unfamiliar with. She laughs back while leaning over the paraplegic with a stethoscope in one ear and the diaphragm pressed against his chest like an artificial umbilical cord. He is asleep in the wheelchair, slumped over with his mouth agape. All but his father appears unfazed.

The son looks dead but the nurse removes the stethoscope and nods to herself. I decide if I ever work in a hospital, I will drink on the job, and keep a flask taped to the inside of my leg like a firearm.

"Henry Gallagher?" The apathetic nurse calls me up to the desk.

There's no chair so I stand next to the paraplegic.

"This is Dr. Michaels," she says. "Do your best to explain why you're here."

The psychiatrist sits and waits. I can hear him breathing and it's making me sick. He must be aware of how loud his breathing is. It's all I can hear.

"Are you able to communicate?" he says.

"Do you have a deviated septum?"

"Okay, so you talk. What're your symptoms?" He looks up from his computer to show me he cares. The nurse eyes me as one would a homeless person crouched on a dark street, cautiously scanning my body language for signs of psychosis.

I don't know what to tell him so I start with the most direct answer. "I can't think straight." That's good. That was a good start.

He watches me for a moment, joining the nurse in assessing my eyes and demeanor. He doesn't appear to gather anything from that. "Have you been diagnosed with any mental disorders? If so, are you on medication for any of them?"

I tell him yes. I tell him I was taking pills and they made me go crazy and my girlfriend is mad at me and her name is Riley. I'm here because I'd like a bed, please.

"What're your diagnoses? Can you tell me what you were taking?"

I tell him these things. I'm honest with him but immediately regret it. I don't trust him. It's the eyes. You can tell everything you want about a person by watching the eyes in good lighting. I'm slipping.

"You have allergies?"

"What?" I say.

"I'm looking here on your file and it says that you're allergic to pollen and animal dandruff. Are you taking anything for that?"

Before I can answer, something stirs next to me. The paraplegic is waking up.

He's coughing and then his eyes open. Then they open very wide. He begins screaming. The paraplegic is screaming and no one can understand what he's saying. He sounds like, "AHHHHWOOOO OHHHHGAWWWW AHHHH AWWWOOOO AAAHHH." His arms wave around like strips of paper in a breeze. He's gasping for breath now.

Nobody is saying anything. Nobody is looking at him. His father puts his hand on his shoulder but it doesn't calm him. The nurse has returned to her desk, focused on her computer. Nobody is paying any attention to him.

His screams echo, bouncing off the walls as they carry down the hallways, but no one is doing anything. Is he in pain? Is he dying? What is happening?

The psychiatrist hasn't looked away. He repeats himself, "Are you on any medication for the allergies?"

My head swivels between the screaming paraplegic and the psychiatrist. "Ah—no. I mean. No. I don't understand what that has to d—"

"I have awful allergies," the psychiatrist says. "Just awful. I have this nasal spray that I use every day. I swear by it." He raises his voice more with each sentence to talk over the paraplegic. "Is that something—"

"AHHHH WOOOO AWWWGAWWWHHH AHHH—"

"—YOU'D LIKE TO CONSIDER?"

"AHHH AHH AHH OOOOOWWWWWGAWWW AHHH."

"BECAUSE I REALLY THINK THAT COULD HELP—"

"OOOOWWWWHHHAAA AHHH OHHHH—"

"—YOU OUT."

I'm going insane again. This isn't real. "No I don't want your fucking nasal spray," I tell him. I want to scream at the paraplegic to stop but I know he can't. None of us can. It must be freeing to scream like that on the outside instead of keeping it inside.

I've upset the psychiatrist. His eyebrows lower and the upturned corners of his lips settle back into indifference. He looks at his computer, then says, "Alright then. Are you suicidal?"

The nurse has finally decided to act. She walks out behind the paraplegic and wheels him down the hallway. The father follows without a word. He must be used to this or no longer cares. This has become a duty to fulfill, not a son to care for. Maybe he's the opposite of his son: He's screaming on the inside. The screams fade into a high-pitched hum as their source is taken farther and farther away.

"Did you hear the question?" the psychiatrist asks.

"Yes," I say. This is a moment I'm prepared for. The answer to this question is the difference between a 72-hour hold in a padded room and a straightjacket—and getting a bed. I want a bed. I just want to rest. I haven't been this tired in a long time. "No, I'm not suicidal," I lie. "But I'm sick. Do you understand? I'd like help. I'd like a bed. I don't want nasal spray or a lobotomy or a straightjacket or more drugs. I'm tired and I want a bed. I've been up for four days. I need rest. That's all I need."

The psychiatrist types something into his computer and looks up at me. He frowns because he thinks it mimics sincerity, but he frowns with his mouth and not his eyes. I see through him. I know what he's about to say: "Look, Henry. I'd love to help you with that, but unless you or I believe you're a danger to yourself or others, I can't do anything like that for you. You aren't going to hurt yourself, are you?"

I can't tell him. He's untrustworthy. He'll have me locked up. He'll have me arrested. "No," I say.

"Then, in that case, I'll tell you what I can do." He pulls out a pen and prescription pad, writes something down, tears off the paper, and hands it to me. "That's a prescription for a different mood stabilizer. This one should do the trick. And I put in that nasal spray for you too, Henry. Just in case." He winks at me.

I want to kill him. At least then I could get a bed. I look down at the piece of paper. It's blue and the writing is illegible.

The psychiatrist smiles at me. He's waiting for me to leave. He's done his job.

I think about the time last summer when I was sitting on a dock over the river. I'd gone out there to read but the sun was going down and the mosquitoes were beginning to swarm in dense, black clouds, looking for a host. I kept hearing this sound behind me, like the soft pitter-patter rain makes when it falls onto water, but it had no consistent rhythm like the rain. I put down my book and looked out over the river for what was creating the sound. After a few seconds of silence, I saw the first displacement of water. Then another and another, small circles carved out from the river's surface that bloomed out and expanded like maturing sunflowers. I stood up, fascinated, and walked down to the edge of the dock to get a better look. The circles popped up at random, dancing around each other, overlapping the ripples created by the one before it, all alight and alive across the river like musical notes plucked by the strings of a guitar. It took a moment of awe to recognize what they were: Swarms of mosquitoes flying low over the water were attracting minnows. The minnows were leaping out and catching the mosquitos. I understood this logically but the minnows were too quick. No matter how hard I focused, I couldn't catch a glimpse of the fish, only the evidence lingering behind told me they had, for a split second, made themselves visible. Like the tails of comets. It could have all been in my head and I would never know. But I saw the ripples, whether or not fish made them.

I walk back out into the waiting room, where the sea cucumber looks up from her iPhone. Her gray eyes are still there and they look at me when she talks. "I hope you got the help you needed. Feel better, honey."

"Thank you," I say. "I feel much better." I walk over to the chair with *One Flew over the Cuckoo's Nest* resting atop it, sit back down, close my eyes, and fall asleep.

MARCH, 2018

I woke up to screaming. My friend, Nadia, was on the phone. Absentmindedly swatting at the phone like an alarm clock, I put the screen close to my ear to keep the violent white glare from tattooing itself behind my eyelids. She was wailing about how she had done something terrible, something horrible, should she kill herself? She was going to kill herself. She strung her sentences together in one long twisting howl: "Myboyfriendfoundout I didheroinmylifeisoverIwannadieldidso methingsohorriblehe—*deep breath*—"HATES ME."

"Listen," I explained to her. "You need to please shut the fuck up." I pulled the phone from my face and squinted to catch a glimpse of exactly when my friend decided to disrupt my life: It was 1:15 AM. I'd been asleep for ten minutes. I'd gotten out of the hospital an hour ago. "Firstly, you need to breathe. Secondly, I hate your boyfriend. He's a piece of shit. Third—"

"HENRYYOUDON'TUNDERSTANDILOVEHIM"—*deep breath*— "MYLIFEISOVERI'MGONNAFUCKINGDOITI'MGON—"

"THIRDLY," I continued, "lots of great people have done heroin." I looked at the plastic bracelet on my wrist, my head still swimming from the dose of Ativan. "Look, I really can't do this right now, Nadia. I just got out of Good Sam."

Nadia's demeanor shifted to subdued curiosity. "Wait, what's the matter?"

What was the matter was I had just been discharged from the hospital after sustaining a prolonged and inefficient four-day manic episode after upping the dose on my Lamictal. I want the record to show that this was as per instructions by, and under the supervision of, a licensed mental health professional. I'm not a loose cannon. I do my taxes.

That part won't be in this book but what does need to be taken from those four days is that my girlfriend left me sometime between that Friday and the Monday night whereupon this encounter I'm describing occurred. I couldn't know specifically when or why, given the nature of manic attacks, the Saturday I spent drinking a revelatory amount of whiskey over twelve hours, the emptied bottle of Ativan (divvied out over the four days for safety—I'm not an animal), and the state of near hallucinatory exhaustion I'd skidded headfirst into by the end of the ordeal.

But what stands is that I was coming down from the tumultuous results of poor medical advice, and readying myself for the dead-end job I was to report to in five hours.

I didn't make it to that dead-end job five hours later. Nadia refused to give me her word that she wouldn't throw herself and the toaster into the bathtub if I fell asleep, so I danced around opiate-assisted unconsciousness by slapping myself awake until the sun came up, talking Nadia off the proverbial ledge until I quelled enough of her self-loathing to know I wouldn't wake up to a tragic news clip in my text messages.

Waking up four hours past my clock-in time, I had no choice but to answer one of the seven new voicemails and explain that I am mentally ill, that I had had an episode of some kind, and had checked myself into the hospital for my own safety. So I'm sorry I wasn't at your morning fucking lineup.

This was met with a long and quiet pause from my boss, before the eventual and hesitant response that maybe I should take a few days off. Or weeks. Just don't shoot up the office, please.

So, let's recap: manic episode, hospitalization, breakup, friend's heroin-inspired suicide attempt, triumphant victory over friend's heroin-inspired suicide attempt, and suspension from a dead-end job.

Good, that's everything.

This has been what's called the prelude.

That night, I attended an AA meeting. This wasn't an attempt to overcome one of the symptoms of my illness but just something to do. My girlfriend had sent me a lengthy email earlier in the day explaining that, beyond all my flaws and shortcomings—which she could and did put up with—the only one I had made no attempt to alter or diminish, was my relationship with alcohol. She made it clear that she would no longer condone this long-lasting battle I was waging with my liver. This wasn't necessarily a direct threat nor an ultimatum, but I did take it as a challenge, a challenge I would win. In every aspect of my life, I always employed a firm streak of stubbornness, so I decided to apply that to something that could benefit my health for once.

So AA was less a way of getting her back or taking initiative with my own wellbeing, but more of a strong-headed retort a child might make towards a neighborhood bully's taunting. The meeting was in the basement of a local Alano Club. I walked in late, choosing a spot next to a gray-haired woman in her mid-fifties who reminded me of my mother. As I sat down, the reality of how much stress my body and mind had been under for the past 96 hours slammed into me like a baseball bat, my stomach cramping and forming a tight, fist-sized stone that dropped into my abdomen.

I scooted my chair closer. She managed a smile and nodded, allowing this intrusion. Based on my sweat-drenched and trembling appearance, she may have assumed I was going through withdrawal, and so allowed herself to be of some comfort at arm's length.

A dread-headed man, rough in the face and built like a grizzly bear, led the meeting. He talked about blacking out and waking up, smoking crack in back alleys. He now built amps for a living. He had been sober for eight years. There was a light in his eyes and the way he talked spoke to the validity of what he was saying. He was a man who had been through much and came through the end of it. His energy put me at ease. I decided I liked this man.

The second thing I noticed at this meeting was that the people who claimed to have over five years of sobriety all had a quality missing from the others. They enunciated, spoke smoothly, were articulate. Their stories didn't meander and had twists and punch lines. They laughed. Their faces showed a weathered past but they wore it well, like tasteful jewelry. They glowed. I didn't understand it until that moment, but I didn't have what they had. I wanted what they had.

But the first thing I noticed was a young woman sitting across from my new, gray-haired surrogate mother. Her hair was short but voluminous and wild. It was the same color as her eyes—a light, golden brown. She had one of those faces where you can't tell if they're 25 or 45. Like the others carrying more than half a decade of sobriety, her face was adorned with grit that added an element of beauty and style. Her body was hidden beneath a draping sweater one might wear if they were rushed out of the house with no time to change. I soon lost track of the meeting and became invested in the art of shooting glances at this woman without her noticing.

I was then called on to share my story.

"Hi, I'm Henry. Alcoholic." I'd seen movies.

"Hi, Henry," said the room of strangers.

I wasn't sure where to begin. Public speaking was never a strong suit, and I wasn't sure where the line was at these things. I went with the short version: Just got out of the hospital for mania. It was the psychiatrist's fault, not mine, I swear. Lost my girlfriend, might have lost my job. I normally drink when these things happen. Doesn't everybody? Didn't wanna drink today. Went to a meeting instead. End scene.

The young woman's ears perked up when I explained this. I wasn't yet sure for which part. The dread-headed grizzly bear instructed me to choose someone else to speak.

I chose who you think I would.

"Hi, I'm Jenny. Alcoholic."

"Hi, Jenny."

What next came out of Jenny's mouth only solidified my fascination. Jenny was bipolar type 1. She smiled at me when she said this. She had found camaraderie. Jenny had recently suffered a psychotic break, and soon thereafter became a born-again Christian. She didn't want to sell her soul to the Devil. Alcohol would make her do this. She realized the world was ending—not in the philosophical sense that all things eventually come to an end, but in the literal sense that the Biblical Rapture was approaching. She didn't want to speak on it anymore, for fear of revealing too much. But she was happy to be here tonight, thank you, everybody.

That was it. I had found my focal point.

After the meeting, she came up to me. I could see the lines drawn out from above her lips when she smiled. "So, you're bipolar?"

"Yeah," I said. "Or that's what they tell me."

"Me too," she said. She pointed to the cigarette tucked behind my ear. "You wanna smoke?"

"Sure."

Outside, Jenny talked about how she had taken a great interest in conspiracy theories since her last episode. She wouldn't elaborate on which ones. She took long, hungry drags from her cigarette and spoke carefully, like each word might be her last. Her fingers trembled and she fidgeted every few seconds in an abrupt and rhythmic manner that made it appear to be a nervous tic. She talked about how she needed to take a shot of Haldol every month, as well as two separate anti-psychotics and another medication to aid her sleep schedule. The psychotic break occurred last month when she failed to take that Haldol shot.

As her words tumbled over me, I began to ache. This person was spilling things about herself to a stranger as if I were a trusted confidant. I admired that level of openness. Jenny was a person in pain. We were two people smoking cigarettes in pain. It dawned on me that making sexual advances on other recovering addicts is frowned upon.

It also came to me that I was perhaps not recovering but simply an addict, and wondered if that voided the unspoken agreement. I was pondering making a move on a mentally ill person I had just met at an AA meeting after leaving the hospital, losing my job and my girlfriend. I am a very sick person, I realized. One of two people smoking cigarettes in pain. It should be left at that.

This was what's called in the business, Act One.

Mornings are, and always will be, the worst. For some reason, there's this romantic notion documented in bad poetry and Tumblr posts that lonely nights are the true witching hour when the demons of your past and future expel themselves into the empty, dark space to wreak havoc. This is untrue and the people who are saying this obviously don't drink.

Nights are the only time the mind quiets. Even on nights where I hadn't retreated to the bottle, the moon and stars had an unexplainable, tranquilizing effect on my psyche.

The world slows and the people I fear are tucked away from the streets (for the most part). The reason some people find the evening unbearable is the very reason I was always put at ease. Finally, after the chaos of the day, I had silence.

No, it's the mornings that break me down to my base fight-or-flight instincts. You come screaming back into the blinding light, jolted awake from the depths of a Kafkaesque nightmare or a whiskey-drunk blank, and, within seconds, every regret and memory you left beside your pillow comes swirling back down the clogged drain that is you, and you are consequently and without fail, miserable.

This morning, the sunlight hit through the branches of the trees outside my window, the birds screeched and cried for me to face what I was, and the knowledge of what had happened in the last few days struck me like a sucker punch before I could gauge where I was.

Engulfed in a deep black terror, I doubled over into the fetal position and began to shake, unable to breathe. As someone never well-equipped to cope with adversity, this was a healthy dose without the numbing effect of alcohol to lean upon. In all my life, I had never faced trouble without running to a substance, a medication, or the first name in my address book I felt would tolerate my babbling through choking fits and agonized grunts. But something about the memory of my friend, Nadia, screaming and wailing about suicide over the phone as I wrestled through half-consciousness made me sick to my stomach. Reality had turned the mirror on me, allowing me to see how pitiful and unsympathetic someone in the throes of such a state actually is. How pitiful and unsympathetic I had been for the entirety of my life. Wallowing and drowning in the torment I alone had created. If one were to take all the mental states I had ever experienced and add them up, based on the duration of time spent in each, any onlooker would probably conclude that my current state was my baseline. This frustrated and disgusted me.

I wasn't going to self-medicate away this feeling. I would sit in it, feeling every vibration of terror as if it was a dentist drilling into a nerve. Whether this decision was out of self-determination, or yet another form of self-punishment, I didn't care to ponder. I laid in bed and felt the sickness in sharp waves until it was all my mind could occupy itself with, until I hated it so much that I wanted to find its wet, black center and destroy it with my fists.

And then the feeling passed.

I lifted myself from the bed and walked to the bathroom. I found that the image in the mirror was less pathetic now. This man had some form of strength. Or a tenacious sort of weakness, but this was better than our previous encounters. I saw the brown, patchy beginnings of a beard. He had let this go unchecked. An uncomfortable reminder of a time years ago when I'd given up with all my being—one of the few endeavors I had ever put so much effort into. This was a time that culminated with a fifth of whiskey defeated in bed each night, fifty extra pounds gained, and a thick, scraggly beard maintained purely to demonstrate my deep depression to the world without them having to ask.

I couldn't explain why I wasn't going to return to this state—in fact, this seemed like a perfect time to—but I wasn't. I was going to shave the beard and I was going to be sober and I was going to go to another meeting.

I didn't feel any sense of accomplishment. I was driven by anger—anger at the shameful, ghost-like memory of my sick, cowardly hands, eyes, mouth, mind, and fuck-the-world beard. But I was going to run on whatever fuel I had.

For those keeping score, this was what could be considered Act Two.

The next meeting was less beneficial.

As I walked through the doors of the dilapidated Baptist church, the feeling that at once washed over me was not of hope. A pervasive sense of desperation floated across the overcrowded room like a thick mist. I came in late and was greeted by the stuttering whine of a woman attempting to tell her story through thunderous sobs.

I sat in the corner next to an elderly, overweight black man so affected with vitiligo that he could be mistaken for a white man with black splotches. This reminded me of a zebra and I wondered if this thought had ever occurred to him, or if anyone had ever mentioned this comparison.

The woman's story was surprisingly unremarkable, considering her issue was beginning to drink two glasses of wine a night instead of one. Everyone appeared sympathetic to her, however, and thanked her after she finished her tale of suburban, stay-at-home-mom woes. There were shouts of "Keep coming back!" and "Surrender to your higher power!"

I began to get that cult vibe I was always told about by angry, recently relapsed drunks at bars.

The next woman was visiting from San Bernardino for the weekend while her husband was at a job interview, and it became apparent she had simply switched one habit for another. She had started to feel uneasy during the two-day car ride because she had gone longer than 24 hours without a meeting. She said this with a dismissive chuckle to give the impression that she was kidding, but she was not. I could see how the addict will always be addicted to something, and that replacing something self-destructive for something much less destructive—if not boring—is an understandable jump in logic for the chronically addicted, but the unrest and craving in this woman's face made me uncomfortable.

The next woman to speak appeared to be about my age, with blonde hair down to her shoulders, wearing a baggy jean jacket and a red beanie fit loosely over the top of her head. She had not been smiling the entire meeting. She sat slumped in her chair, chewing gum and bouncing her knee with the intensity of an inmate awaiting the electric chair.

As she began talking, the San Bernardino woman's husband and small child walked in. The child was about four, with some type of cold or flu virus. His mother lifted him onto her lap, where he moaned each time he coughed and sneezed, making no attempt to cover his mouth. Instead, he aimed his phlegm rockets directly at his mother's face.

The young woman across the room got about two sentences out before explaining through tears that she hated AA, didn't want to be here, didn't like any of us, in fact she hated us. She was 25 and wanted to get fucked up with her friends and it wasn't fair that she had to be a fucking alcoholic. She didn't want this life and she was tired and unhappy and sick, and after being sober for two months, she could now definitively tell all of us that being drunk all the time was a better decision.

Most of this tirade was drowned out by the screams and coughs of the small child, completely unaware of the fascinating mental breakdown occurring to his right.

There were more shouts of "It works if you work it!" and "Let go and let God!"

The young woman then stood up and screamed, "FUCK YOU, you fucking SOBER ZOMBIES," and stormed out.

This, for your pleasure, has been what we'll call Act Three.

The trembling energy and hyper-focus of the lingering mania had by now worn off as I sat at the corner of the bar, the closest I could find within proximity to the meeting.

Part of me expected to see the AA dropout sitting there three shots in, but that fantasy was dashed. The place was empty, save a mouse-faced woman sitting at a table behind me.

The bartender approached, his barrel chest eclipsing the light shining through the window at his back. "Whatdyawant?" he asked.

Shaken from my daze, my eyes scanned the shelves of brown and green bottles, every one of them harboring the ability to subdue the buzzing sickness gathering second wind within the walls of my skull. "I'll have a...whiskey. Shot'a whiskey."

"Well?"

"Uh. Yeah. Yeah, well."

Sensing my hesitation, he said, "I can just get you a glass of water if you like. While you think about it, brother."

I was surprised by this response, what I took to be a moment of compassion but could have just been indifference. "Yeah, water is good. I'll just have the water."

Later, I realized he'd overheard a conversation I'd had with Nadia, who had called to complain once more about her boyfriend, the coke addict who drew the line at heroin. "I can't take it anymore," she said. "I hate him. I barely ever do it. I smoked it, I didn't even inject. He's a fucking hypocrite."

"Okay," I said.

"You wanna get a drink? I need someone right now."

"I'm not drinking."

"What do you mean?"

"I mean, I just..." I lowered my voice so not to be outed as a fellow hypocrite. "I just got out of an AA meeting."

"Gross."

"You really fucked me, you know that? I might have lost my job because of you." The blame was mine but I didn't feel like taking any of it at this moment.

"I don't know what you're talking about. I didn't do that," she snapped. "You're so fucking selfish, Henry. Think about other people for a change."

And *click*.

I contemplated the glass of water in front of me, placed atop a ringed stain in the wooden bar. Whether it was water or whiskey in that glass, it wouldn't change how I felt.

But that was probably just a lie I had to tell myself.

Outside, the rain was picking up. I could hear the soft white noise it created against the windows. People new to sobriety talk about excruciatingly long days. Hours drag by as if held back by a rope, only giving the time an inch of slack once you've let your focus on the clock dissolve. Businessmen die by the thousands of exhaustion and work-related heart attacks. But boredom is the lethal disease of the addicted.

My attention drifted to the mouse-woman behind me. She wasn't attractive—a scowl was screwed into her face as if she came out of the womb like that. Her facial features, framed by black, uncombed hair, condensed in the center like her face stopped growing but her head carried on. She couldn't have been taller than five feet or weighed more than ninety pounds.

But she was the only company I had.

Before her sat two plates of food, which she was devouring at a staggering rate. My eyes burned through her, making no effort to hide that I was staring. Her focus was compelling. I wanted her to see me, to acknowledge me, to nod or wave. I wanted to wash away the feeling that I wasn't a ghost haunting this place but a person like her. I wanted this more than anything.

The longer I stared, and the longer she failed to make eye contact, the more I wanted to make physical contact with her. This wasn't a sexual impulse but something deep-seated welling up inside me. The clogged drain was spilling out its putrid insides across the bar and over the floor, and I saw this but she didn't see this and I knew nothing of how or why this was happening or how I would clean up what was gushing out of me, but I knew only that I needed her to touch me. To see that her fingers would not pass through me like motes of dust floating in a ray of sunlight, but would stop and connect with something that existed. Something of substance. Something that told me this all hadn't been for nothing. I needed to believe that I had passed through a gauntlet and returned with limbs and heart and brain intact. I needed closure and I needed this woman to give it to me.

As I began to drown in the rancid mess accumulating around my chin, my eyes screamed and the woman did not hear but finished her meals. I sat and waited for a moment of recognition, my knee trembling so hard that I had to steady myself to stay in my seat. My field of vision became a visor of thick, black slime.

The woman stood and my heart jumped. She reached into her jacket pocket, pulled out a cigarette, and placed it between her lips. Her movements were in slow-motion and I followed the hand up to her mouth and back down, where it rested beside her hip. I watched her legs propel her body forward, watched her eyes fix upon a target I couldn't see, still unable to break my gaze, tethered by anticipation of the moment she would return it.

I just need you to look at me.

Just look at me. Tell me I'm okay.

The woman extended her arm and pushed open the door. From behind the window, I watched the flame from her lighter touch the end of the cigarette, the blue-gray smoke expel in a transparent cloud from her lungs. I watched the rain fall upon the white paper and form dark splotches just beneath the glowing ember. The woman looked upward as if to check if the rain had come from the sky, took another short drag, and walked down the street.

My eyes lingered there for a while, on the empty space behind the window's glass, where a person had once stood.

I can't recall for how long.

Now take a bow. Close the curtains.

APRIL, 2018

"Do you know how easily I could kill you right now?" He pointed the barrel of the .22 revolver at my chest from across the table.

"You keep that thing loaded?" I asked. "If you're gonna point that at me, you better hope to Christ that it's loaded."

"I keep two empty. Then the next two are loaded. *Click, click—bang, bang.* Like Russian roulette. In case I accidentally shoot myself."

The ice touched my lips and the whiskey went down with a warm sting, eyes trained on the black hole staring at me.

James's glare fought to command my attention as he reached for the bottle between us to pour more into his glass. "You understand that I thought we had an agreement," he said. "You sat here—just like this—right across from me last week and you said you didn't have any intention of doing it. You seemed sincere and I trusted you. You understand that, Henry? You shook my hand and looked me in the eyes, just like you're looking at this pistol now, and you promised me."

I lifted another cigarette from out my front pocket, exhaled, lit the end, and inhaled the smoke. I watched it curl underneath my nose. "I wasn't lying to you," I said. "I think there was a miscommunication. I thought—"

"You promised me, and I went to sleep that night, and you stayed here and slept on the couch—and this is the funny part. You wanna hear the funny part?"

"I like to laugh," I said.

"Don't fucking push this, man."

I scanned the objects strewn across the back porch table: four empty packs of American Spirits, an empty beer bottle stuffed to the brim with cigarette butts, an empty fifth of Buffalo Trace bourbon, another beer can with the top sawed off by the hunting knife sitting beside it to create a makeshift ashtray. James had not been taking the breakup well. I had my own problems and reasons for dereliction, so I sympathized—

although it hadn't stopped me from furthering his regression with my actions. The guilt was there but I was doing my best to drown it and everything that led to it with the gauntlet of a bender I'd embarked on for the past week.

I returned my attention to his sunken eyes and the black barrel. "Look, just say it. We both know why I'm here. I took the invitation—I'm not running from anything. This is something I'd like to talk about."

"The funny part," he continued, "is that I woke up to you on the couch next to her. The funny part is later that day I was cleaning up the apartment and found an empty bottle of wine and an opened box of condoms sitting out on the table."

I remembered that wine. Rotgut shit, two liters for eight dollars. Merlot. It was the only bottle that didn't require a corkscrew. Nobody drinks merlot.

"Shit." I mumbled the word out the side of my mouth and took a deep drag until my lungs burned. "She's not very smooth, is she?"

James was shaking now and the pistol clinked against its metal insides. "We had...an understanding. And that night you fucked my girlfriend. You fuck my girlfriend in MY APARTMENT...the SAME NIGHT that you LOOK ME IN THE EYES and TELL ME that wasn't your intention."

I finished the whiskey, poured another. Rebecca had bought it for me for driving her to the airport that day. With her out of the way, James was free to invite me over, point a loaded weapon at me, and speak openly. It had taken about half the bottle and a half-hour of small talk before he gained the courage to ask if I'd like to see his gun collection. He'd been drinking long before I came over, and stumbled back onto the deck, fumbling with the safety, holding the gun up to the light to double-check where the bullets were in the cylinder.

I realized this was a critical point in the conversation. The next thing I said could be the difference between walking out of this alive or being wheeled out with a bullet in my sternum. A part of me welcomed the thought of dying—a bullet, especially from an outside party, would be a quick and easy solution—but I recognized that most of my suicidal thoughts were a result of the Zoloft I was tapering off of. In times like these, it was imperative to think objectively.

After a moment of silence, I arrived at, "Ex-girlfriend."

"What?" James's eyes became brown slits, his lips contorted into a gnarled grimace.

"She's your ex-girlfriend," I repeated. "I fucked your ex-girlfriend."

"DO YOU THINK THAT REALLY MATTERS?" He thrust the pistol closer to my chest.

"Yes, I think it does."

"Do you love her?" He stuttered and choked on a muffled sob as the words left his mouth.

"No," I said. I studied the etchings on the handle. I had never held a gun before. I imagined it must be heavy. Something capable of ending a life must be heavy.

James lowered the weapon. I felt nothing when he did this. "Why did you have to do this? Upend my life?"

"I don't know," I admitted. "Self-destruction, probably."

"You can't escape into self-pity now. Maybe with her you can but not now. Life has consequences." He put the pistol down on the table. "I should hit you in the fucking face."

"You can if you want. Would it make you feel better?"

James ignored the question. "I knew it the first time we all went out together. I knew you would be the guy. I remember seeing you talking. It was like watching two of the same person. I knew she would gravitate towards you. I know what she sees in you."

"What's that?"

"You're this damaged piece of shit. You revel in it. I know people like you. You'll never change. You'll be a broken piece of shit all your life and you know it so you own it. You wear it like armor. You'll never attract anyone but sad, broken girls who will always leave for the next guy with the better suicide attempt story." He sat back and chuckled at his insight. "Maybe that's enough of a punishment. You'll never have anything in life that lasts longer than a bottle or an orgasm. You'll never accomplish anything."

"Does that make you feel better?" I said.

"It does."

"Then you can have that." I picked up the whiskey and drank from the bottle, clicked my tongue, and frowned to wash down the sting. "What I meant when we talked was that my intention wasn't malicious. I wasn't trying to rub this in your face. I'm not proud of any of this. I'm not trying to hurt anyone. I'm just trying to keep my head above water. Until I find a better way out—or until I decide to want a better way out—I'm utilizing every vice I can to keep breathing air. It's not the healthy way to handle things but it's my way. I'm sorry my downward spiral involves wrapping you up in it with me. I didn't intend to drag anyone else under. But I didn't ruin your life. Whatever happened between you and Rebecca happened between you and Rebecca. All she did was crawl out of the rubble and fuck me afterwards."

James recoiled at my bluntness, and I prepared for a tirade or sucker punch but he remained stoic. He extended a hand. "Can I bum one of those?"

I tossed the pack on the table.

He took a cigarette, resting it between his lips, and staring at the wall with its peeling paint as he lit up. The glow from the sun tinged the smoke yellow as it floated up. "What happened with Riley?" His tone had softened.

"She couldn't take it anymore," I answered. "This shtick I have wears on people. Rebecca was the closest person next to me, so I grabbed on."

"What do you think Becca would think about that?"

"I don't think she would care." I noticed the pistol was still pointed at me from the table. "I imagine she's doing the same thing I am."

"She probably is," he said. "She'll leave you too."

"She probably will. I'm not really thinking about that."

James watched me eyeing the pistol. "Wanna hold it?"

"Yeah," I said.

"Pick it up."

It was heavy and solid and cold in my hands. I ran my finger down the barrel and let it rest in my open palms. I couldn't stop staring at it. I was fascinated.

"If you really want to self-destruct," he said, "you can kill yourself right now."

My eyes widened and the lingering fascination poured out in a single word: "Really?"

James smiled. "The option is there if you want it."

I thought about it, gliding my thumb back and forth over the trigger. I made sure to really think about it. The idea flared and grew and grew. Then it fell away. "Ah, you'd like that too much." I placed the pistol back on the table, the barrel pointed at my chest. "I'm supposed to make your life harder. If I can't find an easy way out, then neither should you."

We both laughed at that—a loud, morbid laugh. The grins stayed on our faces, obscured by the dying light and the smoke twisting between us.

"Yeah, you're probably right," said James. "You're right."

MAY, 2018

Rebecca climbs off me and pulls the flowy, tie-dye summer dress back around her thighs. She reaches into the undone mess of blonde hair made greasy by enabling the alcoholism I nurse better with the promise of company, scratching at her scalp and letting it fall back down her shoulders.

"I have a gift card to Applebee's," she says. The semen drips down her leg as she stands. "Have you been to Applebee's?"

"No," I say. "Do they have liquor?"

She's let me come inside her despite the fact she isn't on birth control. I wasn't aware of this but she assured me she has a plan and it seemed like I needed it so she didn't tell me insemination wasn't an option. We've been fucking for three weeks but almost every time I've been unable to finish. I tell her and myself that it's only a result of the antidepressants, but I also know this is an easier answer than the obvious, which is that every time I'm inside her, the idea of ejaculation only comes after strenuous focus on memories of Riley.

"Yeah, there's liquor," she tells me. "Tons of it."

What I perceive as the inside of a national family restaurant chain is the most soul-sucking place I can imagine, but within the depths of a depressive fit, there's nothing I enjoy more than stabbing an open wound. "Then we're going to Applebee's. Let's make our little anti-Christ retarded."

Escaping the storm of severe psychosis often brings on the same lease on life that I imagine born-again Christians experience. It's the feeling that you've been cleansed of something dark, something frightening and all-consuming. You've come out on the other end of something that could have easily resulted in your demise, spiritual or otherwise. You have a newfound sense that you're free to explore the blank pages set forward for you and write a new narrative. The difference between the outcomes of the two experiences, however, is often the difference between seeing the opportunity to create something beautiful from your moment of cleansing, and the realization that you now have an entirely new playbook to reference for fresh and creative ways to destroy your second life with refined purpose.

Getting drunk for free and performing a pseudo-abortion by way of alcohol poisoning at a local Applebee's may not sound like the most fresh or creative method of self-destruction, but it's been a long few weeks and you need to crawl before you run in the wake of a spiritual awakening.

Applebee's is the gatekeeper to the entrance of the graveyard that houses the death of the American Dream. Giant flat-screen televisions line the walls, blasting whatever major league sport is in season loud enough to drown out the screams of infants bouncing up and down on their obese mothers' laps. Colorful advertisements are superimposed into the tabletops, decaled across the walls and ceiling, and over the horseshoe-shaped bar sitting unprotected in the center of the crowded room:

MILLER HIGH LIFE: THE CHAMPAGNE OF BEERS
MCDONALD'S: I'M LOVIN' IT
FLAVOR-BLASTED DORITOS: DIABETES, ONE $3 BAG AT A TIME
JACK DANIEL'S BOURBON WHISKEY: DRINK A BOTTLE AND RUN OVER YOUR NEIGHBOR'S CAT—WE WON'T TELL

To help direct your eyes from the overwhelming glare of commercialism, the proud owners of your local Applebee's have gone to the trouble of outfitting every single fucking table with a personal tablet. If total isolation from any and all human contact is your prerogative, you can order and pay for your meal through the device and avoid that whole facet of social etiquette entirely. And for those days that all you want to do is watch the goddamn fucking Patriot's game in peace like the good, God-fearing American you are without the distraction of that two-year-old, shitting, pissing money pit crying over John Madden's take on Tom Brady's fourth-quarter, 50-yard Hail Mary spiral, not to worry! Just swipe over on that trusty tablet and you'll find a world of placating video games to shove down the kid's throat for a much deserved break—for a nominal fee, of course.

This all is set before you for one result: sensory overload. With every distraction thrust onto your direct environment, you become the perfect customer: a docile, brain-numbed consumer ready to spend as much money as they deem necessary, unburdened by the troubling concept of free thought. In this way, Applebee's is the vanguard of modern American culture. They have perfected the equation that western society has been built upon, an equation that can be best boiled down to one simple sentence: Shut up and give us your money.

Though, there are ways to sidestep this trap. We felt that paying for liquor—and only liquor—with a prepaid gift card provided by an estranged family member was one of those ways. Being aware of this before becoming part of it can give you the perspective one may get by strolling through the zoo, idly gazing at the stupefied creatures as you pass. They will never be able to escape, and that is the difference between the two of you. This is often the case for habitual drug users, BDSM enthusiasts, et cetera that soon find themselves on the other side of the cage—sprawled across a downtown drug den with an empty needle erect in the crease of their arm, or hunched over a table with a leather-clad gimp cracking a three-pronged whip across their assless chaps—wondering, "How did I get here?"

But one can only surmise what side of the enclosure they'll end up on once they get close enough to make eye contact. One can only hope, when participating in activities that trigger the pleasure of self-deprecation we all crave to some level, that we will come out unscathed, only tourists.

Rebecca and I are directed to a booth in the center of the chaos. Our server also happens to be named Rebecca. She stands with a hump in her back, hand pressed against her hip, and a sunny disposition masked across her face like wallpaper. If it isn't a façade, she has no idea how lucky she is.

She asks what she can get us started with, and I answer, whiskey—whiskey with a little soda in it. Go light on the soda though, darlin'.

Rebecca the server goes to write that down, then pauses and trains her eyes back on us. "Is that all?"

Rebecca the blonde alcoholic looks up and says, "Oh, and I'll get... What is that called, Henry? The one you really shouldn't drink if you're pregnant?"

"Well, I've heard you really shouldn't drink anything if you're pregnant, Rebecca."

"Hey, your name's Rebecca too?"

"That's right," says Rebecca One. "Since I was a baby."

"How do you spell it?"

"An E and two Cs."

"I think you're thinking of the Adios Motherfucker," I say.

"Hey, me too!" says the server. "Small world."

"I guess," says Rebecca. Then pivoting to me, "Is that what I'm thinking of? Is that the blue one?"

"Yeah, that's the blue one," I say.

"We call it the A.M.F. here," Rebecca the server informs.

I pick at the dead skin adhered to my bottom lip. "Right. Wouldn't wanna offend our conservative sensibilities."

Our server forces a chuckle. "So how 'bout anything far as food?"

"None, thanks," I tell her. "I'm here to get drunk at an Applebee's. Nothing more, nothing less."

She nods. "Well, sir, we can do that for you." Rebecca the server's support fills me with a fluttering warmth and I realize that I now love this woman in some fashion I can't yet articulate, so I respond with, "I appreciate that."

She turns to walk away and my chest becomes hollow and cold. I'm reminded why I am where I am and why I am hollow and cold and why did I do this? In the same way that some people must always be angry about something to keep the anger they feel towards themselves at bay, I too constantly feel the need to create problems that require fixing, because once my self-inflicted messes are all cleaned up, I have nothing left but to look inward at the messes I have let fester for two decades or more. If I can spend my life leap-frogging from disaster to disaster, then I will never have to look upon the real damage done—the damage that may be unfixable.

Rebecca the alcoholic sets a black-and-white notebook on the table between us. "We're going to write a story," she tells me. "I'll start." She eyes an elderly couple sitting in silence across from us before her hand glides down to the lined paper. Her handwriting is clean and legible and the words come fast:

A sullen, dragged-out couple sits together. They have so many years on their faces. The woman wears a Life Alert necklace like a family heirloom. They inform the server that they are in a rush, and order salads, sirloin, and broccoli. They haven't said a word to each other. They just sit and stare at the baseball game relayed on half a dozen TV screens, heads swiveling back and forth, unsure which screen to stick with.

She hands me the pen and pushes the notebook in front of me. "Now you."

Rebecca the server returns with our drinks. I take the brown-tinged glass out of her hand before she can place it on the table, acknowledge the returning warmth that comes with her reappearance, and take a sharp swig. "I don't taste anything," I mumble. "They water the shit down to nothing. This won't work."

Once the server leaves, Rebecca says, "Don't worry about that. Write something."

I scan the room, shaking off the feeling that I've been thrown into a therapeutic exercise. A man walks by and I study his movements as he hurries through the open corridor between booths. The pen finishes my thoughts before I can eliminate the sentences with self-doubt:

An aged server walks by, balancing an assortment of plates on two hands. His hairline is receding, his face detailed with crow's feet and worry lines. His eyes give the blank expression of a man acutely aware of the pit he exists within.

I swallow the rest of the drink and wrap my right arm around the notebook to hide my thoughts from Rebecca:

I am depressed and the drink either does or does not help, but I decide that this unnamed server is the most depressing ornament in this restaurant and I am reminded of how there are always worse places than the ground your own feet stand upon.

I push the notebook away and wave our server over once we make eye contact.

"Keep it going?" she asks.

"Yes. Between you and me," I say, "how much do I need to tip you to get a decent amount of liquor in a glass?"

"Enough to get me outta this job."

"How much is that?"

"I'll bring you a shot."

Rebecca begins writing again as Rebecca Two comes back with the carefully measured whiskey.

I drink it in front of her to show my dissatisfaction with the job she's done. She must know I can't tip her enough to get her out of this life. "I need another," I tell her. "And then another. Just assume that once you put the next shot in front of me that you should then go get another one."

"Look," she says, "there's only so much I can do. You really wanna get drunk, go to the bar across the street."

"Maybe I will, Rebecca. Maybe I will. But right now I'm at Applebee's and I'm going to get drunk. When you make a plan, you need to follow through with it. Otherwise, what do we have?"

The server says nothing.

"Exactly," I say. "We have nothing. A person is only as good as their word."

The server leaves and Rebecca pushes the notebook back in front of me.

I don't read what she's written. "So, about the pill."

"I've got one at the apartment," she says. "But it's in James and I's bedroom. I'll have to wait until he's out to get it."

"Okay, but you only have a few days. You need to make sure—"

"I'll take it, Henry. You think I wanna have a little freak with your genetics popping out of me?"

Despite knowing that she's kidding, a twinge of pain runs down my spine. It's hard to offend me but that must be what it feels like.

"And plus with all this suicide talk you keep rambling about, maybe I should wait a day or two in case you feel the urge. Our child can take over where you left off."

I laugh. "And where's that?"

"Rock bottom, right?"

"Well, only one way up from there."

The server returns with a double shot. She winks before turning around. I want her to have my children. I want to impregnate every woman in the world and pollute the gene pool like dumping radioactive waste into the Pacific Ocean. I take the shot in a gulp. "You'll be a great mother one day," I tell Rebecca. I mean that. Rebecca is more of a mother to me sometimes than my own.

She fills me in on the details of the pill she'll be taking to kill my child. It's newer and safer than what we used to have to buy. I've only ever had to buy Plan B once before.

Communication prior to ejaculation is key.

I begin to think of incest porn, and so shake off the guilt by filling up another page of the notebook:

Rebecca may be impregnated (not the server) and she says there's a pill—a pill like Plan B but without the painful, physical reminder that you are flushing out the little would-be sea monkey-turned-fetus-turned-infant— and sans the heavy flow that follows. She makes jokes that she is carrying my child and she will carry on my legacy after I kill myself. I laugh, but I also make the mental note to remind her after we are done getting drunk at an Applebee's to take the fucking pill.

Rebecca drains her A.M.F. and curls into my shoulder, burdened by the damage we've dealt our bodies in the hopes of numbing memories of our exes. "Do you think it can feel what I'm doing to it already?" she asks. "Does a fertilized egg know it's being poisoned?"

"I don't know," I say.

She looks around the room, takes the notebook back and writes something. I call over to our server for another A.M.F. and double. The drinks come to us as Rebecca gets up to use the bathroom. "I'll be right back," she says. "Read what I wrote. Let me know what you think."

Once she turns the corner out of view, I look at what she's done. It's a short paragraph, saying she's fighting the urge to either throw her glass against a wall or come back and fuck me in our booth.

Grief does strange things to people. It's as if it triggers a survival instinct. Any logic and hesitation is thrown to the wind as long as what you have in mind has any chance of lessening the pain. I suppose, though, that survival is a more apt word than I realized. More people have committed suicide over a lost love than for any other reason. So then, anything goes. Anything is fair game if it can carry you to the next day in the face of heartbreak.

A couple approaches and sits at a booth ahead of me. They are overweight and pink with bloat. She wears a dress with flowers on it. He wears a Budweiser T-shirt. They sit on the same side of the booth. She grasps at his hand and smiles. He kisses her and pulls her into him with his free hand around her waist. They sit there smiling. They don't watch any of the television screens.

They don't bring their attention to the tablet beside them. They don't bring their attention to anything but each other. They hardly even talk. They just sit there, holding on to each other, smiling big smiles. At times, she strokes the ring on his finger. My stomach begins to twist and throb but I can't look away. I feel as though I am about to vomit or collapse into a panic attack but I can't bring myself to look away.

"So what do you think?"

I look up. Rebecca is back. She pushes me aside and slides in next to me.

"Good," I say. "It's good."

"Write something or tell me what to do."

I take the notebook, take down the whiskey, and cough. My throat burns and my chest feels as though a knife has plunged through me from the inside. The couple smiles and smiles and holds hands.

There are words that want to leave the end of my pen but there is a survival instinct screeching in the deepest part of my brain. It will not allow me. It needs me alive.

My eyes break away. I search for a distraction. Anything.

The couples' server appears. On his chest is a nametag that reads Mike. He leans over, talking with an animated grin and eyes with life in them. Suddenly, the panic and sickness is replaced with hatred. There is nothing I can do to get to that booth.

I touch the pen to paper:

Mike is young—too young to feel the brunt of life, and so he smiles at customers when they order food, and when the children cry, and the families ask to be relocated as the children elevate their violent screams. He wears large, sparkling earrings in both ears, and he will probably go to college and have many experiences and discover his malleable sexuality after a drunken, coke-fueled freshmen orgy with many body parts swinging and mashing and grinding, and he may overdose on fentanyl-laced molly, or get alcohol poisoning pledging for some frat—but for now he is smiling and serving food at Applebee's and I don't like him.

It's hard to relate to people who exist within the space prior to the death of hope. I don't need to blame him, but I do.

Survival instinct. Grief does strange things to people.

Rebecca reads what I've written and snorts. She puts her mouth on the straw and the blue cocktail empties down like the temperature on a thermometer. "One day we won't feel anything," she says. "There will be pills and injections that cure sadness and regret and guilt. We'll all be happy and nothing will mean anything anymore."

"They have that," I tell her. "It's called a lobotomy."

"Yeah, but this way there won't be a scar."

A burning, acidic flash of pain tears through the center of my abdomen, as if a wound is being cauterized on the inside of my stomach. My body crumples over and I turn my head away to wince so she won't notice. I can't remember the last time I've eaten something. How long can someone go like this?

I straighten myself out and place my hand on her shoulder, rocking it gently until she falls out of whatever daydream she's entered. "You need to take that pill, okay?"

Rebecca pulls the notebook close and leans against my chest. "Yeah, Henry. I know." She writes something quickly, and looks up at me, closing the book. "Do you wanna go?"

"Yeah," I say. "I'm ready."

Eight months later, I will borrow the notebook to read what we wrote that day, hoping I can turn it into the words you're reading now. I will remember that I never read the passage she wrote before taking it away, and I will not know how to react:

In an instant, I think I ought to push all the past away and commit the rest of my existence to you. I think about really having a baby of our own and being fucked up, depressed, world-traveling journalists, floating together from one moment to the next. Maybe it can be okay.

Grief does strange things to people.

III.

ABYSS

JULY, 2018

I spoke to myself as I drove, expending the minimal effort necessary to stay on the road ahead of me, with the majority of my attention focused on the mental image of my ex fucking someone else. "Okay, now don't look away from it. When you twitch and try to distract, don't. Really look at it. Look at his cock! It's huge! He's really fucking her!"

I watched her legs wrap around his waist, her mouth open, crying out, grabbing at the back of his head and sticking her tongue down his throat. On her back, her body vibrates in ecstasy. The bed shakes, sweat runs down their faces, then he's coming inside her, grunting as she says the words she used to say to me, "Take it. It's yours."

I pieced her face together in as much detail as I could when she said it. I needed this to be as graphic as possible, or else I'd be cheating. I had to watch it all. It was like sitting through one of those animal torture videos vegans use to convince you you're a bad person. The scenario seeped into every corner of my mind until it flooded my senses and I forgot I was driving. "Okay. Now sit in it."

I dug my nails into the side of my head and wiped the tears out of my eyes. "This is an inevitable reality. You can't stop this from happening. Feel that sting in your chest, the sinking feeling, all of it. Don't run away from it." The big-cocked porn star pulled out of the woman whom I was in love with. "Now accept it. Accept it and let it go." I suppressed a sob that came out somewhere between a cough and a yelp. After came a heavy sigh. "Okay, say it: I accept it."

I clung to the image of Riley naked on the bed. Her eyes glowed green like the last day I saw her. She was smiling. Wider than she had with me in a long time. Then I shook my head and she dissolved like my anxiety was an Etch A Sketch. "I accept that Riley will fuck big-cocked porn stars who are well-versed in the *Kama Sutra* and don't get panic attacks when they're about to fuck. Yes, I accept that."

The sting pulsated a moment, hanging on for that last opportunity to feed upon me, then faded into the pit of my stomach and died. "That was good, buddy. That was good. You're doing great. You're okay." I recognized that I was talking to myself like a child but I was new at the act of self-love, and it still felt like an awkward, unnatural exercise. I figured I would get better.

To my surprise, the image didn't return to my head, but I was uncertain if that was the pint of tequila clouding my mind. But I had never made the decision to run towards these thoughts before. I had always fought back like a child whose toy is getting ripped from his hands. My favorite method was to drown these thoughts with whiskey, though a cigarette was a quick, albeit more temporary, distraction. Masturbation worked but could backfire. This method was interesting for that reason.

In almost all scenarios where jealousy and self-consciousness overtook me, the thought of Riley with a more capable man disgusted me to my core, to a worrying degree. But when I imagined her cheating while I masturbated, I became unexplainably aroused. I would picture her getting fucked from behind by someone, anyone, it didn't matter—as long as they could satisfy her. I would imagine her screaming, face screwed tight like she had tasted a lemon, yelling out, "You fuck me better than him! He can't fuck me like you! It's so fucking big! " And she would come and come again, and the mystery stud would come and then so would I. Then I would lie there with my cock in my hand, confused why I liked that as much as I did.

Even as I drove, heartbroken with tears leaving red streaks across my face, talking to myself like a mentally disabled child, there was the gentle spark of arousal that emerged from the most terrible scenario I could imagine. Maybe it was a punishment complex. Maybe I knew I deserved to be punished, and took some perverted pleasure in that humiliation. Either way, being drunk stopped me from exerting the energy to figure it out.

I coughed up nicotine-stained phlegm and decided maybe it's just hot for the time being. Put a pin in that one.

Sometime during my therapeutic exercise, the road had taken me into the outskirts of the city. Empty lots, broken windows looking in on foreclosed houses, strip malls, fast food chains next to fast food chains next to gas stations next to strip clubs. Flat roads. Areas like this always felt more dismal on bright, hot days like this one. Gas vapors evaporating off the street like risen souls. The malnourished homeless glistening on the sidewalk with cardboard signs that say truths or untruths for food, money or drugs. Under the glare of the sun, areas like this were stripped naked and the unnaturalness of it all became obvious. It takes the form of some kind of desolate, alien landscape.

I chose to exorcise my preoccupation with sex first because it was the aspect of post-breakup depression that most bothered me in a superficial—and thus more easily rectifiable—manner.

Before she broke up with me in front of a couples' therapist, Riley and I hadn't fucked in three months. She hated when I said "fucking"—she preferred "having sex." It felt less aggressive, that's what she said. But she wasn't here anymore so, Riley and I hadn't fucked in three months.

It began like I imagine most ill-fated relationships do: with us meeting up once a week to get drunk and fuck in the back of her car on a dark street. We would roll off each other, our nakedness hidden behind the fogged windows, and she would giggle and say, "We're gonna kill each other." And like any good example of foreshadowing, that almost became a truthful statement for less enjoyable reasons.

One day, we were sitting on the patio of a bar we'd return to again months later to cry and discuss my mental illness, but today we were talking about putting down dogs. How it was important to take the back exit after the vet did it so the people in the waiting room wouldn't see a man holding a large box who had walked in with a dog and no box. Riley agreed, and so this seemed like a good time to tell her I didn't want anything serious. I just wanted to be friends who fuck, and she said, "Friends who have sex," and I said, "Yeah," and then she said, "Me too. That's all I'm interested in." So naturally, three months later, we made the most popular mistake that people make, which is to fall in love.

This was the next order of business. "Okay, now you need to picture this—" I gripped the steering wheel and came to an abrupt stop at a crosswalk. The pedestrian I almost killed slammed on the hood of my car and gave me the finger. I ignored this and returned focus.

"Picture this: She will not love you anymore. She will fall in love with someone else." I forced up the image of her smiling with a man's arm around her shoulder. She squeezes against him and reaches up to kiss him. He has no face. It doesn't matter what he looks like, it matters that she is in love and she has forgotten me. She rises on tiptoe as he leans over and they embrace for an awkwardly long time because they're in public. She did not do this with me but she does with him because he is not me. He takes her hand and chews on her fingers like I used to. She looks into his eyes and her eyes narrow and the ends of her lips curl into a subtle smile and her dimples show and her nose crinkles because that's how she looks at someone when she is in love. I watch her mouth open and she says, "I love you."

"There. That wasn't so bad, buddy. That's good. Don't let it go away now." I felt the sharp jolt in my chest that comes with self-pity, and inhaled hard until I thought my lungs would burst. "You don't have to like it. But don't go anywhere. This will happen. Accept it." I thought about the softness of her hands, how I may never feel that safe again. "I accept this. People fall in love all the time. I wasn't the first and I won't be the last. These are things that happen. I accept."

I let the image drift off behind my eyes and the knife in my chest dislodged. The thought occurred that I was beginning to paint myself as the victim, but I understood that it was either deal with the reality of the situation head-on however I could, or continue to bloat myself with alcohol every time these epiphanies presented themselves. So far, running away from them resulted in little more than a feedback loop of increasing hopelessness and a kiddie pool's-worth of vomit.

I glanced at the empty bottle of Jose Cuervo rolling beneath the passenger seat, and decided that I would blame that bottle. Fuck you, bottle. I'd blame the pedestrian I almost killed. I'd blame the Yankees, the stock market, Scientology, chicken pox, McDonald's, Ecuador, raccoons, bad breath, cancer, the fucking world. I decided I'd put some of the blame on whatever I could if it alleviated an ounce of the self-hatred I felt for knowing I lost the love of my life. Fuck it all. Fuck the world. Take some of this weight off me and I'll take some off the tab you owe for putting me here in the first place. Anything had to be better than knowing you were the villain.

This was the part where I would talk about what the relationship was like when we were in love, when things were good. I'd tell a story to illustrate what it was about Riley that made me love her, something to add depth to the character in this story who was a very real, three-dimensional person. But I realized, as I swerved between semi-trucks and oblivious dog walkers, that I couldn't think of a fucking thing. This person I'd spent a year of my life with was nothing more than a ghost. Always just out of reach. I thought, maybe that's what happens when *you* walk through life like a ghost, a few seconds behind the moment. Maybe we were a ghost couple that floated through life together. Maybe I would never know who she really was.

I'll talk about New Year's Eve, when Riley and I went up to the mountain to stay in some friends of hers' cabin, when I realized I loved her. I brought a grocery bag full of everything I'd written up to this point, and she stood beside me as I burned it all in a stranger's fire pit. He watched with impatient eyes and a beer in hand. The stars were visible and the night was cold, and I wore the improper shoes to be standing in three feet of snow. Our silhouettes were lit up orange and gold next to the flames and I watched three year's drunk, depressed ravings wither away into black soil.

I looked at Riley and she smiled. I smiled, and for the first time in my life, I was hopeful. Hopeful for a future in the eyes of this person, hopeful I could leave behind the past and find happiness with her. Hopeful that the darkness of the night was the only darkness that would remain in my life, because if this person loved me back, then maybe I wasn't broken but simply cracked. And cracks could be mended. Golden fillings in otherwise fragile porcelain, like the Japanese teacups I'd heard about and put far too much merit into the metaphor they represented.

That night, I had my first panic attack in front of Riley, and this was when I knew for certain that it was love. The stakes were real, and somewhere deep inside, I knew there was no gold to put me back together. The ticking clock was set, counting down until the gravity of life pulled my pieces apart and left me scattered in the dirt.

Of course, this was all in my head, I reminded myself, but self-fulfilling prophecies were as real as anything else if you believed them. I didn't understand that that night. Feelings didn't exist in a vacuum, though, and one person was never to blame in these situations. I put that idea into practice by slamming the steering wheel and screaming, "LOVE YOURSELF. FUCKING LOVE YOURSELF, YOU PIECE OF SHIT," and I knew this wasn't the correct method but it was the closest I could get because memories were forcing their way through unmended cracks like a failing dam.

I could detail our downfall: how the panic attacks and depressive fits increased, how Riley lost patience and grew cold. How, subconsciously or not, she saw the self-hatred glowing beneath my skin and allowed me to take the blame for everything she did to avoid taking any herself. How I thought my unhappiness was inherent and not a result of her unwillingness to compromise or treat me like I treated her, not a result of her anger and manipulation. How the sex dried up as her respect for me drained, as I became so desperate to hold on to her that I let her treat me how she wanted, because if she stayed with me then there was hope that I wasn't, at the very base of me, unlovable. But this is a story, not a goddamn journal entry, so I dropped these thoughts and lit a cigarette next to a homeless man reaching through the window to ask if he could bum one.

Accumulated in a pile on the passenger seat was a small cache of items Riley had given me. It dawned on me that I could not spend another second with the knowledge that they remained unharmed. I pulled beside a dumpster situated against a porno store. On the inside of this establishment, men crowded together, separated only by thin stalls, masturbating in tandem to rented videos of women recorded doing things for these men's pleasure—women who were daughters and mothers and sisters, now no less daughters and mothers and sisters, but who were now all those things while also fucking themselves with GMO-grown cucumbers and dishwasher-safe dildos in front of a camera.

I thought about if Riley had ever made a sex tape—and if so, how I could find it—while I threw the lavender spray into the dumpster. She had gotten it for me to spray on my pillow before I slept to help with the nightmares. It didn't help but I liked that she got it for me. I threw away the Guatemalan worry dolls she got me on a business trip in California. They were supposedly used by real-life Guatemalans before bed to combat anxiety. They were voodoo doll-looking things that came in a little, wooden box. You pulled one out before bed, and tell it all your worries. When you were satisfied with the amount of fear and shame you vomited upon an inanimate object, you placed it underneath your pillow. In the morning, allegedly your worries would be gone, taken on by the little twig-and-straw worry doll. This didn't work but I liked that she got it for me.

I continued throwing objects away, banishing the memories that came with them, until I reached the last memento of Riley's existence in my life. It was an old business card from when she worked as a pole-dance instructor. Not a stripper, she reminded me. A pole-dancing instructor. She gave it to me when we were still friends who fucked to prove to me that when she was my age, she used to be skinny.

On it, was Riley with her head back, straddling a pole in nothing but black lingerie. She pointed out the tattoo of the 1600s ship visible on her waist so I knew it was really her. I told her I needed to keep it for research purposes, and used it for the rest of our relationship as a bookmark. I would stare at it every day, in awe that this person loved me and found me attractive.

Looking at it now only reminded me that I failed in an immense fashion by letting this go. So I decided that I would pretend I was a character in a movie, the protagonist in the pivotal scene where he moves on with his life and forgives himself, instead of continuing to masturbate to his estranged ex. I lit a cigarette and held up the card for one last good look, then pressed the red ember against the center of her chest, anticipating a dramatic circular burn to appear, imagining the triumphant orchestra that would play in the background when they made a movie about my life.

But the result was a dark smudge of ash glazed over her body and the smell of burnt wax. She was unharmed. Disappointed, I placed the cigarette back between my lips and took the more direct approach of a lighter. A weak flame coughed out at the bottom corner and fizzled away, leaving nothing but a stronger scent and a blackened edge. I frowned. Riley was indestructible. I would never get away from her. I sat in the dirt, thinking about the unnerving metaphor, folded the card and tore it into as many pieces as I could, leaving them scattered on the burning, flat ground.

There. Close enough.

I got up, returned to the car, and forced myself to drive in the direction I'd been avoiding. I would still be on time.

Next exercise: You will never be friends again. You will forget about each other until the day you die before her.

I pictured my life alone.

This wasn't as difficult: I pick up my phone, text Riley hey, and the message doesn't go through. I call her to wish her a happy birthday and my number has been blocked. We see each other on the street and she walks past me as if I am already dead, a ghost haunting her space. A harmless, pointless, impotent ghost.

"Now accept it," I said. "She hates you. Accept it and let it go." This wasn't as hard as the others. I saw this one coming from the beginning. I had never remained friends with any of my exes, and though we told each other we were best friends, I knew a bond like ours with the strings of attraction and emotions attached was bound to be broken. "I accept," I said under my breath, calmer this time. Tears came but no sounds escaped with them. "I accept that I have lost my best friend and we will never talk again."

Our first three months together were some of the best months of my life. I kept waiting for the moment my mental illness would erupt through the cloak of sanity I'd fashioned, but it didn't. We were happy. We took trips to the coast, drank in bars until the sun came up, fucked in hotels, and recognized that each of us was the best partner we had ever had. We were very, very good to each other. She was good to me. After two months of bliss and low commitment, I started to believe that I was no longer crazy. That I might be able to hold down a relationship after all, and the only reason they hadn't worked in the past was because my partners were the crazy ones. I was just the victim of poor choices.

We had met at work, a place we were hoisted into by necessity, a simple job that paid little and demanded less. Every day after clocking out, we would leave together and go to the bars to drink and talk while the sun still shined outside the heavy, blacked-out doors. I was recovering from a violent and tumultuous relationship, one I had taken the blame for, so made the point of hiding the deeper issues beneath me with the rationalization that if I could pretend to be normal, then maybe this one could work.

Her mother was an abusive, bipolar alcoholic who dragged Riley across state lines whenever the warrants were about to catch up. She told me stories of being locked out in the family room as a child while her mother fucked anonymous men from bars or in exchange for pills. One of these men Riley had met a single time was the man she was named after. She stole Riley's ID to run up every credit card she had. The reason she gave for this was, "You are my child, and your money is my money." Riley is still crawling her way out of the hole her mother dug for her, a decade later.

She would tell me all this, a little more each day as she became more comfortable, as she sat closer to me until we were holding hands everywhere we went. She hated her mother and never forgave her—but she laughed about it, joked about it. She was the best actor I'd ever seen. I began to believe her childhood hadn't affected her. I would nod and say her eyes were pretty, repressing the urge to share any trauma that may have hinted at the person I really was. Riley knew I would lie and hide things—I was not the actor she was. But she was falling in love with me. She didn't care about any of that. To her, I was the best in a long line of abusive relationships that always ended in abandonment, and we both knew I would never leave her.

I think she loved me for that more than anything. For the first time, she would be the one to break a heart. And we both knew I would let her.

Riley was the most beautiful woman I'd ever met. The sex was the best I'd ever had. Those days all blurred into a single liquor-spattered, euphoric night. This was the woman I was going to spend the rest of my life with. I felt safe. I was encompassed by her maternal instinct, forged in the absence of her mother's. She was everything I'd always wanted.

Then there was the night of the company Christmas party. It was a week after our trip to the mountain, and I had been panicking and morose since we'd gotten back, fearful that my cover of sanity was blown. She was on to me.

I'd been drinking at the Guilty Sparrow before Riley and her sister picked me up—the latter I'd only met once. The resentment was bubbling inside me. *She knows you're broken now. You couldn't hold it together. This is who you are. You'll destroy it all like you've destroyed everything else.* I was terrified of what my behavior at the cabin meant for me, what it meant to Riley. I was cracking.

The entire night was spent avoiding Riley—talking to her sister, talking to coworkers, drinking everything I could get my hands on until I was well on my way towards blacking out. I would walk out of the room every time she entered. It was my way of sabotaging what we had in anticipation that my actions had already set in motion the doomsday clock. I wouldn't let it happen to me, I'd do it myself before she got the chance. I was angry with her for the *possibility* of an outcome. Crazy.

Riley soon began to notice that something was wrong. I held my alcohol to a staggering level of professionalism, but when drinking to numb a bad mood, I become vitriolic. The words came out like a sober person's, but they were tinged black. Pessimism and irritation slid off my tongue. She pulled me away from the party and asked what was wrong, but I don't remember this. Apparently, I refused to answer and insisted on heading to the bar down the street. "Fuck all these people," I told her. "I don't wanna be around any of them."

So Riley, her sister, and I ended up seated together at the end of a bar. No one wanted to be there. I don't think I even wanted to. I just wanted to leave where I was.

After having a conversation with her sister about how great it was to meet her, and how much of a bummer it was that I would never see her again because Riley was going to break up with me soon, I was accosted by a man I didn't recognize. Or I thought I was accosted, but it was more likely a polite introduction that I took as aggressive. I don't remember what he asked. But my response was, "I hate people."

"That's cool, man," he answered. "Totally, me too. But like, I was just asking if you saw the game." Or something to that effect.

"No," I said. "I fucking hate people." I was becoming irate, raising my voice more each sentence that escaped. "I fucking hate people and I hate the world. I hate myself. I want to die but I can't do it because I'm a fucking pussy. I hate myself." From here on, I don't understand how it escalated to where it did, but the interaction ended with me screaming at the man, threatening to beat him the fuck up, as Riley and her sister stared on in horror. The bartender kicked me out before I could lay a hand on him though, and Riley ran out ahead of me, bawling. When I caught up to her, the regret tore through the center of my chest. Her mascara was ruined, her eyes puffy and red, fear and confusion rippling across her face.

"I'm sorry, I'm sorry," I said. "I don't know what's happening, I didn't mean to hurt you. I didn't mean to."

After that, I made her drop me off at another bar where I drank until closing, somehow able to keep ordering despite my state. Someone later found me on the street, babbling and falling to the ground over and over again like a newborn horse.

I should have died that night.

The next day, I was shaking and sick, and after work, Riley and I walked to the bar where months before we'd decided to just be friends who fuck, and I was forced to explain to the woman I loved that I was major depressive, had an anxiety disorder, had PTSD, and was probably bipolar. I was an alcoholic and an addict and I didn't like myself. Actually, I hated myself. I was very unstable and it was too difficult to hide it. That I loved her though, and I was sorry I never told her and would understand if she wanted to walk away.

She still wouldn't.

The biggest regret I had about that night wasn't anything that would have changed the outcome. I would have found another night to fuck up. No. I just wish I told her how pretty she looked in that dress. Instead, I got out of the car and walked away from the most beautiful woman in the world without a word. I hate that.

After that night, Riley began to worry. At 31 years old, she left our job and got a better one: 401k, salary, medical benefits, real responsibilities. She was transformed into a career-oriented adult. I was knocked down as a priority. I was becoming a problem she didn't have time for. This hard-drinking, fighting, nihilistic 24-year-old she had fallen for was becoming a burden. Our ages were showing and we began to grow apart. She worried that she was making me grow up too fast, but I told her I wanted to. I wanted to grow up with her, grow old with her, and leave behind the flaming path of destruction I'd been on for a paved road of domesticity. She didn't buy it and, deep down, neither did I.

Our nights became slow—less euphoric, less frequent. I wanted a drinking partner I could fuck, and she wanted a boyfriend with more concrete goals than being a writer and surviving the night. She would get angry with me more often for behavior she had enjoyed before. I began to feel guilty and resent her for it. She was moving forward with her life, and I was unwilling or unable to move with her.

It turned to every ending in a fight about my drinking, my depression, my anxiety. We would be sitting in a bar, my face buried in a drink, unable to speak through the shroud of malaise, and she would sit there beside me, crying, knowing that there was nothing she could do any longer to help me. I was too far-gone, and I would drag her beneath the water if she let me. "We love each other so much," she told the therapist on the last day I saw her. "But I just can't do it anymore. I've got nothing left."

Sitting here, I realize I'm having difficulty writing about the good times, what made us friends, how it started that we fell in love. But it was just a look, a feeling. This unimaginable warmth and safety I experienced when she was next to me. When she had her arm around me, I honestly believed that I would never die. For a time, we believed we would be together forever. I can't describe it. Some people just connect.

I could tell you about my favorite night with her. I've told her it was one of the best nights of my life, and Riley said, "All we did was wander around bars, getting drunk and eating food." And she wasn't wrong. I guess I'm a cheap date. But there was this moment long after midnight. We were in a small college town to spend the night in an Airbnb. It was the first trip we took, no longer than a month together.

We'd been drunk for hours, and while waiting for a cab to take us back, stumbled into a dive bar somewhere on the strip of road that this place called its downtown. We sat at the bar, holding on to each other and kissing like we'd known each other for years, and she ordered our drinks. Then somewhere beyond the fog of my drunk, a burlesque dancer came onto the stage across the room, wearing the traditional feathers and fishnets, like a flapper girl. An old, sleepy ballad from the '40s came on. Over the dizzying piano and lilting violins, the woman began to sway and twirl across the stage in her high heels, removing clothes only to cover them expertly with decorated fans. She sang with the low and sultry voice that echoed out into our ears. We watched, mesmerized by the performance. I looked at Riley, smiling past me, at the woman, and I returned to watch, holding out my hand. She grasped me and pulled me closer to her body, and I thought, there is no one in the world I'd rather watch this with.

"*Bali Ha'I*" by Peggy Lee. I'd never had a song with a girl before. You know, like *our* song. I remember it came on in the car one night towards the end of the relationship as I drove her home and she yelled at me for being depressed and always ruining the night. I tried to stop it from happening, recoiled and apologized for not feeling well. I turned up the music and whimpered, "Listen baby, it's our song. Remember?"

Riley grew quiet and looked down at her legs. A tear was running down her cheek. "Yeah. I know," she said.

The streets were returning to a wholesome ambiance: green lawns and full trees lining clean houses. I was getting closer. The drunk was wearing off so I looked around the back of the car for any stray bottles I may have left the night before. There was nothing. The fear was returning, bringing along a rapid heartbeat and sweaty palms that made it difficult to keep my hands on the wheel. I watched the people in the cars next to me as I sped past, hoping to catch a glimpse of the pain in their faces that I felt inside me. I tried to remind myself that everyone goes through this. Everyone doesn't feel good sometimes, even if it's all the time. I waited for that insight to sink in and help, but it didn't.

"Okay, buddy—most important thing now. You gotta do this." I held a hand against my chest to steady the trembling. I would be there in less than ten minutes. That was ten minutes to figure out how to fix it. "Forgive yourself. I know this is hard but I need you to do that, okay?" I tried to picture something that I could then let go of, but found it difficult to compress the entirety of my mistakes with Riley into a single image.

Then it came to me. The personification of everything that was wrong with me, why I destroyed everything good in my life that I ever touched: Rebecca.

Rebecca and I started hanging out when I got out of the hospital. She was another coworker. (I know, I know. I know how to pick 'em.) I'd been out of work for a week, hanging on to my sanity alone or as alone as one could be while in the company of barflies. She texted me, asking if I was alive and if Riley and I wanted to hang out. I told her Riley and I weren't seeing each other and I was alive but didn't want to be.

We met up at a bar by her place. She told me everyone at work thought I tried to kill myself, and I said it inspired confidence that that scenario was the first people would jump to if I disappeared for a few days. I told her Riley backed off because I was unfixable and she deserved that break. Rebecca told me she was breaking up with James, her boyfriend of two years she moved with from Utah. He also worked with us. (I KNOW. I get it.) That night, it became clear that I'd never met someone so similar to me. Our minds were the same. Our souls followed the same frequency. We had known each other for years before we'd ever met. She fell in love with me the first day we talked.

Sometimes that just happens. She attempted suicide at 20, filled the hole in herself with anything she could (but to her credit, largely with more positive things), wrote like I did, thought of the world like I did, felt the despair I did. More than anything, she shared the flame I held inside me—the flame glowing within that special type of stubborn person who is painfully aware of the anguish of the world but still has the need to find some meaning in it. She was my friend and I needed her.

My health deteriorated. I crashed my car, spiraled further into excessive drinking and smoking, and failed to return to work for several more weeks, choosing to lay alone in an empty apartment, failing to feed myself, swirling into panic attacks and manic episodes every time the phone rang. I begged Riley to help me, to come see me and feed me the love I so desperately needed from someone, but she refused. I was not her problem. She needed to focus on her life, and I needed to suffer alone. I was abandoned. I shouldn't blame Riley for this, but the agonizing memory of those weeks still bring a burning anger to my chest as if I'm putting a cigarette out on it.

Then Rebecca came to see me. She saw the state I was in and refused to leave. We would spend every day together as soon as she got off work, where she would slowly nurse me back to health and take me out of the house, tolerating my suicidal ramblings and moans with a smile and comforting words. I would hold her hand and began to feel the love that I needed. She was filling a gaping hole, unaware of the crack at the bottom where her affection steadily leaked out, requiring more and more to satiate. But she didn't care. She loved me.

Soon enough, I grew the strength to return to life with the hope that Riley would take me back if I wasn't the person I was—if I was better. A new man.

To my surprise, she did.

I worked my way back into Riley's good graces, a tedious process involving the illusion of friendship until it briefly evolved into the sexual relationship we'd once had. But she knew something was different. The looming specter of Rebecca's love and influence remained as shadows on the walls of our repaired home.

Rebecca and I continued to see each other while Riley and I were at arm's length. I was open about this, and Riley wouldn't do more than raise an eyebrow and make jokes about how I had "a second girlfriend."

Which wasn't as far off as she may have thought. The day Riley instigated the break, and Rebecca and I were free to begin our sexual relationship—we did. So I had to sit down with Rebecca once it was clear that Riley was willing to accept me back, and tell her I couldn't see her anymore. Her ex had threatened to kill me (a story you're now familiar with) and I felt myself slipping back into the nihilist hedonism I exhibited during a time where I was even more ashamed of myself—a time I vowed never to return to.

With Rebecca, I had given up on living well, seeing no point in bettering myself because no matter how hard I tried, I was nothing more than the cracked shell of the human I'd been born into. For reasons beyond me, Rebecca accepted me.

But now that Riley was willing to give me a chance, I saw a light at the end of whatever hole I'd fallen into, and left Rebecca—quite literally—sitting alone in her own tears. I told myself it was for the best, that it was my only way back to a place where I could be deserving of Riley's attention, but somewhere in me I knew the truth: All I had done was trade one source of love for the another, unwilling to admit the damage I was causing.

So back to my comeuppance. I was more unable than I'd hoped in masking the guilt of my actions, and Riley— always able to see through my acting—knew exactly why I was behaving strangely. The domestic bliss we'd fought our way back to lasted no more than a month. We promptly returned to the fighting and paranoia and lack of sex that had marred our relationship for half a year.

By the end, it had been three months and I'd been complaining. Riley finally gave way and told me, "Have sex with whoever you want, because I'm not going to with you for a long time. But don't tell me about it."

I took this as, "Have sex with Rebecca again."

So I did. My drunken logic was that I could have the hedonist and the saint, the excitement and the domestic life, and I would keep them separate. Never having to ask Riley to drink and fuck, but only to love me—and never having to be in love with Rebecca, only to drink and fuck. I thought I'd figured it out, the great conundrum. I could have all I needed, and no one would care. Everyone would be happy. Riley and I could work. Of course this was the worst decision I ever made. This decision blew up in my face. Save your applause.

The last night Riley and I spent together as a couple, we were not happy. We were walking on eggshells at all times to avoid getting the other upset. It was the end and we could feel it. We were sitting out on the patio of a jazz bar, letting the trumpet and drums roll over our heads with the soft, summer wind, and Riley asked, "Did you and Rebecca have sex?"

I wasn't going to lie. "Yes," I said. "But I thought we talked about this?"

That was when the relationship ended. We broke off from each other at that moment and floated away like icebergs in the night. She accused me—all humor and sarcasm gone from her voice—of having a surrogate girlfriend. That it could have been anyone but her. Why did it have to be her?

I was almost relieved. A part of me knew the whole time what I was doing was wrong. I was finding a loophole in the contract to fill the loneliness that Riley couldn't or didn't want to. The right thing to do would have been to break up with her the minute I met Rebecca. I was never 100% hers after that night, no matter how hard I tried to tell myself I was. But the fear of being alone outweighed the knowledge that I was forcing the heads of others underwater so that I may float

for just a minute longer. I was a weak swimmer. And never
accepted the fact that some people should just drown.

To be honest, I think I wanted to tell her about
Rebecca. Because maybe then I could extract out of her the
attention and love that I wanted so fucking much.

The love that I was crying out for. The love that she no
longer made the effort to give.

Maybe then she wouldn't abandon me again. I would
have abandoned Rebecca right then and fucking there if I could
have gotten that back.

Weak.

Don't leave me here. I can't swim.

"Now please, let go of it," I said to myself. "Let go of this
and move on. Go be a human." I took the exercise as seriously
as possible, forced myself to sit in the stink of my bad
decisions. I saw it all run behind my eyelids like a movie reel:
every moment I'd gone wrong, every disagreement and
depressive fit and Rebecca Rebecca Rebecca. I let the memory
of Riley spin circles around me until I became dizzy. "You
fucked this up. You destroyed the most beautiful thing the
universe was ever kind enough to grant you. You will never
see her smile, hear her laugh, feel her hand, be inside her, be
enveloped by her, watch dumb movies with her, drink bad
whiskey with her, listen to the silly health podcasts in the car
with her that she likes and you try to because she does. You'll
never hear her say your name again. She's gone. She's gone
and it's because you drove her away. Now accept it. Forgive
yourself and accept it."

The tears were coming again, and I stifled the urge to
reprimand myself for it.

One memory at a time, with each flash of regret and
despair, I threw it all away into the imaginary dumpster in the
back of the porno store that was my mind. Like they were
nothing but corrupted files on my computer, one by one. Drag
and drop. Drag and drop.

Delete delete delete. Until all that was left was the
image of Riley smiling, looking at me with narrowed eyes and
curled lips and dimples and crinkled nose because that's how

she looks at someone when she is in love, and at one time she was in love with me.

"Let it go, Henry. Please let it go. Forgive yourself, buddy. We gotta keep going, I won't let you not keep going. Please." The tears burned salty and hot like acid across my cheeks. The noises started coming. The whines and chokes and sobs. They all came rushing out. The crack in the dam had burst open. "Let her go. Please."

Someone was honking. *Honk honk HONK HONK HOOOOONK.* I looked over my shoulder. A man in the car behind me was screaming and flipping me off. His face was scarlet and twisted up in rage. I turned back around and saw that the light had turned green. I apologized loud enough for myself to hear, swerved across the intersection, and skidded into the parking lot, pulling up in the corner spot. I was here.

I got out and stretched in the abrasive sunlight, letting the wavering drunk acclimate to solid ground. I climbed up onto the hood of my car, lit a cigarette, and took out my phone. The parking lot was empty. I scrolled through recent calls until reaching her name. It had been a week since we talked. I breathed in the smoke, pressed dial.

There was no ring. Straight to voicemail. I hung up. I began to feel nauseous.

Okay, send a text—say anything. **Hey,** I said. **Hey.** The message failed to send.

Again, call again. The phone trembled against my ear, and the familiar robotic voice told me Riley was unavailable. It hadn't rung. I waited for the beep.

"Hi, Riley. I'm at the therapist's and you aren't here. You said last week we could meet here next week and that's today. So we can work on being friends. So I can still be in your life. I would like that. I would—ah. Fuck." I breathed out smoke and let the realization wash over me. "But you, uh, you blocked me. I'm talking to no one, aren't I? You aren't coming." I let the phone slide into my lap while the wave of panic rattled my insides, then I returned the phone to my ear to continue. "I get that." I wasn't sure what to say so paused and let the pregnant silence between her ghost and me undulate before repeating,

"I get that. Yeah. Goodbye, Riley. For a while there I was honestly happy. That was nice to have. For what it's worth."

I hung up. The sun was setting enough that the orange and red began glowing through the leaves and branches hanging above me. Like the tree was on fire. The wind was calm, just soft and cool enough to wipe the exhaustion from my face. It was a beautiful day. It was nice out.

I dragged the last of the cigarette, tossed it on the cement. "Forgive yourself, Henry," I said. "Please forgive yourself. Please, buddy. Forgive yourself." I pulled out another cigarette, lit it, and sat on the hood of my car. "Please."

It was warm out. I'd sit there as long as I had to.

AUGUST, 2018

It was between my drunker friend and me. Well, maybe not drunker but I held my alcohol better than Colin, so she chose me. Sometimes I could pull off the illusion of charm despite the quantity I've consumed. Sometimes.

I noticed the scars on her forearm once we were all in a circle, talking and smoking in Ellen's backyard. Ellen was the mother of the children she babysat. She was the daughter of a woman who was a regular at my bar. I hesitated to say my bar, thinking the bar might help me save face, but if I was going to be honest about her, the least I could do was treat myself with equal honesty. It was my bar. I went there a lot. The money I'd spent alone at the Guilty Sparrow could, and probably did, pay for a renovation or two. I tried not to think about the amount of dollars I'd stuffed into empty whiskey bottles.

Her mother was beautiful, and she looked like her mother. She was 19. Her eyes were brown and her hair was black and hung just above her shoulders. She complained because she cut her bangs too short but I told her I liked them fine.

Her stepfather was an asshole. He went to the bar too. He had tattoos and a long beard and black, beady eyes that suggested fear, which explained why he was an asshole. I told her I didn't like him and she agreed but it was her mother fucking him, not her, so she didn't have a say in any of it. I liked her mother's ex-boyfriend though. He was smart and charming and also had a long beard and tattoos. He rode motorcycles and was a ward of the state for many years as a child. He said he wrote and told me he was good. I believed him. He liked that I wrote. I liked him better than her stepdad and she agreed, but told me he used to beat the shit out of her mother. I remembered that after she said it. Her mother would come into the bar tearing up, with makeup poorly concealing a black eye or a cut or bruises on her arms. She still liked him anyway.

The scars were a deep reddish-purple and crisscrossed over each other all the way down her left arm. They were raised high on her skin like mountains on a relief map. She made no attempt to hide them. It was warm out but most people hid those kinds of things.

There were no scars on her right arm. She was right-handed.

I told the group I was getting my first book published. They were excited for me and we toasted to my success, and she looked at me different then. I told everybody I knew as soon as I got drunk, despite the fact that I was trying to keep a low profile, and despite the fact that the publisher who accepted it was a sketchy, small press whose main export was bad sci-fi and fantasy—the kind that sold ten copies and only got reviews from family members who were the only people who bought them. The editor wrote vampire fantasy novels, and published his work through his own company.

The editor didn't like me. He thought I was a prima donna because I refused to make any social media accounts to help sell the book, and I required threats of voiding the contract before I would give them a picture of myself for the back cover. He hadn't read the book, and thought I was an entitled fantasy writer—not a paranoid, alcoholic depressive. Here, I realized that I was setting my first book up to flop, and that had been setting in. I didn't tell them any of this though. I smiled and said thank you and drank.

She grabbed my knee and pulled herself in closer to me while Ellen's neighbor Chris talked about his well-endowed son. His son was aware of this and refused to wear clothes around the house. He was studying to become a yogi and move to India. He and his girlfriend fucked in the shower while Chris was home, but he wouldn't listen when Chris told them to stop. She and his son are both 19 so Chris had tried to set them up before he met the shower-fucker. He was awkward though, and they didn't get along, but she said that she should've taken him up on the offer, knowing what she knows now.

Riley broke up with me a month ago, and I'd been fucking anyone I could to forget about it. I drank too much every day, blacking out every night, and snorted up anything that wasn't Flonase. I was unemployed. I was fired bright and early the day after our aborted second visit to the couples counselor. That same day was when I found out I was going to be published, while taking shots at the bar at eleven in the morning and contemplating the most direct method of suicide. This part will come later.

I fucked a bartender until we ran out of condoms, and then went without after she told me she was clean because her fiancé she had broken up with a week prior had only been with one other girl in his life. I continued fucking Rebecca until things got uncomfortable and I didn't like looking at her anymore. She reminded me of why I don't like myself. I fucked my friend Marcus' partner, Rita, but was so blacked out that I couldn't get it up for long enough to come, so we fucked once more after that. We spilled an entire bottle of red wine on her carpet but I came then. Now I wanted to fuck the 19-year-old pressing her leg up against me in Ellen's backyard.

I traced my finger along the scars while she talked. She didn't seem to mind. Today was the best day I'd had in a long time. I'd been drinking since the early afternoon, and from across the apartment complex's parking lot, I could still hear the blues band playing, the last reminder of the street fair that'd been going on since the morning.

I met her earlier in the day, outside the Guilty Sparrow with Ellen, while a homeless woman let me hold two kittens she was trying to sell because she couldn't afford to spay the mother cat that wouldn't stop fucking. The woman chain-smoked as she held the kittens and watching it made me uncomfortable. It was loud and bright out, and the kittens were so young. They cried and meowed in my arms. I worried that I was scaring them and wanted them to be safe, so I asked the woman to put them back in their carrying case.

It was the end of the summer. I could feel it dying at night under the stars. The air was growing colder again, and the sun disappeared an hour earlier than the last time I noticed. I was trying to hold on to the summer, but didn't know why because it'd been a horrible summer. This was the best day I'd had in a long time. I don't know why.

Colin weaved his way around the circle of people, on his phone calling other people. He did this when he got drunk. He needed to be somewhere new, always. Always moving, always where other people are. Marcus and Rita were here earlier but they left to go to our friend Lauren's graduation party at a different bar. That was where he wanted to go. I didn't want to go there, though. I wanted to stay and trace my fingers along the razor scars on this 19-year-old's arm. So I did that instead.

The book I was getting published was all about the choices I made. How I got stuck in a cycle, a pattern of self-destructive behavior, and how it would eventually lead to my death. The idea was I would write the book, and through the self-exploration that writing the book required, I would cure myself of the self-harm and sabotage that plagued my entire life up to that point. Eight months later, the book would be on shelves across the country, and I would be no closer to breaking that cycle. In fact, I was deeper in it. I lost everything. I clung to the bottle in my hand and the girl beside me harder than ever to grant a respite from my thoughts. I was not better. This book would do best to remain unpublished. I should check myself into rehab or leave the country to dry out or chop off my balls and become a eunuch, but tonight I wouldn't. I was leaving with her.

At around one in the morning, people started clearing out. I stood and she asked if I'd take her home. We walked out and I looked up at the stars and told her how I'd gone out to the country 30 miles south of the city last weekend to see the meteor shower, but because of the smoke from all the forest fires, I couldn't see anything.

She nodded and went *hmmm* but was uninterested in this. I took her hand to try to be charming. It was working and she tried to be charming back. She was much more confident. We stopped at a street corner and she said something else charming and we kissed. Our tongues slid inside each other's mouths at different times. Our rhythm was off but I liked her, I didn't mind.

Her house was a couple blocks down from Ellen's place. She could have walked but wanted me to take her because she wanted to have sex, and I thought about how life would be easier if we all just said what we meant, but I thought about it again and decided it might not be as interesting that way. We needed games to occupy us. Mystery was part of sexual attraction. It was only once we started opening ourselves up to another person that the attraction dissipated. Well. At least in my experience.

Her roommate was a 60-year-old man. Before I could ask something inappropriate, she told me he's also her landlord and she pays rent. He leaves for weeks at a time so she often gets the house to herself. The house was nice. We started kissing again and she led me to the bedroom, her hand gripping mine behind her back like a mother elephant with her tail wrapped around her child's trunk. Every woman I'd ever met who invited me over told me not to judge how dirty her room was, and every time it wasn't. So when she said this I scoffed and walked in. It was neat: books stacked atop a dresser, books I'd read but didn't tell her because I was distracted by sex.

"I'm not kidding," she said. "It's gross. Don't sit on the bed." I asked why, and she lifted the blanket to reveal a faded, red stain covering the mattress and a grainy, white substance spread over it. I assumed that she had her period in bed but she told me she fell asleep with a glass of wine in her hand and threw salt over the stain to soak it up. "I don't know how long you're supposed to let it sit for," she said, "so I'm leaving it there and sleeping on the other side until something happens."

I followed her back into the living room.

"We can fuck on the couch or on a bed of salt, it's up to you," she said.

I was indifferent but she seemed inclined towards the couch so I sat while she poured us boxed wine in the kitchen.

We took a drink and got back into what we were doing. She straddled me and I took off her loose tank top. The right nipple was pierced with a barbell. Stage left.

"Why do you only have the one piercing?"

"I didn't have enough money for the second one. I came in thinking it was two-for-one but it wasn't."

"Nipple piercings should be like shoes."

She stuck her tongue in my mouth to shut me up. I tried to hike her dress up her thighs. "No, it's a skirt," she said, and stood in front of me to slide it off. It was long and black and had constellations of little red roses on it. But it was gone now. I was staring at her naked body. A tuft of black pubic hair stared back at eye-level. I pulled off the rest of my clothes, wrapped a hand around the small of her back and waist, and let my weight guide her to the carpet.

She gave me soft, moaning vocal cues to keep doing what I was doing with my hands or tongue or teeth. "Bite me," she said. "Harder. I like that." I bit her neck just above the shoulder and tasted sweat, then bit her earlobe and she made the noises I'm listening for. I ran my hand over her breast to play with the barbell, then back down along her torso. I stopped at something crusted across the side of her hip, about two inches long. Beneath that, I felt another patch but deeper, the depression in the skin like a trench above her bone. I lifted my hand and looked down, and she began sucking on my neck as her hand found my cock. I saw four long scars across her hip, each above the other like etchings on a prison cell. The top two were deepest. I saw dried blood still filling the open space inside the gash. I sat on my knees and deliberately stroked the healing wounds with my middle and index fingers. The blood was a vivid black through the shadows of the living room. The hairs on my arms stood up but I didn't know why. The scars didn't bother me.

"These ones are new," I said.

She sat up. "Why don't you mind your own business, sweetheart?" Her voice climbed to a higher, playful octave but I could see that this made her uncomfortable. "Now fuck me." She handed me the condom to put on, and I made a comment about trampoline-ing but that word was lost on her. She raked her nails across my back once I was inside her. She said, "What do you want me to do?"

I was happy with the situation so didn't say anything, but she said it again, her legs lifted towards the ceiling in a V, "Baby, tell me what you want. I just want you to be happy. That's how I get off. Tell me."

"I want you to talk to me," I said.

"Yeah? That's good, honey. Keep fucking me. Use me. I want that."

I listened to her voice bounce and break when I thrust into her. I felt her.

I felt her nails and her warm breath on my neck. I felt her scars against my hips. It occurred to me that this was the first time since the breakup I hadn't thought about Riley while fucking someone else.

"Henry, use my pussy. This is for you. I wanna be sore after this. I wanna lay here and take it for you. I wanna pleasure you."

I spoke back and was there with her. Not three days ago. Not three months ago. I wasn't five seconds, five minutes, five years, five girlfriends ago. I was inside her and nothing else existed. Fucking. Zen.

I let go. I rammed into her as hard as I could. Stabbing her with it.

"Oh God, it hurts," she said.

I was about to stop but she kept going, "I'm gonna be sore for days. I'm gonna feel you for days. It hurts so much." She liked it.

I went harder, exerting all the energy I had.

"Henry, it hurts. It hurts so much. You're stretching me out."

I couldn't tell what was real anymore. I stopped. "Are you okay?"

I pulled her out of the spell. Her eyes returned from the back of her head. Wild and wide eyes looked at me. They were only brown. Most eyes had specks of black or orange or yellow floating around in them, but hers were pure brown. Lit up brown, like looking at the sun through a beer glass. "What're you doing?" she asked. "Keep fucking me. Hurt me."

"Hurt you?"

"Choke me. Fucking choke me." She was screaming now. "Do whatever you want with me. I want it. Fucking use me. Let me be your sex doll."

I pressed my dominant hand against her neck until she coughed, so I eased up, but she told me to keep going. I couldn't. The scars scratched against my skin like sand paper.

"Do you wanna come on my face?" She wrapped her legs tight around my waist, pulling me in as far as she could, as if she needed it—all of it.

"No, I wanna come inside you."

"That's good, yeah. Fill me up. I want you to be happy. Whatever makes you feel good. I want it. Take it, Henry. It's yours."

Riley didn't even enter my mind.

I came. I grasped at the carpeting and pulled her hair, holding on to the sides of her head as leverage as I thrust long, deep strokes inside her. I wanted to be as far in as I could. I wanted her to envelope me.

It didn't stop. It kept coming in waves. My whole body twitched. I was swearing, being loud, I could tell. I buried my face against her neck and bit down so she won't see the ridiculous face I was making. The room disappeared.

The walls fell away. The carpet burns on my knees floated down beneath the floor. There was no Riley, no unemployment, no failure, no depression. There was nothing else. I needed this.

"I'm sorry," she said, standing with wobbling legs and collapsing back on the couch. "Sometimes I go too far into the sub thing." Her hair stuck up in all directions like she'd been struck by lightning. The bangs were long enough to cover her eyes. Beads of sweat ran down the insides of her legs.

"Sub thing?" I asked, and sat beside her. The wine tasted better than before. My head was clearer. I couldn't remember why I'd been depressed.

She curled her legs over my lap and stretched out with a glass in her hand. "Sub. Like submissive. Some guys don't like it. I get carried away sometimes. You weren't hurting me yet."

"Oh. No, I like it. I'm not sure where the line is though. I couldn't tell there towards the end."

"That's alright. That's why I have safe words," she said. "Green, yellow, red.

Green..."—she reached over and kissed me with the edge of her lips—"means you're good. I like it, keep going. Yellow..."—she wrapped her small fingers around my neck and squeezed enough that I felt the pressure on the inside of my head—"means this is okay but don't get any crazier yet.'"

"And red," I said. "Red means—"

Her hand slid from my throat to cup my balls. She tugged hard and I winced, almost spilling the wine. "Red," she said, "means stop."

"Got it," I said through clenched teeth.

She let go.

"I got it."

"We probably won't need that system until you start tying me up, hitting me, things like that. But I'm telling you now so you know."

The room was coming back into focus. On every wall were photographs of a woman. She had white hair and glasses. Wrinkles were starting to take over in the corners of her eyes and cheeks and forehead. She wore typical, unassuming clothing for someone her age. All the photos looked recent. "Who's that?" I asked, pointing to the picture that seemed to serve as the room's centerpiece.

"That's my landlord's wife."

"So that's your competition?"

"No," she said, ignoring my joke. "She's dead."

"Fuck," I said. "This room just got a lot creepier. She didn't die in here, did she?"

"No, at a hospital. Long, painful, drawn out death at a hospital. Cancer."

"It's always fuckin' cancer," I said.

"I know, right? It's like, be more creative."

"So no ghosts?"

"No ghosts."

Now that I was aware of the woman's fate, it was as if the eyes of each photograph were following me from every angle of the room. The air felt static. Funny, how a single piece of information could alter your surroundings. I paused before saying what I was thinking. "Can I tell you something?"

"Yeah," she said, taking the glass out of my hand to refill it in the kitchen. I saw red streaks going down her back as she walked away.

"I'm not a happy person," I said. "It's hard for me to feel good unless I'm doing something bad to myself. I don't know how much longer I can keep this up."

She talked into the box of wine from across the room. "What's that, honey? I couldn't hear you."

I looked at the pictures of the dead woman watching me. Through the window, the faint red halo of the sun peeked over the purple horizon. The stars within the belt of orange it created were fading away. I wouldn't get this back. "I said, I haven't been fucked like that in four months."

She came back with two full glasses, put one on the coffee table, and stretched her arm to hand me the other. I looked down at the scars. They could've been years old. They weren't going anywhere. "Glad you're happy with it," she said. She leaned over, laid her palm against my cheek and kissed me. It stung when she bit my bottom lip. "Do you wanna go again, Henry?"

"Yeah," I said. "Before the sun comes up."

JULY, 2018

I step out of the car and recoil beneath the morning light. My eyes have difficulty adjusting through the hangover. I'm ten pounds lighter, retching from stomach pain, and have allowed my beard to grow out for too long, giving me the appearance of a dope sick street kid. I am back to displaying my discontentment for everyone to see. Forever a "misery loves company" kind of person. I'm not proud of it but it's a reality.

We all have weaknesses.

The bender has persisted like a virus since Riley left me, and I have no intention of letting up. I've just got on a good roll here. I intend to walk into the office, smelling of misery and pussy and six different liquors. This is me giving up. This is my "I couldn't care less if you fired me" face. Look at that smile.

Walking along the parking lot towards the door, I wave at the homeless woman screaming and banging her fists against the chain-link fence next to the sidewalk. She mostly comes out at night and screams about the government, her sweatpants dirtied from soiling herself, slapping herself in the face out of a frustration, but today is one of those days she's amongst the working class.

Like a raccoon so sick with rabies that it's unable to return to hiding until the moon comes back.

I catch the eyes of my two bosses through the glass door. Their eyes are wide and frightened. They tear through the entrance before my hand touches the knob and line up side-by-side, blocking me from coming in, as if I would bust through with force. One is Kyle. He doesn't like me and I don't like him. He's 30, overweight, with a bald patch at the crown of his head that's been eating away at the black hair but no one will tell him. It looks like a clearing in the middle of the forest. He hands me an envelope and I'm aware of what's happening.

Tom speaks first. "You can't come inside. Here, walk over this way with us."

They don't want people to see me getting fired through the window. It would be bad for morale. Rebecca is in there, working with her ex who has a micro penis, and I know this because she tells anyone willing to listen. Norman is in there, pinching Rebecca's ass every time he's alone with her. Joseph is in there, drinking pinot noir out of a can of La Croix. Alex is sitting at her desk, eyeing Joseph in the hopes that she can catch him in the act and snitch her way up the corporate ladder. Harold is in there, recovering from last night's coke binge. Everybody hates everybody else but no one says it until someone leaves the room. But *I'm* bad for morale.

There's a long pause. I hold the check in my hand. Two years wasted at this place. The best thing I got out of the experience was fucking two of my coworkers. The bosses know this. They have no real reason to fire me, any more real than why they could fire any of the others. They just don't like me. I know this. They fire people when they don't like them. They don't like me because I don't like them.

"Look," Tom says, "we all knew this was a long time coming. You haven't been pulling your weight for months. You come in late and sulk around and ruin the mood of the office."

What else, Tom? What else? Tell me. Tell me you smell the pussy. Tell me you smell the liquor on my breath.

"And it's time for you to move on. I don't want you making a scene, and we need you off the property or we'll call the police."

Kyle hides behind Tom's wide frame. Tom is one of those golden boys: handsome, built, played football on scholarship, got right out of school and started a business. Fucks his girlfriend who looks like a Barbie doll until you get her face wet. I've suspected that he fucked Riley before me. We stopped getting along after he found out I was dating her. I'd fuck his girlfriend for equilibrium but she's not my type.

"Is there anything you wanna tell us?" Kyle pipes up.

"No," I say. "You made your decision already. I'm not begging for anything." I begin to turn around.

"Oh wait," Kyle says, "you need to sign this." He hands me a clipboard and a pen.

On the clipboard are some words about me.
Underneath is a line for my signature.

"It's just to state that we lawfully terminated you and
you got your last check."

"Of course," I say. I sign and hand it back with my
signature: **Fuck you**. "Hope that works." I spit on the ground—
an unsatisfying glob of viscous white from dehydration—and
walk back towards my car. I know what I'm going to do.

Chaos. I want chaos. Give me chaos.

"Henry, wait!" Rebecca's voice stops me as I'm getting
into the front seat. She comes running up and pauses before
speaking. "What happened?"

"Fired," I say. "Got the boot. Terminated. Voted off the
island." The heat is getting to me. I'm uncomfortable standing
under the sun like this. My legs feel like they won't be able to
support my weight soon.

"They can't do this," she says. She seems visibly hurt.
"This is bullshit."

"Fuck 'em."

"Please don't go drink."

"Of course I'm gonna go drink. I've been broken up
with, blocked, and fired all in the same flaming shit-pile of a
week and change. This is the prime example of when someone
should go drink."

"Henry, it's 10 in the morning."

"Good, then I'm getting a head start."

"This is just gonna make things even worse. Think
about the morning."

"You don't get it," I say. "I've got nothing. I'm fucked.
I'm sure in a few days I'll have some clarity and see that things
will be fine and I've got something to live for but right now I've
got nothing. And maybe things won't be fine. Maybe this is it. If
I'm ruining my life then let me enjoy it for a minute. I don't
care anymore.

"Don't give me that shit," she says. She's getting angry.
Her face grows narrow. "You've been enjoying this the whole
time. You like destroying your life. You see that, right? You're
not as big of an asshole as you think you are, but for some

reason you keep trying to live up to how you see yourself. Get better. Stop doing this."

I step back into the car and turn the ignition. "You got a cigarette?"

Rebecca ignores me. "I'm gonna call you after work, okay? Be safe. I'm serious."

"Yeah."

Stupid piece of shit idiot you don't deserve her you deserved to get broken up with you deserved to be fired you deserve to hurt yourself you're broken you're unlovable everyone hates you everyone should hate you do it do it do it hit the car hit that car faster you pussy do it no one will ever love you you'll destroy everything you ever touch your brain is broken drink until you're sick then people will see you're sorry punish yourself until people know you're in pain I hate you.

The beauty of dive bars is that they remain dark no matter what time of day it is. I sit in the corner beside two older women. One recognizes me. She's the mother of a girl I slept with. She doesn't know that though; she thinks I'm gay. I can't remember why she thinks that but I'm not interested enough to clear it up. Telling her I fucked her daughter might do it, but again, this doesn't seem like the time.

"Hey, it's you... Harry!" There are lipstick stains on her teeth. She drinks the same beer I always see her drink. She comes here every day.

"Henry," I say. "Yes."

"We're celebrating!" She points to the bartender, a short, balding man with discolored teeth. "Get Harry whatever he wants. I'm not dying!"

The whiskey shot lands in front of me and I drink it before speaking. "We're all dying. Don't fool yourself."

"No!" she shouts. "I got the blood results back, I'm not gonna die!"

The woman next to her coughs up something onto her sleeve, wipes it underneath the bar, and slams down her hand. "Well, goddamn! Margaret, you dumb slut, I told you it'd be alright!"

"I know, I know! I'm gonna be okay!" She smiles wide, revealing the receding gum line that's turning black from age and cigarettes. "Today is gonna be a great day!

Another one for Harry and Tammy!"

Hurt yourself. Drink until you hurt yourself.

Another one goes down.

I order a third. My head swims. I drink and am reminded I no longer have a source of income. I am unemployed. My 31-year-old with the 50-grand-a-year salary and the fear of intimacy is gone. There is no rope to climb out of this.

I step outside and the contrast between the darkness of the bar and the light of the outside world strikes me behind the eyes, like looking at the reflection of the sun on a piece of metal. I sit down next to the soup can people use for an ashtray and look for her number. It stares at me for a long time before I dial *67 and call. Six rings come. They are long and painful and with each pause, my breastplate dislodges itself farther away from my chest until all that exists is the heavy, fluttering heartbeat. It bounces against the inside of my body like a bullet in a steel room. Then the familiar robotic voice: Leave a message after the beep.

"Hi, Riley. Yeah. It's Henry. I know you hate me and you never wanna see me again but I just got fired and I need that money you owe me. So unblock me and call me back. Or don't. Just send the money in some other way that doesn't require communication. PayPal. Venmo—well, I don't have that one. Send a carrier pigeon with a check if you want. I don't care. Anyway. I'm gonna stop talking now. Bye."

Unsatisfied with the message, I call to clear up any confusion that may get in the way of me getting my money. It doesn't ring this time. "The number you are trying to reach is unavailable," says the robot. A young couple walks past me with their child. She wears a pink dress and has a hairband with Minnie Mouse ears on it. She holds a balloon in her right hand and her father's index finger in the other. The mother smiles when she sees me looking at them.

I get up and go back inside the bar.

The only problem is that if I'm not going fast enough or I hit the tree at the wrong angle, I may survive and wake up as a quadriplegic. Or brain dead. Then what? You're depressed and crippled. Or if you kill someone on accident while you're on your way over the cliff. Then you wake up depressed, crippled, and handcuffed to a hospital bed.

Then you're really fucked. Can quadriplegics get prison time? Where do they go? Are they let loose into the general population like everyone else? Do vegetables get prison time? Or is that a free pass if you go into a coma after whatever crime you commit?

Someone must know this shit.

"What're you thinking about?" Margaret asks.

"Nothing." I drink down the next shot. I've lost count. The world is blurry. It's easier to find the humor in dark things now. That's always a sign. You get that warm, fuzzy feeling when you think about punishing yourself. That's another sign.

"What happened to you, man? You look too sad for someone your age. You're not supposed to look like that for at least another...twenty years. You'll give yourself wrinkles."

I look at myself in the mirror. I hate you.

My phone vibrates inside my pocket, filling the space where a proper answer would have to go. There you are. Right above the bottles, under the clock you can't read, all lit up in neon. Nothing's changed. What're you going to do about it?

"Hey! Are you gonna get that, Harry?"

Kill yourself or run away and do something with your life or go to rehab. Get another job. Do anything. As long as it's not nothing. You can't sit here and do nothing. You did nothing for three years and got a book out of it and now you need to change. Nobody wants to read another boo—

"It's buzzing, man! Don't you hear that?"

Nobody wants to read another book about a guy who never did anything with his life. You're writing the same goddamn story over again—you see that, right? This isn't an option. You've lost all the ties that were keeping you here. Either kill yourself or—

"Hey, Harry!"

"YEAH FUCK, ALRIGHT."

I answer the phone without looking at who's calling.

I don't recognize her voice at first. Through the poor cell service, her words come out garbled and masked in static. "Henry. Helloooo. Henry?"

"Yeah, Rebecca."

"How are you?"

"I'm good. Margaret isn't dying. We're all good."

"Where are you?"

"Say hi to Tom and Kyle for me."

"Are you at a bar?"

"Tell them 'fuck you' for me. Tell Tom I fucked Riley better. Make sure to tell him that."

"What are you talking about?"

"Did you know that? Tom fucked Riley and so he doesn't like me. He thinks he can fire people for being Eskimo brothers but you can't do that, Rebecca. We live in a society. We have laws. We have laws to maintain order, Rebecca."

"Jesus, Henry. You're drunk."

"Bingo."

"I'm coming to get you in an hour."

"Nope."

"Yes, I am. You've been getting drunk at the Sparrow for four hours. You're gonna come help me run errands."

"Shit. Has it been that long?" I look up at the clock with one eye closed. The hands' doppelgangers fall back into themselves then come back into focus. "Well, how 'bout that? You're right. I guess time flies when you're having fun!" I hold my hand over the bar until the bartender high-fives me. "Hear that? I'm making friends, Rebecca. Companionship. Don't worry about me. I'm fuckin' aces, baby."

"I'm gonna be outside in one hour. Answer the phone when I call."

"Yes, ma'am." I lean in towards Margaret, pointing at my phone with one hand over the speaker, and whisper, "She's mad at me."

"Bye, Henry."

"See ya later, home-wrecker."

"What?"

I hang up and order another drink.

Could you even find a gun? You could ask James, I'm sure he'd love to help you out with that. His was nice too. But what about those stories about guys who aim a centimeter off and blow out a chunk of their brain to survive as disfigured freaks. Or miss entirely and their jaw explodes. Shelve that for now. You have Ativan. How many Ativan does it take? There's no way they gave you enough, they're not stupid. But what if you drank enough with what you have? Like a lot. Like a fifth. That would have to do it. I've heard pills are the most painful way to go though. But that's what you're looking for, aren't you? If you wanna be hurt so bad. Are you a pussy now too?

"During couple's therapy?" repeats the bartender. "That's heartless, man."

I clap and throw my hands out by my sides. "I FUCKING KNOW, RIGHT? It's not just me—she's a bitch, am I not alone in this?"

Nods from the group.

"Tell me at least you didn't have to pay for the session," Tammy cuts in.

I look down at my drink and smile with my teeth, embarrassed.

The room erupts, "AW, MAN, C'MON."

"I think I'm the only person in history that had to pay 50 bucks to get dumped."

"Jeeeesus, Harry," says Margaret. "Well, we know why she left you then... You got no spine!"

The room erupts again: "HAHAHA!"

Tammy reaches over Margaret to place her hand on my shoulder, knocking over an empty glass on the way. "Look at it this way, kid: You got plenty more years to mess up. Best to get 'em outta the way while you're young."

"Okay, okay, I'm not done though." I shoot down the whiskey, click my tongue to diminish the burn. "And...and! Wait for it... I got fired today!"

The group emits a long, collective groan.

I'm laughing, struggling to get out the words. "And—hahaha—and! The girl who destroyed it all is coming to get me right now! I'm friends with the home-wrecker! Hahaha. The girl who tore apart my relationship still has her dirty, home-wrecking claws in me! I can't even come while I'm fucking her unless I think about Riley! Ha! ...Ha."

The laughs slow down. The bartender's eyebrows raise and he bares his teeth in an awkward grimace. Tammy looks at the bar and pats my back. Margaret drinks from her beer until it empties.

Reality washes over me and I slump forward. "Shit," I say. "There's a real fine line between funny and depressing."

There's a pause, then the bartender comes with another full shot. Some of it spills over the glass when it touches the counter. "Hey, man, you're lucky. You know why? You're free! You can do whatever the fuck you want! My girlfriend won't let me do anything as long as she's around. It's a prison. I can't smoke, I can't drink, we can't fuck unless the lights are off—and even that's once a week at the most. She's got my balls. But you know what? Right now we're here! We're off the hook. I come to work and I play country music—"

Margaret interrupts, "I've been meaning to talk to you about that, Bill."

"I play COUNTRY MUSIC"—the bartender turns up the volume. Hank Williams fills out the corners of the room until his voice echoes—"I smoke as many cigarettes as I want, and I get to talk to people like you. While we're here, there's no worries in the world. What's her name?"

"Riley," I say.

"Fuck Riley!" he shouts. "Drink that and forget about it. It's that easy."

I take the shot. I sit in the burn as it slithers down the center of my body. I try to stay with the pain for as long as it exists. The bartender is wrong. We aren't free. We're more trapped than most people. It's just easier for us to forget that.

My phone vibrates again. It's too soon to be Rebecca. I take it out of my pocket and on the screen reads, UNKNOWN CALLER. This should be sending a stabbing panic up through my stomach. My pupils should be dilating. My palms should be sweating. My face should be going pale.

Unknown caller means someone found me. It means someone wants to kill me. It means there's a death threat on the other side of this conversation. It means my life is about to be torn apart. My delusions should be sending my body into shock.

But it doesn't. I don't care anymore. Come kill me. Great timing. Bring it the fuck on.

I answer the phone. "What the fuck do you want?"

A long, uncomfortable pause drowns the space where my paranoia should go.

"Um. I—uh. This is Henry Gallagher... Correct?" The voice lilts to a warm chirp to disarm my aggression, then back to a weathered growl like sandpaper against rock, the way a man talks to another man in a professional setting.

"How do you know that?" I say. "Look, you know where I am: the motherfucking Guilty Sparrow like always, so come down and put one right between the eyes, big guy. I fuckin' dare you. Give it to me, baby. One-way ticket to Dead Town, population: HENRY. Let's do this."

Confusion thickens the voice on the other line. "Excuse me, Mr. Gallagher... I think there's a misunderstanding here."

I look around and realize everyone is staring at me, so I get up and walk outside.

When the sun hits, I suppress the vomit at the back of my throat. "Alright... Who is this?"

"Ahem... This is David West, editor for Lighthouse Publishing. You sent us a manuscript a few months back; we apologize for the delay in getting back to you. ...You're the author of *The Skipping Record Waltz*, correct?"

I stare out at the row of buildings in front of me. People go in and out with bags in their hands, children on their arms. Dogs are tied up and left at streetlights while their owners buy things they don't need. I don't understand what's happening. Was *Lost Weekend* real? Can you drink yourself into insanity? Could I reach out and touch these people if I wanted, or would everything fall away into the padded wall of an institution?

"Yes, I wrote that," I say. "Who did you say you were?"

"David West, editor for Lighthouse Publishing. Look, Henry—Can I call you Henry?"

"Sure, Dave."

"Great. Henry, I'm gonna cut to the chase: We've read your manuscript and are offering you a publishing contract."

"You're fucking with me."

"No, I'm not... *joking* with you. We'd like to publish your book. We'll have *The Skipping Record Waltz* in major bookstores across the country, in libraries, military bases; audiobook is another option, along with the opportunity for book signings if that's something you're open to. We'll print, market, and sell your book. You'll get a 25% royalty rate for all books sold, which will go up to 30% once..."

I realize that this is an important phone call. I'm wasted for one of the most important phone calls of my life. The voice on the other line drifts away behind a shrill ringing in my ears, but the ringing doesn't hurt. It's not alarming. It's like violins. Thousands of violins playing inside my head. I feel a smile rising across my face. I feel like screaming, crying, laughing, dancing, singing—anything other than melancholy numbness. I feel present again. It's like my blood remembered that at some point it stopped flowing, and with one burst of electric life, every vein erupts with vibrancy and returns to its forgotten purpose, like watching the power come back on in a major city after a blackout.

"Hello? Henry? Does that all sound good to you?"

"Yes, yeah," I say. "That sounds fine."

"Great," David says. "I'll send you over the contract by Wednesday and once you sign, we'll get started. What kind of work do you do?"

"Nothing," I say.

"Oh. For how long?"

"A couple hours."

"Well. I hope this turns that around for you. Congratulations, Henry. I'll be in touch."

"See ya, Dave. Sorry for the murder stuff."

The call ends. I'm shaking. I sit in the sun for a while, my mouth hanging open.

This is one of the best and worst days of my life. This calls for celebration.

I burst through the door and sit back down in the corner. The reflection in the mirror is grinning a big, fat, stupid grin. Everyone is looking at the reflection in the mirror.

"Well," says Margaret, "who's coming to kill you?"

"No one, Marge. No one is. I'm getting published."

"I don't know what that means," she says.

"I'm getting published," I say again. The words inflate and barely fit out my mouth as I say them. They're the best three words I've ever spoken. "I'm getting my book published."

"Book?" says the bartender. "I didn't know you wrote."

"I'M GETTING...MY FUCKING BOOK PUBLISHED." I can't contain the weight and size of the words any longer. They crawl out of me like a great beast. "FUCK THAT JOB! FUCK RILEY! I'M A PUBLISHED FUCKING AUTHOR."

"Wow, that's something," says Tammy. "Y'know, I just love that Stephen King fella. Now that's a writer, I'll tell ya."

I ignore her. My body is on fire. This is the happiest I've ever been in my life. I'm 24 and this is the happiest moment of my life. "ROUND OF DRINKS ON ME," I shout. "YOU'RE MY

BEST GODDAMN FRIENDS, WE'RE IN THIS TOGETHER NOW. BILL, YOU DRINK TOO. C'MON, MAN!"

We spend the next half hour drinking and laughing and slapping each other on the back because we're drunk and I'm getting published and we're friends now. Even Bill sneaks a Jell-O shot once he's out of view of the camera.

Then it happens. Like a black wave of sewage water, it strikes the back of my muddled head and pierces through the contentment. The elated lightness floating up through my chest is pushed down, and cobwebs are rebuilt in the darkness that replaces it. The universe gave me thirty minutes.

And now I am back. While the people around me laugh and spill their drinks, my attention is brought back to the face in the mirror.

Look at you. This won't work out. This won't change a thing. You will still find something to hate yourself for. You are still you. No matter what you accomplish, no matter who you trick into loving you, you know who you are. You are still broken.

I am sinking further now—no, spinning—as if I'm attached to the end of a great big drill, and I'm being ground into the hard earth until sunlight barely peeks behind the soil and worms. There holding the drill, looming above me, is God, and at that moment I become completely submerged, until I can no longer draw breath, until it's all I see. I am left there, a corroded screw serving no purpose but to infect the roots of the plants above with my rust.

The one thing that I have wanted my entire life, the single accomplishment that I always told myself would save me from the pit, what I told myself would finally make me happy, has happened. And I am still miserable.

The greatest thing I have ever done in my entire life made me happy for thirty goddamn minutes.

My head sinks back into the drink in front of me. The smile fades. The world turns eight shades darker. I no longer have something to celebrate. I have another tragedy to drown in liquor.

My phone rings. Rebecca is here.

I close my tab, stumble out across the sun-glinted street, and collapse into the passenger seat.

Rebecca is there staring at me, trying to gauge at what level of inebriation I reside. "You have fun?"

"Yes. I made friends."

"You told me."

"Good, I'm glad. Let's get a bottle."

Rebecca turns off the corner, heading for the freeway. "No. Not until we go to the mall so I can return some clothes. Today you get to practice self-restraint."

"Clothes? CLOTHES? This is no time to return CLOTHES!"

"It is for me. And obviously I can't leave you alone."

"I'm not a child," I mutter, picking at some lint stuck to the collar of my shirt. It's not until this moment that I realize I'm still wearing my uniform.

"I didn't say you were." She slaps my shoulder. "Now put on your seatbelt."

The mall is one of the first places I think of when it comes to reinvigorating my suicidal tendency—along with strip clubs at two in the afternoon on a weekday, classrooms with florescent lights housing masses of insects like state-run morgues, and the intake room of a county jail—so today of all days, a particular prickling excitement pulses inside my chest as we pull up to the Jefferson Square Mall.

Rebecca grabs my arm and leads me towards the entrance as an obese couple holding overfilled tote bags lumber past us. They smell like grease, like they were standing over a deep fryer for an hour, letting their odor waft over and sting my nostrils. They are a perfect encapsulation of what I picture awaits inside, and the prickling warmth intensifies.

Rebecca says something about needing shoes and hangs a left once the doors open. The smell of heavy perfume assaults my nose and twists around the greasy residue from the couple outside. I don't know what store I'm in but there are mannequins everywhere and they wear cashmere sweaters and high-waisted shorts and I hate it here. Women are staring at me so I follow Rebecca into the aisles. Hundreds of shoes.

The aisles aren't tall enough to hide between so I plop on the carpet, at Rebecca's feet like a hound and light a cigarette.

I can see the wheels spinning in her head before she turns around to identify the smell, dropping a pair of boots. "Henry, what the fuck are you doing?" she snaps, horrified. "Put that out."

"It smells awful in here. I'm clearing my palate."

A puff of gray-white smoke floats over the aisles before Rebecca snatches the cigarette out of my mouth and smashes it into the carpet.

My eyes widen and my face lights up. "That's destruction of property! Look what you did! *Ooooooh*, the mall cops are gonna arrest you!"

"Shut up. C'mon." She pulls me onto my feet and hurries away before the old women catch on. "Please just behave yourself for twenty minutes, can you do that?"

"I can certainly try, home-wrecker."

"Stop calling me that."

I follow for a few minutes before taking off towards the exit, where the mall opens up and my fear of open spaces takes hold. I wander along the storefronts, wearing my sunglasses as a shield to combat my social anxiety, until reaching a Starbucks. I order a tall black coffee ("Whatever the small one is."), and mention to the barista something about how I'd stick my head underneath the espresso machine if I had to work her job. I then say something about how the urge to end one's life is totally normal, and follow that up by asking if they're hiring.

They aren't.

I shuffle back through the aisles of lingerie before spotting Rebecca at the checkout desk. She's talking to a pretty blonde who stands straight and looks like she's never been dirty in her life. They're talking about how much she can get taken off the price of new clothes for selling the old ones. It's painfully unriveting so I jump up and sit on the counter between them.

"What's your name?" I ask.

She's can only respond with an uncomfortable chuckle and a tap on her nametag with a manicured fingernail.

I lean in and close one eye until the name comes into focus. "Do you like your job, Alicia?"

She shrugs and returns to the transaction, but I continue with the drunken belief that what I have to say is more important than their capitalistic endeavors.

"You should quit. You don't need this job. This job needs you. Empty that register, pocket the cash, and let's get outta here. You and me, let's go get drunk. What do you say, Alicia?"

Now that I'm unemployed and thoroughly intoxicated, I've decided that the American nine-to-five job is slavery of the masses, and it's my duty as a newly enlightened radical to set free the Great Unwashed, one young, attractive, working-class woman at a time. Content with my enlistment speech, I lean back and pull out another cigarette.

A look washes over Rebecca's face like she's watching a man gouge his eyes out with a spoon. Nobody speaks.

I try to elicit a response after recognizing that the silence will go on until I fill the uncomfortable space I've created. "So," I continue as I light the cigarette, "you mull that over, Alicia. Decisions like this are a hard choice to make, I get it." I drag the harsh smoke in and cough phlegm into the back of my throat. "But look at me! This is a free man you're looking at! You're looking at pure happiness, Alicia. Let's break those shackles!"

Rebecca grabs me by the shirt, pulls me off the counter, and whispers, "Get the fuck out of here and wait for me outside. You're gonna get us arrested."

"Good!" I walk backwards towards the exit, the cigarette limp between my lips and the middle finger on my good hand pointing to the ceiling. "Let 'em! I'll become an icon for the free man! I'm Nelson fuckin' Mandela, Rebecca! See these wrists? No shackles, baby, no shackles!"

With that, I crumple onto the sidewalk to sit underneath the dull white sunshine and wait for Rebecca. With no audience left to witness my antics, the humor drains away. The thoughts and memories I'm trying to suppress bubble up and spin like a merry-go-round, and the overpowering urge to drink returns. I recognize, as I sit on the hot cement in front of a Macy's in the middle of a summer Monday, there is nothing short of suicide that will free me from this bear trap of a life I've stepped into.

I tell Rebecca that I'm not getting back into the car unless she drives me to a liquor store, so she does and I pick up a pint of Jim Beam. Typically, I'd go for Old Crow to punish my body as much as possible, but today I'm still trying to hold on to the vague notion that I'm celebrating. The image of my arm outstretched through the car window fades in and out behind the formative stages of a blackout.

The coffee splatters across the passenger door and wicks off in the wind.

"What did you just do?" Rebecca asks.

"Nothing," I mumble, refilling the half-empty coffee cup with whiskey. I sip the bitter drink as we move at a glacial pace through rush hour traffic down the highway. Rebecca tells a story about how she thinks a guy she's been seeing is ghosting her because she let him fuck her in the ass and she accidentally shit on his dick, but I'm tuning in and out because I've found a bump on the inside of my lip and realize it must be cancer. My tongue runs back and forth against the protuberance as I catch some of her monologue:

"It was everywhere. It was all over him, all over the sheets. I'd heard about that kind of thing happening but that never happened to me before."

I indulge her. "So, then what happened?"

"I mean, he was cool about it. He was like, 'It's totally fine, I can change the sheets,' then he jumped in the shower."

I laugh. "And then what did you do?"

"I waited until he got out and he said I could still stay but I was like, 'I think I'm gonna go home now.'"

"And then you did?"

"Of course I did. I couldn't even look at him after that." She grimaces and moans, "Ohhhh my GOD, Henry! That's so fucking embarrassing, of course he ghosted me."

"No, see, that's where you fucked up," I say. "You have to stand by that shit.

Literally."

"That's not funny."

"No, listen to me. You should have owned that shit. Owned it. Said, 'Yes, I shit on your dick. That's my shit right there on your dick. You defiled my ass with that thing and this is an all too typical consequence. Now embrace this situation and accept me.'"

Rebecca keeps her eyes forward and remains silent. I pull down on my bottom lip and lean over to study the bump in the rearview mirror. "Hey, Rebecca," I say, eyes trained on my reflection. "What's the survival rate for oral cancer?"

"Not low enough. Where do you wanna go?"

I forgo the liquor mixture in my cup and pull straight from the bottle. "Bar."

Rebecca exhales like she's blowing out a cloud of cigarette smoke. "Henry..."

"Look," I snap, "either you can come with me or you can drop me off and I'll go somewhere by myself." I hear the anger coming through the words slogging off my tongue but can't stop it, my mind too muddled by the mist growing thicker from the alcohol.

"Alright, Henry," she sighs. "I'll come with you to a bar."

"Okay then." I sit back and drain the contents of the little, white cup. "Thank you."

The bar's walls are an unattractive shade of white tinged yellow after decades of cigarette stains. The booths are a deep forest green that leaves black splotches where patrons spilled drinks or bodily fluids. The floors are carpeted.

This was a terrible choice by the owners. One should take the same consideration that a pet owner would before bringing home a dog that isn't housebroken. If I owned a bar, I would line the linoleum with layers of newspaper. This would cut down on custodial costs and present the ambiance of a hamster cage, but the trade-off would be worth it.

These are the only details that I can differentiate at this level of drunkenness: obtuse and abstract details, the kind of indistinct shapes and visuals that make up the world through the eyes of an infant. I don't recognize this place.

To cut down on the cost of a heavy drinking habit, I order a tall glass of soda water and situate myself in the last booth at the end of the bar. I pour half the glass under the table when no one is looking, and fill up the remaining space with the whiskey pint hiding underneath my shirt like an unregistered firearm. I must be dancing between levels of consciousness because I know my eyes have stayed open, but when I turn to the right, Rebecca is there looking at me.

"How long have you been there?" I ask. I feel my tongue swelling and struggling to form consonants.

"I've always been here." Her answer is ominous and I feel uncomfortable. Her lips are moving again. She starts to say something but I blink and an abrupt fog overtakes me, and when my eyes settle back into my environment, I'm at the bar with a drink in my hand. I've forgotten about the whiskey concealed in my clothing, or perhaps I've drank it all because when my hand slides down next to my balls, I feel nothing in the space where a plastic bottle should be. My back is to the bartender, and as I scan the sparse crowd for Rebecca, my line of sight is drawn back to a pair of eyes watching me from across the room. The eyes are piercing and yellow in the dirty glow of what little lighting this bar can afford. They belong to a large man. He stands, hunched over with a hand leaning against the pool table. These are the facts I know.

After a moment, I recognize the form of another man standing beside him. His eyes must not have been trained on mine when I first scanned the room because I didn't notice him, but now the large man is talking to the other man, and directs his attention towards me. Now there are two shadowed figures, large males, staring at me from across the bar.

I'm not unfamiliar with these looks, whether they're for good reason or just an assumption funneled through my skewed perspective. In either case, though, this moment demands action, and I vow to fulfill that demand. Whatever my response will be it, it requires a deft and diplomatic approach.

"What the fuck are you looking at?" I shout.

A few heads turn.

I'm not being clear enough. I point at the shadowed pair who refuse to break eye contact. "You! And you! What the fuck do you want?"

The larger of the two is first to speak: "Just checking out the view."

What kind of threat is this? Are these mind games? I can't think of anything clever or threatening enough so I settle on: "Well, stop it. It's creepy."

I look away. Where is Rebecca? Rebecca will be able to make sense of this. My feet make contact with damp carpeting and I set off on a mission to leave this place and find calmer waters. But as I search, all the faces look the same. They meld into one swirling soup of eyes and mouths and eyebrows and ears. The people become as inanimate as the walls and carpeting that reminds me of walking through a shallow bog. I'll never find her at this rate—she's become furniture.

Before I can communicate this to the man with the handlebar mustache and cowboy hat standing next to me, I feel the firm grasp of a hand on my shoulder.

"I have a question for you." It's the large man. His eyes are no longer yellow but a light brown. He isn't blurred like the rest of the bar. He's larger up close and the intimidating energy he exudes demands my attention.

"What do you want?" I try to appear formidable despite our six-inch size difference and my inability to keep balanced.

His face softens. I can make out the shape of a strong jawline beneath his beard. "Well, more like a proposition." His voice is light and bounces across the syllables, almost like he's singing a song.

"Where's your friend?" I ask, ignoring his invitation to inquire further.

"He's waiting." He points to a corner and waves, but all I see is a small gathering of similar-looking people crowded together like livestock. "Brandon likes me to interact with our potential business partners; he stays behind the scenes. I'm—"

"Creepy," I interrupt.

"The star." He smiles a subtle, crooked smile. This fucking guy is flirting with me. "Have you ever been on camera?" he asks.

"Well, I heard the government watches you jerk off through your webcam."

"Sure, that counts."

"Then probably."

"What's your price?" he asks.

"Excuse me?"

"Do you like blowjobs?"

I hesitate and squint at the large man. "Is this a test?"

He reiterates, "Do you like getting blowjobs and getting paid for it?"

"That's a loaded question. Who's doing the blowing?"

"Let me clear this up: We'll pay you a thousand dollars to let"—he points back to the corner and one of the faceless livestock waves at me—"that guy Brandon over there film you getting head. That's it. One grand to get a blowjob."

"Yes, but—"

"Tyler. Pleased to meet you."

"Tyler, who is doing the blowing? Who's doing the blowing, Tyler?" I don't know why I'm repeating myself. I already know the answer.

"I am." He winks. "The star."

"Right." I look over my shoulder: Blond hair, short, freckles. Where the fuck are you?

Tyler grasps my arm and pulls me back to focus. "Is that something you'd be open to? You'd be in and out in thirty minutes tops, dude."

"That may be a conservative estimate."

"You'd wear a mask," he assures me, as if this makes the offer less creepy. "Nobody would know it's you."

I study the man's physique and try to gauge how difficult it would be to imagine Scarlett Johansson is sucking my dick instead. Shit, I've always told people I'm about 6% gay anyway—13% if I'm drunk. I'd make out with Frank Ocean. And there was that bartender at the Blue Dolphin with the choker and that ass in those capris that elicited a certain unanticipated reaction out of me. A thousand bucks is a thousand bucks. A hole is a hole, right? "Are you gonna shave that small mammal off your face?" I ask. "I feel any stubble and I'm out, man."

Tyler laughs and rubs his chin, and before he can answer, a small hand touches my waist. Rebecca's voice twirls over the Motley Crüe song blasting across the bar: "Hey, Henry! Where the fuck have you been?"

I whip around. "Oh, hey. I'm talking to my friend, Tyler. He wants to blow me on camera for a thousand dollars."

Tyler waves.

"That's nice," she says. "I think we should go now."

"Well, hang on, we're negotiating." I turn back around and finish my liquor, misjudge where the nearest table is, and drop the glass on the floor. It hits the carpeting and remains intact. So that's why it's there. "Fifteen hundred plus 33% of the sales revenue... 33 and a third. You, me, and Gomer over there." I wave to one of the cattle. It doesn't wave back. I must have waved at the wrong one.

Now that a fourth party has entered the equation, Tyler becomes more reserved. "You know what? I don't think this is gonna work out. You have a good night, man."

Before I can reevaluate and renege on my counter-proposition, Rebecca pulls me towards the exit. She's saying something but I can't make it out. I'm fading again. It occurs to me that I can't recall how we got here or where we were before this.

The last thing I remember is tearing my hand away from her grip and yelling, "I'm buying a shot for the road." Then I blink.

"You know what your problem is? You need to lighten up." The man is bald with a trimmed, black goatee. His eyes are sunken and dulled. By the inflection, it seems like he didn't introduce the conversation with this point. He must be responding to something I said. When I fail to answer, he elaborates on his advice to fill the space: "I look at you and all I see is me when I was your age. How old are you?"

"24," I say.

"Jesus. You know what I was doing when I was your age? I was shooting heroin on a mattress in a foreclosed house with four other degenerates believing we were gonna be rock stars. Now, I can see you're not as far gone as I was. You've still got some of that light in your eyes, though you're doing everything you can to kill it. I'm sure you know that. But I'm gonna tell you something I wish someone had told me before I ruined it all by being a stupid fucking kid. I want you to listen to this. Really listen to me, Henry: Hating the world does nothing but make the world hate you back. I wasted my 20s being angry and sad, thinking the world owed me something—thinking I'd never grow old and eventually it would all make sense once I got X, Y, or fuckin' Z. But it doesn't work like that. I destroyed what could have been my happiest years because I thought it made sense to feel bad. And now I'm 50 years old. 50...Jesus. 50."

His eyes trail away, looking past me into the memories he wishes he could change or relive or erase altogether. Decades of memories this blacked-out 24-year-old has forced back to the surface. When the glaze over his gaze fades away, he refocuses. "You know what I know now? Despite everything I did to destroy my life and feel sadness and hate the world, those were still the best years of my life. Because I was young. I had the whole world ahead of me. There was hope, despite it all. That's why I thought I could throw it all away. I would never have admitted that at the time, but it was true. No matter how much I destroyed my life, there was this little flame inside me that said, 'Don't give up. There's still time.' But now I'm 50. There's no hope anymore. There's no time."

He lifts his beer glass in one smooth, mechanical motion through muscle memory, and drinks until it's empty, the bottom of the glass pointed up towards the ceiling, the foaming backwash that escaped the sides of his mouth running down his shirt.

"So lighten the fuck up. Appreciate what the fuck you have. Get your head out of your ass and smile, before you wake up one day and see a bitter, miserable old man staring at you in the mirror. And trust me, it will happen. Faster than you think. This whole depressed alcoholic shtick is a lot less charming when you're fat, middle-aged, and bald. You have hope. Do something real with it."

I blink.

The walls are blood red. The stools are red also, and they have tears in them. My stool wobbles when I sway too far to the right. Black lights glow in phosphorescent blues and purples across the graffiti tags covering the ceiling and walls like invasive mold.

Erratic punk music explodes all around me and drowns out any voices. There are paintings of naked women next to framed black-and-white photographs of midgets standing by slain bears hanging upside-down from ropes.

The bar is busy. The people look like me—they look like they're my age—but they have spiked Mohawks and facial piercings and wear black leather jackets with patches sewn into them that say things like "SUCK MY CUNT, I'M A FEMINIST," and "BORN TO PAY TAXES AND FUCKING DIE." I feel as though I've stepped into what Hell looks like to a Motörhead fan. I don't mind this place.

Rebecca must be here somewhere but I don't care anymore. It's become far too interesting to play time-traveler and see where this takes me.

"WHAT WAS THAT?"

My head jolts up from the wood counter. Someone is screaming at me over the music.

"CAN YOU HEAR ME? I DIDN'T HEAR WHAT YOU SAID, MAN."

I look over. It's a man. The man is trying to talk to me. He looks like Zakk Wylde. He looks like he sells drugs. Am I buying drugs from him? "I FORGOT WHAT I WAS SAYING," I scream back. "I DON'T HAVE MUCH MONEY THOUGH. I GOT FIRED TODAY." I pull on the collar of my shirt and point to my ex-employer's logo.

Zakk Wylde looks at me for a moment. He seems confused. "WHAT ARE YOU TALKING ABOUT, MAN?"

I point again. "I GOT FIRED TODAY SO I DON'T HAVE MUCH MONEY. CAN YOU FRONT ME? I'M GOOD FOR IT, MAN, I'M GONNA BE A PUBLISHED AUTHOR. YOU CAN BE MY PERSONAL DRUG DEALER. LET'S GO FUCKIN' HOLLYWOOD TOGETHER, MAN."

He pauses to sort through what I'm saying for anything discernable. "YEAH, NO— WAIT, WHAT? NO, I DON'T HAVE ANY DRUGS. YOU WERE TALKING ABOUT THE BOOK, MAN."

"FUCK THE BOOK!" I scream reflexively. "THE BOOK IS SHIT. PRINT IS DYING ANYWAY, FUCK IT. BUNCHA PIECE-A-SHIT MILLENNIALS TWEETING NUDES AND SKIMMING *BUZZFEED* HEADLINES INSTEAD OF READING A GODDAMN NOVEL. FUCK IT."

"BUT YOU'RE A MILLENNIAL, AREN'T YOU?"

"THAT'S BESIDE THE POINT."

"THEN WHAT'S THE POINT?"

"THE POINT IS…" I think about my answer. What has me so bothered? There's this drunken, little voice growling something inside my chest. He's hiding between my lungs, nestled up against my sternum. I allow the world around to grow quiet, and when I can make out the words, the drunken man inside me is growling so intently, I mimic the words to Zakk Wylde as if I'm the magnified voice filtered through the other end of a megaphone. As the first word falls off my tongue, I can already feel the avalanche of a booze-soaked diatribe forcing its way up my throat. It's too late now. "…THE POINT IS…NOTHING HAS EVER GONE RIGHT FOR ME. IT'S BEEN ONE MASSIVE FUCKING MISSTEP AFTER ANOTHER. I DESTROY…EVERYTHING I TOUCH. I'M LIKE THE SHITTY, BOTCHED, DOLLAR STORE VERSION OF KING MIDAS. AND ALL I WANT IS TO BE BETTER. I WANNA BE NORMAL, MAN. I REMEMBER I USED TO SAY, 'I'D RATHER BE FUCKED UP AND INTERESTING THAN NORMAL AND BORING.' BUT THAT'S FUCKIN' BULLSHIT, ZAKK WYLDE. I WANT A WIFE AND KIDS AND TO WAKE UP AND SMILE SOME-GODDAMN-TIMES. GIVE ME THE NINE-TO-FIVE AND THE BEER IN FRONT OF THE TV AFTER WORK AND A YARD WITH THE WHITE MOTHERFUCKING PICKET FENCE AND THE COCKTAIL OF ANTI-DEPRESSANTS AND MOOD STABILIZERS TO KEEP ME FROM SWAN-DIVING OFF THE FUCKING ROOF. ANYTHING HAS GOTTA BE BETTER THAN THIS.

"BUT NOW THERE'S THIS BOOK. THIS IS THE BEST THING THAT'S EVER HAPPENED TO ME—IT'S ALL I'VE EVER WANTED, ZAKK WYLDE. BUT YOU KNOW HOW I ENDED UP

WITH THIS BOOK—THIS GIANT FUCKING BLESSING FROM
THE HEAVENS? BY BEING A SOCIOPATHIC, MENTALLY ILL
ALCOHOLIC FOR THREE YEARS. NOW, WHAT THE FUCK DO
YOU EXPECT ME TO TAKE FROM THAT, ZAKK WYLDE? THAT
THE ONE GOOD THING THAT EVER HAPPENED TO ME WAS A
DIRECT RESULT OF BEING THE WORST HUMAN BEING I'VE
EVER ALLOWED MYSELF TO BE. IT'S LIKE THE UNIVERSE IS
GIVING ME PERMISSION TO CONTINUE BEING A PIECE OF
SHIT. IT'S SAYING TO ME, 'DON'T CHANGE, HENRY. DON'T
GET BETTER. IF YOU STAY MISERABLE, THEN YOU CAN
FINALLY BE SOMEBODY. IF YOU JUST KEEP DESTROYING
YOUR LIFE, THEN IT'LL ALL PAY OFF IN THE END.' AND IT'S
NOT LIKE I HAVE ANY EVIDENCE THAT WOULD PROVE
ANYTHING TO THE CONTRARY. THE UNIVERSE IS PATTING
ME ON THE BACK FOR THE FIRST TIME IN MY LIFE FOR,
ESSENTIALLY, BEING A BAD PERSON. SO I'M ASKING YOU,
ZAKK WYLDE, NOW THAT THIS HAS HAPPENED, WHY THE
FUCK WOULD I WANNA STOP NOW?"

The man stares at me for a long time. "JUST WRITE
ABOUT SOMETHING ELSE," he says. He drinks from his beer.
"WHO THE FUCK IS ZAKK WYLDE?"

I blink.

My face is twisted into a sob. I can feel the heat on the
surface of my face as the skin puffs and tightens through the
tears and stress. I am curled into the fetal position on
Rebecca's couch. Rebecca is there next to me, her arm loose
over my shoulder. She is uncomfortable and doesn't know how
to handle this. Neither do I. I don't know what's caused this.

Her image fades in and out between blinks, and once
the brief blackness is traded for the familiarity of her
apartment, Rebecca appears in different positions, sometimes
standing across the room, and I call out between terrified wails
for her to return by my side.

An exercise occurs to me that my therapist had once
taught me to use when amidst the throes of a panic attack. He
called it a grounding exercise. I'm not sure if what's happening
to me is in fact a panic attack but it seems similar enough, so I
focus on anything tangible around me, but I'm so drunk that
the most I can glean from the concept is to call out the name of
the object closest to me, so now I'm screaming, "TABLE TABLE
TABLE TABLE," like a mentally handicapped person as the
tears begin filling the insides of my ears and the world
becomes a giant bathtub.

Rebecca is there and she squeezes my arm to stop me,
and says, "Calm down. Tell me what's going on."

"Did you know that penguins mate for life?" I say. Sobs
and chokes cascade across the words like cement poured over
a wilting garden.

"What?"

"Scientists have studied them. They waddle around
and find a mate in the colony. Then they fall in penguin-love
and they never cheat with other, bigger-dicked penguins or get
a penguin-divorce. They stay together forever."

"Henry, what are you talking about?"

"And then they make an egg and the mom goes into the
ocean to find fish to stay strong for the dad and not-yet-baby,
and the dad sits there with the egg on his feet for months,
Rebecca. He takes care of it. He keeps it warm and safe. And
she always comes back." My sobs intensify. I've remembered
why I am crying. "She always comes back. They love each
other."

"Henry..."

"I want the egg. I want my penguin. Everybody else
gets to have the egg. Everybody else gets their penguin. I don't
wanna do this anymore. I just wanna take care of the egg. I
want my own penguin."

Rebecca says, "Henry, I don't know what to say."

And she doesn't. She doesn't say anything else.

I close one eye and order an Uber, asking Rebecca to
type in her address because I've forgotten what city I'm in, let
alone what part of town. "I have to go," I say. "Today is over."

This is the closest thing to a fact that I can think of so it's what I decide to say.

And then I blink.

She has brown hair that looks coarse and brittle. It falls flat over her back and shoulders. Her nose is large and angular like a protruding triangle. I can't see her eyes well enough in the darkness of the car. This bothers me. It's hard for me to trust people if I can't see the light in their eyes. Still, I carry on with mindless chatter, excited that the change in environment has improved my mood.

"Aiidongowantomayva" is what my words come out sounding like, but she responds with, "That sounds like a day," and "Well, you'll be home soon," so I must be making enough sense to sustain dialogue. My tongue feels like it's disconnected from my mouth.

Through the passenger window, shades of black and orange blend and pirouette between each other as we pass through wooded roads and well-lit streets. We drive across a bridge and the city skyline burns with yellows and reds and blues all blinking and buzzing, and below us the river is solid and black. The current doesn't seem to exist and it looks dead. I can't imagine that there is anything alive underneath the stagnant river. All I imagine is a graveyard of motionless, decaying fish. Soon, the whole city of blinking and buzzing colors will be no different, and this thought doesn't feel saddening but only inevitable and I accept this.

The car stops. We're outside my apartment. She looks at me and I say, "You have cigarette?"

"Yeah," she says. "Do you wanna smoke one with me?"

"Sure," I say.

We step out and lean on the back of her car. I light the wrong end of the cigarette so she takes it out of my mouth, turns it around, and lights it for me. Under the natural light of the stars, her facial features become more prominent, and by the wrinkles of her forehead and weathered expression, I can tell she is probably in her mid- to late-thirties.

She stares at me through the glowing cherry hovering in front of my nose and then says, "Do you wanna keep hanging out?"

Today I have not yet been left alone. I have become lost in the tedious storm of booze, barflies, blinding white noise, lackadaisical supervision, disarmingly poor social etiquette, black humor, masochism, and self-hatred to the point where I can no longer recognize myself, all under the guise of either a celebration or a *Leaving Las Vegas*-style suicide mission, but, in truth, it has all only been for the sole purpose of staving off this exact moment. For the better part of a half-decade, I have driven the hollow and numbing possibilities of excess to the brink. And for whatever reason, it has not been until this night, this day of all days, that I have reached that edge and am left with nothing but the apathetic face before me, and the endless, black abyss of realization staring back from beneath the ends of my feet: I am alone. And I am terrified. I am very, profoundly alone.

"Yeah," I say.

She pulls out her phone. "I'll find somewhere to take us."

I'm not sure what this means but I want someone to take care of me so I don't question getting back into the car.

"I'm off the clock," she says. "Don't worry, you're not being charged."

"Okay."

She brings us to a park in the woods. I know this park. When I was little, my best friend and I used to go deep down into the heart of the forest and catch salamanders. They would hide underneath the rocks close enough to the creek that small amounts of water would seep underneath and provide them with comfortable homes. They were small and black and had two stripes running down their backs. Sometimes the stripes were red and sometimes they were yellow.

"This should work," she says. "Come on."

I get out and stumble on the uneven dirt, and she grabs my hand to lead me down the path towards the creek. We stop at a bench and she sits me next to her like a toddler. It's pitch-black and warm, and I can hear the running water just beyond the veil of shadows. This creek is still alive. The salamanders are still alive under those rocks. I know it.

I feel her hand on my face and then her lips on mine, and I kiss her back because that is what you're supposed to do when someone kisses you. Then she grabs me and gropes at me, and her arms are around me and she pushes me onto the ground next to the bench. She begins taking off my belt and pulling down my pants and she takes her pants off.

"Put it in me," she says.

"I think I'm too drunk," I tell her.

"Kiss me then."

I do and it hardens, and she takes my hips and pulls me in towards her. "Condom?" I manage.

"My tubes are tied," she says. "Put it in."

I don't know if I want this. I don't know where the line is. No one ever taught me this. "Are you clean?" I mumble.

"Yeah, yeah, just do it."

I don't feel anything. She is silent as I do it. Rocks cut into my shins and knees until I know the inside of my jeans will be stained with black, crusted blood. I don't want this. "I'm not gonna come," I say.

"Alright," she says, and pushes me off. "Let's go."

We stand and put our pants back on, and we walk back up the trail I had taken a hundred times as a child. This park was my favorite place in the world. Beautiful, little creatures hid underneath rocks for us to find and the creek never stopped running and the trees swayed in the wind and protected us from the elements. Fifteen years ago, this park was the most magical place I'd ever been.

We drive back to my apartment and she stops in the street, letting her car idle. We have not spoken.

"Do you even remember my name?" she asks.

My eyes are having trouble staying open. "Jordan?" I slur.

"It's Jessica. Get out of my car."

I step outside and close the door, and she drives away. I lie on the driveway and watch the stars until I feel the vomit rising in my stomach, and expel 14 hours' worth of liquor onto a bush. I walk up the steps, weave down the hallway, and collapse onto my bed, falling unconscious with every article of clothing still on me.

I do not dream.

Eight months later, the psychiatrist will give me a new diagnosis and I will go back on medication. And I will crash and burn.

IV.
TRANSFORMATION

MARCH, 2019

Borderline Personality Disorder is not a romantic mental illness. There's no creative connotation that comes with this diagnosis. Bipolar is a romantic mental illness. Depression. Anxiety. These disorders walk hand-in-hand with the stereotype of the tortured creative genius. At least in the eyes of those who don't suffer. We as a society revere the artist teetering on the edge of sanity and suicide. We swallow up their pain and erect pedestals in their honor on which to place their work—the labored result of their martyrdom.

We picture Bipolar in the poetry of Sylvia Plath. Her ethereal words forged in the irons of unbearable masochism and a fractured mind at the whim of its own uncontrollable ups and downs, soaring upward and crashing down to earth violently like a paper airplane caught in a strong draft.

See, that sounds fucking romantic, doesn't it?

People don't think about when she stuck her head in that oven and asphyxiated herself at age 30 that she had stuffed towels against the cracks of the kitchen doors so her children sleeping upstairs wouldn't smell the odor and stop her in the act, but instead be forced to find their dead mother lying on the floor after it was too late.

That part is less romantic. That's just mental illness.

We picture depression in the novels of Jack Kerouac. How his suffering led him west on the greatest adventure in America, west to find God itself, to find meaning from his existential pain in the sights and sounds and smells of his country.

That's romantic as hell, isn't it?

People forget that by the late-'60s, Kerouac was a bloated, babbling drunk too afraid to kill himself for fear of violating his deeply engrained Catholic beliefs, and so chose to drink his way to massive hemorrhaging from cirrhosis of the liver. Kerouac never found God and never found salvation. His depression led to vomiting blood and dying a middle-aged, vague shadow of himself.

That is less romantic. That's just mental illness.

I lived with people who were bipolar my entire life: my father and sister. They are two of the most creative, intelligent people I've ever met. There is an undeniable connection between mental illness and creativity. Whether it be due to seeing the world differently—or inability to see it through anything but strained eyes—or experiencing the wider spectrum of emotion that others can't, is difficult to say. What is most important to note, though, is that this is the smallest and by far most profound positive aspect of having a damaged mind. In fact, I'd argue that it's the only one.

That's the problem with the glorification of mental illness in the artist. People read their words or see their artwork or hear their music and all they know is that this was a factor in creating something beautiful. They only catch the best glimpse of what the condition can facilitate. The thin silver lining can be blinding to those unaware of what it contains. They haven't seen their father standing atop the roof of their house when he's gone off his medication, claiming he can fly and that he's about to jump to prove it to you, as you stand watching from the driveway in your uniform, waiting for him to take you to school. They hadn't gotten on a first name basis with the local cops by age 10, after they'd come to your house on a weekly basis to talk your teenage sister out of suicide from behind a locked door. They haven't had to take the knife out of her hands when the cops don't arrive fast enough.

When experienced firsthand, the illusion of so-called romantic mental illnesses quickly dissipates.

In a way then, I was spared that illusion after my diagnosis. Borderline Personality Disorder is not a romantic mental illness. The list of my peers is not comprised of artists and writers. My peers are evil, manipulative monsters. Murderers. Serial killers. Tyrants. O.J. Simpson. Jeffrey Dahmer. People say Hitler had it. Fucking Hitler had it.

Those are my peers. That is less romantic.

I am not creating art in the face of a monstrous disorder, grappling with my own broken mind until I find something beautiful within the cracks. I am the monster.

One of the theories is that the majority of cases are a result of prolonged childhood trauma. Some sort of mental rewiring that occurs in the malleable brain during the formative years. The other camp believes it's simply a matter of genetics. A roll of the dice. But having an abusive childhood is as much a roll of the dice as anything else, so this really doesn't change much.

When I was six, I had a pet leopard gecko. They live in Pakistan in the wild and in an eight-gallon tank at Petco otherwise. I wanted to name it Crawler but had a strong lisp due to my stroke so it came out as Carl when I told my parents, and that stuck. Carl was a female. I was ahead of my time in 1999.

I don't know why it started. I don't know why I did it. But soon after purchasing Carl, I took to torturing her. Resting atop her terrarium was a large heat lamp. Every few days, I would take her out of the tank and place her atop the wire mesh ceiling. I would then place the lamp over her so that she was trapped inside the ultra-heated metal, and stand there for a minute or so, listening to her writhing, wriggling in agony beneath the white-hot bulb, until lifting it and gently taking her in my hands, observing with scientific indifference the cauterized wounds and blisters forming across her bumpy scales.

It's a blurred and sickening memory that I've done my best to hide from—a murder weapon thrown to the bottom of the neighborhood lake. But like Poe's *Telltale Heart*, I can still see it shimmering beneath the surface when I pass by the remaining memories of my childhood. I've never told anyone about this.

That is what psychologists would call a warning sign. I never had an obsession with setting fires, and never had an issue with wetting the bed, so I'm shy of meeting the requirements for the Macdonald Triad, but by 17, anyone could have told you that my behavioral patterns suggested something seriously wrong with my brain chemistry.

After my diagnosis, the psychiatrist gave me a prescription for Effexor and showed me an educational video.

He said it might help with the bite that comes with the stigma
of BPD.

It was a cartoon about a little dog. His name was
Borderline Bill. Borderline Bill had issues with impulsive
behaviors. Borderline Bill engaged in dangerous and self-
damaging acts like reckless driving and drug abuse and
alcoholism. Bill also had difficulty abstaining from
indiscriminate sex. The world was a scary place for Bill. The
only people who lived on Earth were angels or demons in Bill's
eyes. Bill suffered from extreme and sudden bouts of anger
and panic. Bill was often depressed and highly emotional. Bill
thought about suicide often and would sometimes make
attempts on his own life. Sometimes, he would only do it
halfway on purpose. These were Bill's cries for help. Bill had
problems with lying. Bill was always in pain. It never escaped
him. Borderline Bill was married to suffering.

More than anything in the world, Bill loved a little, red
ball. It was all he thought about. He spent his days thinking
about it and thinking about how much he wanted it. But
something inside wouldn't let him have it. As soon as he ever
got close to the little, red ball, he would do something self-
sabotaging. Bill didn't know why he had to ruin his chances to
have his little, red ball. It was all he wanted. But his brain
wouldn't let him have it.

Bill's little, red ball was happiness. Bill could not let
himself be happy. Any time he began to feel okay, Bill needed
to do something to destroy his happiness. Bill was never happy
for very long. Bill's little, red ball was love. Bill could not hold
down relationships. As soon as he began to fall in love, Bill had
to sever that connection. Bill did this sometimes to hurt the
other person before they had the chance to hurt him. And
sometimes he did it because somewhere deep down he didn't
believe he deserved to be loved.

Bill had a 10% chance of dying by suicide.

Bill never got his little, red ball. At the end of the video,
Bill finally got to hold it in his little dog hands. But Bill became
so scared of losing it that his mind became a hurricane. Fear
became his blood, and anger became his flesh, and before he
could realize what he'd done, Bill kicked the little, red ball

away. Bill then sat there alone and cried. Wanting only what he could not allow himself to have.

The video then squeezed in a few positives before 10% of those watching killed themselves: Bill is very good with children. Bill is a talented artist. Bill can be very kind.

This video did not take away the sting. I was Borderline Bill. And I would never have my little, red ball. I sat in my empty body for a while after that and cried. I cried for Borderline Bill. Borderline Bill, who was empty inside but could be very kind.

APRIL-MAY, 2019

Poor Decision #1:

You are drinking at the Guilty Sparrow. It does not matter what day or time it is, as this is the sole activity you participate in if you're not jerking off, vomiting, or fucking—if not all three in quick succession. You are with your old coworker, Joseph, as you tend to be these days. He is a heavyset, Hispanic hopeless romantic—always stooping low over the bar counter like a dying tree to illustrate this—with a serious drinking problem to match yours. In the last few weeks, you and Joseph have taken to each other quite well. You've stayed friends since the day you were fired, but he finds company in misery, and he has been unable to find anyone more miserable than you. His girlfriend of five years left him when he asked her to move in. This was a year ago but he still talks about it. He can drink more than you and you don't like that, but you love him.

He's talking to your friend, Miles. Miles is a gaunt and unpredictable drug addict with an undetermined mental illness. His constant erratic movements and rambling unsettles you until you've drunk enough to ignore and then enjoy his unique brand of company. You've known him since the two of you were four-years-old and he had frosted tips like a member of the Backstreet Boys. He used to mix cocaine and heroin in a needle and shoot that. He wore sleeves to hide the track marks and became paranoid when people asked why he wore his sleeves in 90-degree heat. After the two of you talked, he got on methadone and kicked the junk.

He still does every other drug but at least he doesn't do heroin, and you love him.

Miles and Joseph are talking about the baggie full of pills that Miles has pulled out onto the bar top. "This is Ecstasy," he says. He pops two. "You want some?"

"Fuck yeah, I do," says Joseph. He reaches out and pops one in his mouth. He begins chewing.

You look over at them from the corner of your eye. Before you can ask him why he's chewing an ecstasy pill, Joseph swallows and says, "This is a *Flintstones* vitamin."

"No, it's not," says Miles. "It's ecstasy. My guy told me it was the best shit he's ever gotten."

"Yeah, the best *Flintstones* vitamins he's ever gotten. You bought a bag of vitamins from your drug dealer. Mine was cherry-flavored."

Miles leans in and peers through the plastic like a scientist studying a petri dish through a microscope. "You're fibbing."

"I'm not. How much did you pay for that?"

"A hundred fifty," Miles tells him.

"You just bought 20 dollars' worth of *Flintstones* vitamins. How many have you taken so far?"

"Four, I think."

"And how're you feeling?"

"Nothing so far, but it just takes a second." Miles pauses and ponders this, staring through the shelves of liquor in front of us like he's experiencing a war flashback.

Joseph picks up the bag and pulls out a little green one, shoves it in front of his face. "Dude, it's shaped like a fucking dinosaur."

Miles looks at this and you can see the moment his heart breaks.

"What you've taken has made you healthier. You have literally achieved the opposite effect of ecstasy." He eats the little, green chewable. "Apple."

Miles is distraught. He gets up and leaves to call or stab his drug dealer. This is when the person who's been sitting on the other side of him is revealed to you.

Her hair is shoulder-length and curled and strawberry blonde. Her eyes are large. Her legs are long and bloom out from a pink pencil skirt. She sits erect, almost regal, despite her apparent intoxication, suggesting it's been hammered in at an early age to remain ladylike. She is sitting alone. You lean across the bar. There is no time for hesitation. There are too many holes bleeding from every part of you, and the irony is that the more you fill them with what they require, the faster you are going to die anyway. "You are fucking gorgeous," you tell her.

"Ah, hehehehe." She laughs like that, high-pitched and overacted. You do your best to ignore this. "Well, thanks," she slurs. "You are too."

Joseph butts in to be your wingman. "Y'know, my boy's an author. You ever fucked an author? Do you read?"

"Ohhhh, is he?" This doesn't appear to impress her but she moves a seat closer to you. "And who are you?"

"I don't think she reads," he whispers to you. "I'm Joseph," he redirects toward her.

"Isn't my boy good-looking? Who wouldn't love that face?"

You're not sure if he's just trying to get you laid to live vicariously through you or if he's gotten so drunk and lonely that some feelings are coming out.

"He's gorgeous," she says and grabs your leg.

"I'm Henry." You feel the need to reciprocate, honor the friendship and maybe get Joseph's dick sucked instead. "What about my friend though? You think he's cute?"

She appraises his appearance through one eye. "You're both cute. I'd fuck both of you."

Anna the bartender comes by and rolls her eyes. She's become accustomed to a very different Henry in these last few weeks. "Another round boys...and...lady?"

"Shots," Joseph shouts. "Three tequilas, no training wheels."

"Wooo! Shots," the girl screams, throwing her hands up. "You guys are so much fun. Like ah, hehehehe... so much fun." Her bedroom eyes drift between the two of you.

You realize as the shots are placed upon the bar that you never got her name. This doesn't bother you.

Joseph holds up his shot. "So, what're we cheersing to?"

"I wanna fuck both of you at the same time," she says.

Anna makes a face like she bit into human shit and walks away.

"To fucking both of us," he screams. He looks at you and shrugs as the shot goes down. "So...down?"

If you were sober this would be one of the worst ideas you could think of. Right now you can't imagine why this idea has never been expressed until this moment.

"I want one of you to fuck me in the ass while the other fucks my mouth," she says.

You swallow hard to avoid coughing up your tequila. "Yeah, yep. We can do that." You and Joseph exchange glances.

"We've gone this far," he mumbles. "It would be uncouth to leave her hanging at this point."

"It would be ungentlemanly," you agree.

She eyes both of you. "Okay, okay, lemme just check with my boyfriend."

Her boyfriend.

Joseph launches into a fit of laughter.

"Is this like, an open relationship situation?" you ask.

"I'm not sure. I can't remember," she says. "Lemme call him and ask."

Joseph looks at you, his entire face lit up. You've never seen him enjoying himself this much.

'Call him and ask?' you mouth. "She's a fucking nut."

He shrugs and talks with his hands: *Is that bad?*

"I didn't say that."

She steps away to see if her boyfriend will give her the okay to get double penetrated.

Joseph watches her walk out the door with the phone on her ear. "What would you rather take?"

"I'd rather the mouth but I'll take one for the team if you need me to."

"Not a fan of anal?"

"Not for me, no."

"That's fair. Alright, it's settled then," Joseph decides. "Makes you wonder why her pussy wasn't an option though, doesn't it?"

"I was just thinking that," you say. And you were. You really were.

Before you can dwell on that for too long, she returns, sits next to you, and straightens her skirt. "He didn't answer. Poor baby must be asleep. Wanna take me home?"

"Is this the home where your boyfriend lives?" you ask.

"Ah, don't worry about that," Joseph interjects. "We'll figure that out when we get there, right... Uh, what was your name?"

She throws her head back and kicks up a leg. Her stilettos look like weapons. "Ah, hehehehe. You're so funny. You guys kill me. Seriously."

Joseph leads you down the street in a direction you can't stabilize yourself enough to be aware of. It's nighttime. You wish you were a sailor so you could navigate by the stars, but you're so drunk there are copies of each star so even if you could, fuck all it would do for you. You think about how often pirates must have gotten lost at sea in the 1700s.

The girl piles into the back while you collapse into the passenger seat like someone has thrown you.

"So where to?" Joseph asks the girl. He is shit drunk, but you have done enough tonight to make the bleeding stop and so you could hardly care. You don't hurt anymore and that is all that matters. She gives him vague directions and Joseph tears down the street like he'll win a prize for getting there before an imaginary clock runs out.

Joseph insists on talking while driving, twisting around with one hand on the wheel to make eye contact with her. "So we should just come in, is what you're saying. I'm sure he won't mind. He can watch! Maybe he'd be into that."

"That is true," you add. "Cucking is becoming a more and more universally accepted sexual kink these days. Have you ever typed 'cuck and bull' into PornHub? It's a thriving community. We don't judge!"

"No, not at all," says Joseph. "It might wake up something in him. Maybe he just needs a little push to learn that we accept him."

"I agree. Let us give him the courage to step out of his shell and accept his desires. We'd be doing him a service, I think."

"In fact, it might even be detrimental for him *not* to watch us fucking his girlfriend," says Joseph. "I don't think it's fair of any of us to deprive him of the sexual awakening that this could provide. I'll go as far as to say we'd be doing him a disservice if we don't."

"Just something to think about," you tell her.

"Ah, hehehehe. You boys are too funny. And so fucking sexy. I want you both fucking all of my holes." She starts pulling down her blouse. "You wanna see my boobies?"

Her vernacular is off-putting, but Joseph is unperturbed, and shouts, "Yes!"

You turn around and there they are. Her tits are out in the backseat. She starts playing with them and making orgasm faces like a poorly trained porn star, her tongue sliding across her lips, her eyes rolling to the back of her head. If you hadn't before, you decide that she is insane.

"Oh shit!" Joseph takes his eyes off the road to enjoy the show behind him.

"No, no, no." You wave your hands in front of his face. "You drive, I'll watch for the both of us and relay it back to you through descriptive words."

As you say this, the girl throws her body into the back of your seats and points to a turn you're about to pass. "Oh, shoot, there! Turn there!"

Joseph whips his Ford Explorer on a hairpin turn, slamming into the curb, and launching you three feet into the air. The car lands on its right two wheels, and the left two follow, slamming onto the cement with the force of an anvil.

Nobody moves. The car idles in silence. You stare forward, your eyes wide with the feeling you imagine someone must experience after recognizing they almost died. Joseph says nothing, his hands gripping the steering wheel.

The girl points towards the house you've nearly crashed in front of. "There I am! Thanks, boys!" She takes the phone out of your trembling hands, puts in her number, calls herself, and kisses you both on the cheek before skipping towards the door. "I'll let you know if Boyfriend will let you fuck me! Have a good night!" And she disappears inside.

You and Joseph continue staring forward. "We never even got her name."

A grin stretches across your face. "No," you laugh. "No, we didn't."

The next night, you and Joseph are back drinking at the Sparrow when you receive this text:

Hello. Thank you so much again for the ride home. But boyfriend and I decided that we aren't going to go for the threesome. I'm sorry I showed you my boobies, that wasn't cool. That's not something my dog and I agreed on. Hope you're having a good night! Bye bye.

You show this to Joseph.

"Her dog?" he says. "Well, that explains a lot."

Poor Decision #2:

You are drunker than you ever remember, although you can't recall much of anything anyway. What you are aware of is that you are alone and you are driving and that the car isn't yours. The awareness of your loneliness seems to operate through a game of extremes. That is, you are able to stave off the guilt and self-hatred while living in the happy, gray medium of manageable intoxication, but it is in the overwhelming acuteness of morning sobriety or the suicidal depression at the end of the night that you are unable to focus on anything but the exact thing you've been drinking to avoid.

Tonight, you find yourself at the latter end.

You realize that you need to do something to quell the urge to drive into a guardrail, something that will flood your brain with however many endorphins can still get through.

This is when you get the idea. On a main road not too far from you is a popular strip club. Next to that strip club is what has only been described to you as a brothel. It's called the Cat Club and it has been there for as long as you've lived in the area. It's a tiny shack of a building with multi-colored lights strung up around the entrance, a sign next to the door with the silhouette of a voluptuous woman and the words: **OPEN 24-HOURS. PRIVATE MASSAGES.**

You've never understood how something so blatantly a whorehouse could have sat on the side of this high-traffic road for so long, but you don't know what exactly goes on in there, but tonight you will find out.

You pull up to the side of the Cat Club at three in the morning, open the door, and fall out of the car. It's the only building that still has its lights on other than the 7-Eleven down a block or two. Stepping towards the entrance, you remember the rumors that one of your friends from high school started working here after she became addicted to meth and heroin. It would be nice to see her again.

Inside, the Cat Club is narrow and claustrophobic. The lobby is hardly larger than a prison cell. A desk sits to the left of you with a call bell, and a corridor runs down about 30 feet with two doors on either side that open up to a private room. Small TVs are attached to the walls in the corners, playing softcore porn with the volume off. The video quality is so bad, it looks like two beige squares slamming into each other. The lighting is low and glows red. This is your favorite part so far. You've never liked bright lights. You can hide in this kind of lighting.

Before you can ring the bell, a woman drifts from one of the rooms. She is a little shorter than you, with long, brown hair and blue eyes. She wears an appropriate amount of makeup for her line of work. Beneath it, you can see the age etched into her skin and the fading glow in her eyes earned by pain that would break most people. There is a weathered beauty in her face. You imagine she must be around 35. A see-through black negligée drapes her body, tied together with a satin ribbon around her stomach—underneath perhaps the biggest breasts you've ever seen in your life. They spill out quite on purpose, mountains of white flesh pushing out as if they'll tear open the seams and break free.

There is some kind of brief exchange that you immediately cannot recall, and she smiles and leads you by the hand into the first private room. You smash into the wall on the way in and almost trip on an electric fan sitting on the floor beneath you.

"You okay there, honey?" she says, and laughs.

You nod and try your best to sound reasonably sober, but all that comes out are nonsensical mumbles spoken with a swollen tongue. If she didn't know before, you know that she does now. This doesn't bother her though, and she continues leading you into the room, and sits you down on a wide, cushioned bench against the wall.

The room is just an extension of what you've already seen: Attached to the walls are two small televisions playing porn with the volume off. The walls themselves are decorated with vague Thai designs and paintings of positions from the *Kama Sutra.* Lining a few shelves are dozens of unlit candles and statues of fertility goddesses from different cultures. In the center of the room is a basic massage table. Beyond that, in the corner opposite you is a small bed with a purple curtain pulled back around it.

The woman smiles, standing over you with the door open in case you turn out to be a serial killer with a meat cleaver. "So what're you looking for, honey?"

"How much do you charge?" you manage.

"If you really wanna have fun, I'm $300. But that's full service. You get everything: a massage, hand job, blow job, fuck my tits. Even you'll come once I'm finished." She laughs and taps your nose with the end of her fake nail. "Otherwise, it's $120 for just the lap dance. Then you can watch and finish yourself."

A literary magazine recently paid $400 for one of your stories. You decide that buying a prostitute with money you've earned from writing is simply putting that money back into writing. This is research for your next book. This may even count as a tax write-off.

"Whole thing," you say. "$300."

She grins and strokes her hand down your chest. "Perfect. Ah...I'll just take your card and charge that down the hall then."

You nod and pull out the card, and inexplicably tell her, "I'm a writer. I spend my writing money on you. You cost one story and you are worth one story. Spend money to make money, right?"

She looks around the room and giggles uncomfortably. "Sure, honey. Be right back."

When the woman returns, she hands the card back to you. "It was declined, babe. You got another one?"

"Don't think that's right," you retort. "My writing money. It's in, uh—savings." It is not lost on you even in a state of advanced inebriation that you are attempting to dip into your savings account to buy a hooker. You assign yourself the mental note that cash is more comfortable for both parties.

She takes the card back out of your hand, eyeing you up and down with a flicker of pity. "Alright then. One second."

The next time she returns, she appears a bit less annoyed but the margin is still wide. "It only let me charge $200. You may need to go to the 7-Eleven and pull out the rest of the cash yourself." She pulls you closer into her chest.

You can smell the cheap perfume masking the sweat of whoever was in this room before you.

"Can you do that for me? I'll be right here, babe."

"Yes," you say. "Yes I can."

She takes off your hat and places it onto her head. It doesn't fit right. "Just in case," she giggles. "Now you have to come back."

You stumble under the harsh fluorescent lights of the convenience store and weave to the back, where the ATM awaits your bad decision. The clerk says something as you pass but you just throw your arm up over your shoulder and say you'll give him 20 bucks, to fuck off and get off your back.

The ATM is a foreign construct. You stand in front of it for a full five minutes before you remember how one is supposed to access such a thing. You go into savings, do the mental math, fail, and attempt to pull out $200. It declines.

Without reading what comes on the screen, you try again. Declined. On the screen, pops up the warning you'd ignored: **Suspicious activity on account. Cannot withdraw more funds.**

You've attempted to take out too much money too many times from different devices. You are—as you have been countless times in different ways—cut off. You stare at the screen. You have been defeated.

The store clerk yells at you as you leave, and you charge out the door without answering. You really would have given him those 20 bucks.

The woman is waiting for you in the lobby. "Missed you, babe. You got that for me?"

You explain what happened, and the woman frowns. "Well, you won't get the works. That's too bad."

She leads you back into the room and instructs you to sit back on the cushioned bench. She closes the door. Her bare legs straddle you and she leans back, thrusting against your limp cock. The negligée falls to the floor. Without the clothing's support, her breasts are too large and sag to her stomach under the weight of age and gravity.

You begin to unbutton your jeans, and reach up to touch her hanging tit with a free hand. The second you make contact, as if waiting for this to happen, she jolts up from the bench. "Nope, nope. You grabbed my tit too hard. Get the fuck off me. You grabbed my tit too hard, we're done."

"Wait, what? What?" You're confused. You barely brushed against her.

Her entire demeanor has shifted. "You grabbed my tit too hard, we're done here. Have fun jerking off to porn and get the fuck out." She tosses you a tissue from the table and walks out of the room, slamming the door behind her.

You stand up, button up your pants, and wobble back into the lobby. The woman is there standing alone, drifting into a different room. "Hey, hey," you slur, "what did I do? I didn't do anything to you." You realize you are leaning against the desk for support.

"Doesn't matter," she says. "You're done, goodbye."

"My money, lady."

"What did I say? You're done. Get out. Go ahead and write about this, dumbass." She glides away into the private room, aware of what she's gotten away with.

You are too drunk to form an argument. You have no one to argue with anyway. You are too tired.

After six tries, you are able to get the key into the car door. You throw the keys on the front seat, close the door, and begin walking home. The smoke from the cigarette in your mouth twirls up towards the streetlights and disappears.

A prostitute just rolled you for $200.

Poor Decision #3:

Within five minutes of talking you understand that there's something wrong with her. You recognized her as the airy waitress at the restaurant down the block who always told you your aura was navy blue whenever you ordered. Now you are sitting next to her at the Sparrow, six and a half drinks in, and she's asking, "Where's that cute tattooed girl you always come in with?"

"Which?"

She smirks. "Cockiness doesn't suit you."

"It's not that. I just can't seem to make 'em stick around long enough to make an impression."

She looks you up and down through wide-brimmed glasses that magnify the brown in her eyes. Her face is gaunt and narrow. She is shark-like and the steady, intense gaze she keeps on you gives the impression that she may decide for no reason other than instinct to pounce and bite off your nose. You don't remember ever finding her attractive but figure you must have been wrong because now you do.

"Well it doesn't matter," she says and sucks her vodka soda up through a plastic straw. "Never liked her anyway."

"Yeah. Neither did I, I guess."

"Well, God obviously had different plans for you. You should be thanking Him for leading you away from all that before it got even worse."

You cough. "What was that?"

"God," she laughs. "You thought this wasn't God's choice? He was watching over you, like He always will. I could see the poison she was seeping into you, every time you came in. She was no good for you. I knew it. But He freed you, Henry." She smiles wide, as if she's reminded of the beauty of this reality she's chosen. "And now you don't ever have to look back. Right? Isn't that wonderful?"

You look down the bar to where McEwen, whom you came with, sits at a table with some people he knows. McEwen is a tall, Scottish college grad with a wild mane of red, curled hair, and a deep red beard that makes him resemble what you might get if a pillaging Viking raped one of his ancestors—which may not be so far off. McEwen is your good friend and editor, but when not fixing up your whiskey-soaked ramblings, also serves as your impromptu caretaker, ensuring that you don't get yourself in so much trouble you'll end up dead or arrested, but just enough to keep the pages flowing. He stares at you intently, his eyes wide and locked in distress as if trying to communicate that a live bear is behind you. He is holding up his phone and pointing to it with violent stabs. You grin and give him the thumbs-up, and turn back around to the God-fearing predator.

"Do you not believe in God?" she asks.

"Ah, uh. No. No, not really. I mean, there's always the, uh, possibility but—no. Not really."

There is a brief pause, and her eyes scan you once more. This doesn't give off the feeling it previously did. It's like she's reading your soul to decide if you're already damned to Hell.

Before she can whip out the crucifix and holy water, you add, "I mean, do I believe that there's some kind of force in the universe that's more complicated than we can understand—something bigger than myself, in whatever form that may be? Do I believe in karma? Could you call that God? Sure. I'm not an asshole. Do I believe in the big, all-powerful, bearded man in the sky, the hyper-violent Santa Clause figure, watching you and weighing your sins and good deeds, deciding whether or not you're gonna spend eternity getting your foreskin repeatedly torn off and put back on by red-skinned demons after you die? No. I got enough of that in Catholic school." You stop for a moment, realizing you may have laid it on a little strong there. You backpedal, "Ah, I mean, I don't think there's anything wrong with it, though. Whatever gets you through it isn't my business. I'm glad you have something that works for you."

You have always found religion fascinating, and have studied just about every one out there. It's a vital part of each country and peoples' culture and way of life. Many people have done many horrible things in the name of these religions, but you can't fault the layman who just wants to sing in a building with like-minded people once a week and imagine that infinite nothingness isn't the result of their inevitable death.

Besides, if it weren't religion, it would be something else. You understand that. That's the quintessential aspect of being human, ever since our first ancestors looked up and saw bright white bolts of lightning striking the night sky. Without these stories making sense of what we otherwise couldn't, we as a species never would have gotten as far as we did.

You tell her all this. You just fail to mention that maybe it wasn't such a great thing that we did make it this far, and that religion has turned into nothing different than any other money-grubbing, power-hungry, pedophile-hiding institution that only serves as another way to keep stupid people content, poor people even poorer, and ensuring that we as a whole don't ask too many questions that may not be conducive to their centuries-old, systematic destruction of free thought and healthy chaos.

Yes, seeing as you are planning on sleeping with this good Christian woman, you leave that part out.

"Plus," you say, and take a sip from your drink, "it's not like you're a Scientologist or anything."

There's a moment of tension as her eyes bore into you. "I'm a born-again Christian," she says. "I converted from Scientology."

The whiskey goes down your windpipe. Through the coughing fit, you manage to sputter, "Well... Welcome back!"

She slaps you on the back. "You alright there?"

"Yeah, yeah. Wrong tube."

"Well, good," she laughs. "I can't have you dying on me yet. At least not until I'm done with you." She winks and stands up. "I'm going to the bathroom. But I'd like to keep talking to you. You're smart. And open-minded. A lot of smart guys aren't open-minded. And vice versa. Don't you go anywhere until I'm back. I think we should take this to my place and I can offend you with more of my beliefs."

"I'm not easily offended," you tell her.

"Good. That's good. Be right back."

The second she's gone, McEwen beelines over to your barstool. "Man, you gotta check your texts."

"Oh, that's what that meant?"

"Listen, I'm trying to help you. As your editor, I insist we leave this bar right now and go somewhere else before she comes back."

"Why's that?" you ask.

"She's crazy. Do I need to spell that out? You've spent the last half-hour talking to her."

"Yeah, I gathered. A bit pious, isn't she? But hey, I don't judge, baby."

"A bit? Trust me, Henry, I'm trying to help you here."

"Yes, and I appreciate that." You pat him on the forehead and tickle his chin. "But from what I hear, this is God's plan."

"Jesus Christ."

"Exactly!" You hold up your drink and guzzle the watered-down remains. "She's not a Westboro Baptist or anything, is she?"

"No, but—"

"Yeah I didn't get that vibe. Feel like she would have led with the 'death to fags' angle. She's not gonna try to indoctrinate me into a death cult then? Fuck me and hand me the Kool-Aid for the approaching inter-dimensional spaceship?"

"Don't be a dick," he says. "You just gotta listen to me. I know her. You don't need to get tangled up in that."

"Oh come on, McEwen, now you're just tempting me. At this point, I gotta find out."

"Has she brought up her love of all things Trump yet?"

Your eyes light up. "Oh ho ho, not yet. Should I ask?"

"Yes. Yes you should."

"Well, that settles it then. You've convinced me."

McEwen sighs and grabs your shoulder. "Okay, good. Good. Then let's get out of here then? I'm guessing the convent is gonna be wondering where she escaped pretty soon anyway."

You look across the room and see that she's on her way over. "No, no, you shoo. How can I possibly not go through with this now?"

His face drops to the floor. "I don't know, moral integrity? Oh, yeah. I forgot you're incapable of possessing that." Just before she reaches the two of you, McEwen gives his final warning, like an ashamed father: "Don't say I didn't warn you."

"If I had a nickel." You smile at him with the whiskey sloshing around your head like a storm raging across your brain cells.

He grimaces and shoots you his best frustrated, defeated look before retreating to his table.

Your poor decision sits back down beside you, glancing over questioningly at McEwen. "So, you coming or what?"

"Does Christ have stigmata?"

She forces a snort. "I'll take that as a yes."

You sit with her in a small backyard. The cigarette passes between the two of you, and past the gate, beyond the hill below, is the freeway. It is empty and quiet and dark. A wall of discarded trash like a protective barrier lines the shadowed asphalt. It is all you can seem to focus on. The roads are like veins running down the mangled arm of a dead drug addict. They are dried up and no longer hum with the movement of blood. They are of no use. You prefer it this way—the quiet lifelessness. It allows the beating of your heart to fill the insides of your ears and remind you that there's still time to change. How you choose to take it, though, is that it means tonight you do not yet have to.

"What do you want to do with your life?" she asks.

This knocks you off guard, though you don't know why, as most of your life you haven't had a problem deciding what path to take. Through one way or another, the answers have been glowing in your face and you have wholeheartedly attached yourself to that next option that inevitably presents itself. And when that next path has dried up and halted at a dead-end, you have never needed to float aimlessly in the purgatory between decisions.

You recognize that you are lucky in this regard. Most people wander their entire lives. Purpose has always found you. There has always been some new path to traverse.

Despite this, you respond, "Sometimes I think I know and sometimes I don't." Though you decide there may still be some truth to this.

"I want to do something big," she says, blowing out smoke. "I always knew I would. I'm gonna join the Air Force."

"The Air Force? Why?"

Without the hesitation you imagine a semi-sane person would feel, she proudly declares, "So when the time comes, I'll be first in line to join President Trump's Space Force."

You give yourself a moment to absorb this. "Like, the outer space...force?"

"Yeah, I wanna be the first woman on the moon."

"Well, that's noble."

"So I can see for myself if the Nazis really put bases up there."

"Ah."

"And think about it"—she points the cigarette at you from between two fingers—"how else am I ever gonna really prove Earth is flat unless I go up there and see it with my own eyes?"

You are now fascinated by this woman, and wish for nothing more than to listen to everything she has to say, and then to fuck her. You have never fucked a flat-Earther, and would consider it an honor to try fucking the crazy out of her.

"That's a fantastic point," you say.

Her eyes narrow to slits. "You're making fun of me, aren't you?"

You don't wish to lie to this person, and so are overcome with relief when she doesn't wait for an answer: "That's fine though, it's not like I don't get it all the time. But you have your opinions and I have mine. And we can each respect them, can't we?"

"Of course," you reply, and you mean this. You would rather have an open-minded, ex-alien worshipping, Trump supporting, born-again Christian flat-Earther than a close-minded liberal any goddamn day of the week.

"I figured," she says. "That's why I like you. I'm guessing you're not a big Trump supporter either. No one seems to be in this town. I love the man. I think he's the greatest president we've ever had, and I'm proud I voted for him. I don't have a problem telling people that. You don't feel the same. And that's okay."

You take the cigarette out of her hand and place it between your lips. "How do you know? My MAGA hat's just in the wash right now."

"Very funny. All I'm saying is we don't need to share the same political beliefs to have good sex. Right? Unless that violates your moral codes."

"It would violate my moral codes not to." The smoke cascades from your mouth like the ectoplasm of a trapped ghost. "I mean, I think the guy's a fucking fascist and he's probably on the spectrum, but hey, who isn't, y'know? I can ignore my political leanings for 15 to 20 minutes."

"Make it 30."

"Deal."

She grins and reaches out to slide her hand up your thigh.

"Just one thing," you say, putting out the cigarette. "When you're about to come, call me Donald."

The act is the closest to patriotic you have or will ever feel. You decide this is your duty as an American, and with each violent thrust causing her to scream and convulse, it is as if you are fucking her with the American flag itself. You decide this is a metaphor for every war against bigotry, tyranny, and racism, and what you are doing you are doing in the name of freedom and liberty. With your dick, you are fighting back for the greater good and you will not lose. It is at the moment the King James Bible vibrating on the bed stand finally falls to the floor, and the female ejaculate rockets into your face like a well-aimed Scud missile, that the thought briefly but genuinely comes to you: "I should run for Senate."

Poor Decision #4:

The unfamiliar bitter drip—well, rather what has become familiar in recent times—slides down the back of your throat and you gag as you pace outside a stranger's apartment at four in the morning. The amount of cocaine you've ingested is too much because your body is screaming. You have no choice but to accept that this may be how you die: standing alone outside the apartment of a man whom you met at a bar, waiting for an Uber to get you home, feeling your heart vibrate like a hummingbird's then stop completely, then continue after the excruciating silence fills the inside of your chest—over and over.

The fear that would normally wash over you is dulled by alcohol, and with this boost in morale given to you, you take a moment to understand that if this stranger's coke was laced with rat poison or fentanyl, your heart would have stopped by now and your breathing narrowed to asphyxiation. You have not keeled over and so this is good news.

The headlights of the car cut through the night and burn your eyes. It pulls up and you disregard any notion of social awareness, leaping into the front passenger seat. You are visibly trembling, fidgeting with the zipper on your torn and stained bomber jacket.

His name is Eric. He is a young, handsome African-American with long dreads and a soft face. He appears feminine and speaks with a low rasp as if trying to lull you into docility. You appreciate this and decide to trust Eric. With nothing else to do but expel word vomit to quell the effects of the narcotics, you tell him everything that is on your mind without stopping, with surprising eloquence. You trust the words you are saying because they are said clearly and with certainty. This is what you tell him:

"Sometimes I want to be an alcoholic. I want the darkness to encompass me. I want to feel the tight constriction of dependence. I want to put holes in my body with each stinging swallow. There is a naïve power in taking control of your own mortality, commandeering the wheel and deciding your own death in the face of its inevitability. In a way, it's a form of revolt, of dissent. An avenue to express your anger and desperation that comes with the knowledge of your impending end. Sometimes you just want to give the middle finger to the stardust that birthed you into this explosion of chaos. It feels cheap to be drained of yourself by the very force that made you endure it all without ever asking if you wanted any of it in the first place. Like the Vietnamese monks lighting themselves on fire. With each extra shot you know shouldn't be consumed, you are in protest of the entirety of the universe. And during the whole process, you are thinking, what an asshole you are for thinking this way.

"I am so terrified of death. And yet I do everything in my power to ensure an early witness to it. I can't explain it. I am a biological freak. My brain has been unspared by the Gods or the fates but I am doomed to be a monster, to fuck up and destroy all that's beautiful around me, to roam through darkness until my legs give out and I die at the feet of the villagers and their pitchforks. No matter how goddamn hard I try, I can't fucking fix myself. I don't know why I do this. I don't have any answers." You take a deep breath and turn to see that somehow Eric is still listening. "Do you ever feel like that?"

"I think I do," he says and smiles at you, boring his eyes into the spot below your nose.

"Can I light a cigarette in here?"

"Sure." He rolls down the window. "You can keep talking if you like."

You realize that the car is stopped and is idling in front of your apartment.

"I can turn off the meter, you won't be charged," he says. "You could just come over if you want. I've got drinks and everything."

The dim orange glow of the sun is rising over the trees. You can hear the first morning's birdcalls chiming back and

forth around you. The damage to your body is beginning to
emerge in the sharp pains dancing and pulsing around your
temples. How long has it been?

You want badly for Eric to say something soothing
enough to match his voice, some wisdom to impart that will
dissolve your need to remove yourself from your skin, but
instead, this is what you get.

When you fail to answer his suggestion, Eric confronts
the core of what he's trying to communicate: "Are you gay?"

"No," you reply.

"Are you sure? I keep catching you looking at me."

"I've been taught to maintain eye contact when having
a conversation. I'm polite."

"Have you ever tried though?" Eric describes gay
sexual encounters as if it's a type of ethnic food. This does little
to assuage you but you make an effort to study the details of
his face. The male form does nothing for you but there are
feminine features common in some men's faces that can be
focused on and found attractive enough to blossom throughout
the entire person. "You're really, really sexy," he says. "You
deserve all the attention. I can give that to you. Have you ever
kissed a man?"

You have kissed a man only once. It was years ago,
funnily enough while trading lines of coke with an old friend
inside his car, parked outside the ruins of a high school. He
was a fellow artist, volatile and insane, but made his instability
work to his advantage through his pieces. Together, you had a
habit of drinking to excess and cruising down highways and
downtown streets at suicidal speeds. He owned a handgun, the
first one you'd ever seen, and would routinely pull it out
amongst company, pointing it at his head or others, explaining
the fragility of life and how quickly it could be snuffed out with
one adjustment of his index finger against metal.

That night in the car was the night he introduced you
to cocaine. He drove across town in the middle of the night
while you sat in the passenger seat, chain-smoking his
Marlboro Lights and taking swigs from a fifth of Jim Beam.

"The guy we are going to see is a crazy man, Henry," he told you. "Don't look him in the eyes, and I'll do the talking. He once fucked a severed goat head."

There were many follow-up questions you had to this but you kept your mouth shut and watched as he stepped across the street into a waiting vehicle.

The man in the car was blanketed in the shadows of the back alley. You didn't feel the need to make out his face anyway.

When he returned, he opened up the little bag of white powder, dipped in his car key and held it up to your face. "Now close one nostril with your finger and snort hard."

"Is this shit safe?"

"As safe as it's gonna be."

You remember very little about your first reaction to the drug. It was underwhelming. It was nothing compared to the elation that came from alcohol, and you immediately understood that you would never have an issue with cocaine like you did with booze.

Thirty minutes later you were in front of the foreclosed campus, trading lines cut up with an expired J.C. Penney card.

"Have you ever watched gay porn?" he asked, tilting his head back and vigorously rubbing his nose.

"No," you said. "No, I haven't."

"Then how do you know if you're not gay? How do you know you wouldn't enjoy it?"

"To tell you the truth," you said, "I couldn't give a fuck either way. But I sure like pussy, so I figured that was the end of the road in the sexual spectrum department."

"But what if you're missing out on a whole other side of yourself, man? You could be walking around, living a half-life for the rest of your existence."

You tried to ash your cigarette out the cracked window and missed, letting the gray clump fall into the space between the seats. "Look, if this is your way of coming out to me, my dude, you don't need to spin a whole philosophical yarn to do it."

"Damnit, man, that's not what I'm saying. Here, I'm gonna kiss you now, and you're gonna tell me what you feel. Got it?"

You snorted up another thin, pretty line, sucked at the cigarette as it dangled between your fingers. "This is ridiculous."

"Is it? Is it ridiculous to question things?" he asked. "To want to know more about yourself?"

"Shit, that coke is short-circuiting your brain cells."

He leaned in, the white debris crusted around the rims of his nostrils. "Just fuckin' don't be a pussy and kiss me."

You let it happen. All at once, his dried lips were upon you and you felt the sandpaper stubble scrape against the sides of your mouth. It was quick and impassionate. Purely scientific. You detached.

"So what do you feel?" he asked.

"Nothing," you told him. "I feel nothing."

He grinned. "Well, there you go! We disproved my theory! We gained insight." He leaned back into his seat, picked up the 36 Chambers CD off the center console, and began cutting up more lines.

"So *have you*?" Eric repeats.

"No, I haven't."

He leans in close enough that you can smell the delicate cologne beneath his collarbone. "Why don't you try? You are so handsome. I just wanna kiss you."

You balk. The inescapable truth is that you are alone and painfully in need of human affection. You can't help but be flattered that someone, regardless of gender, finds you attractive. And so you want to give this to him. Maybe any sort of intimate human contact will satiate the lonesomeness. You need someone to show you that you are enough.

"I'm not gay," you reiterate.

"I know," he says. "I'm not saying you are, man. Relax. You're up for new things. I respect that. I totally get it."

All that you can hear is the arrhythmic pulse of your heart. "Okay then."

The kiss that follows is an empty ghost. It is nothing more than a vague physical sensation. Nothing has been cured and no void has been filled, even for a brief moment. You are no more loved, nor accepted, nor whole. As Eric stares at you, expecting some reaction, you wish only to throw your head into a solid wall so you may punish yourself before falling unconscious, and for however long that lasts, you will no longer have to deal with this putrid rot feeling that's begun to climb out of you like a parasite.

This thing is inside you. This thing that breaks your soul and poisons your mind. It is not you, but something that has taken root somewhere within you. You know this. You have to believe this. You have not always been this despicable, miserable monster. You were once a child. You smiled. You were happy—you can't recall any examples of this but know still that it is true. What has happened to you?

You are struck with the terrifying, drug-induced notion that the only way to feel normal again is to take a knife, plunge it into your abdomen, and dig around your insides until you find the invading creature, remove it, and kill it.

"What about head?"

The words pull you back from your own mind. You are not sure if you heard him right. "What?"

Eric's hand slides down and begins rubbing his cock through his jeans. "How 'bout you go down on me?"

You are suddenly much more sober. "Nah, man."

Only bitterness resonates through you. Lonesomeness and depression are gone. You don't know where the anger came from, but would rather feel this self-hatred than what you felt before. You'd like to hurt something, set something on fire. There are holes in the ozone layer, islands of plastic trash the size of Texas floating in the Pacific Ocean, rhinos bleeding to death from the stump where their stolen horn used to be, children dying from exhaustion in prison camps at the border. This is the world and you feel every iota of the pain it screams out into the empty universe. All of it has settled and hardened into a coal-black stone at the center of your stomach, and you recognize that you are no longer in control.

Eric takes your hand with the one not unzipping his pants, pulling it towards his lap. "C'mon. Just do it. I come fast."

You rip your hand away from him, the rage quickening your breath. As you go to pull open the car door, you hear a click. Eric has locked the doors.

"Just do it," he says. "Then I'll let you out."

"You're making a mistake," you say. "You need to unlock this fucking door." You are not frightened. You feel nothing but the stone in your stomach.

"Look, man. Don't make this weird. Just suck my dick." Eric's cock is out. His hand reaches around your neck to grab the back of your head. "I won't tell anyone."

The first punch lands in the pocket between his right eye and nose. You feel the bridge cave in against your middle knuckle and blood spurts out both nostrils onto his shirt. You've forgotten how punching a man feels like punching a brick wall.

Human bone is strong, but the nasal bone takes only seven pounds of force to break. This is why many boxers have noses like a jutting cliff face. The second collides with his jaw, snapping his neck sideways and his head slams into the window. Blood pools out of his mouth like an overflowing sink. He spits out a tooth. You grab him by the hair and bash his forehead into the steering wheel. The horn goes off.

"Let me the fuck out," you tell him.

Eric sits, cowering in the corner with his hands up over his face, spitting blood into his lap. He reaches over and unlocks the doors. He says nothing.

You open the car door and step out into the morning air. Before the door can be closed, the car swerves into the street and is gone. You look down at your aching left hand and see his blood smeared across your knuckles. You wipe the blood against your shirtsleeve and walk into your apartment. You realize at this moment that you are very tired.

A few days later you describe the event to McEwen.

"If you're gonna put this in the book," he tells you, "make him some guy who picked you up hitchhiking or something. No one's gonna believe that this shit happened to you on two different Uber rides."

"Yeah, maybe," you say. "Fuckin' Uber though, man. They really need to vet their fucking drivers."

JUNE, 2019

"I don't believe in many things. Maybe anything. The entire point of belief is that it requires a lack of evidence— evidence that would lead you to trust that belief in the first place. But then it's not a belief. It's a hypothesis. Backed by evidence gathered by logic and experimentation. So for this reason, no, I don't hold beliefs. I hold malleable truths that remain open to adaptation or being trashed altogether when new data presents itself.

So when I say that I believe in karma, what I'm saying is that over the course of my life I have gathered more than enough evidence through much experimentation that karma is in fact, quite possibly, a core malleable truth of the universe.

This is one reason why.

After a long enough point, all negative behavior reaches its breaking point. Past that point the damage done is irreversible.

It started with an itch. The paranoia was there—given my sexual proclivities and hypochondria, the second an ingrown hair revealed itself anywhere near my groin the thought of suicide was the first reaction my mind would claw at—but sometimes you are already too drunk and suicidal to care. It's freeing. Until you're sober again. And the itching is worse. And you can see what's causing the itching.

My first stop on the scenic hike down STI Scare Avenue was the local clinic. The doctor who saw me was a square-bodied mole of an old man. His broad shoulders hunched like an armadillo about to curl into a ball to hide from a coyote. As he asked me to pull down my pants, he rolled up his sleeve to put on medical gloves, revealing the numbers tattooed in aging bluish-black ink down his wrist. He was a Holocaust survivor. This comforted me in a way, because what he was preparing to witness once my boxers dropped was guaranteed not to be the most disgusting thing he'd seen in his life, but once the moment occurred, I felt guilty. Hadn't this man seen enough?

He'd earned the right not to be subjected to the sight of a man's infection-riddled penis. I wanted to apologize.

Before the opportunity presented itself though, the doctor concluded his hands-on investigation of my dick and balls. "It's probably just a skin infection," he said, straightening up to throw the gloves into the medical waste bin.

"That's it?" I said. "But...look at it."

"I did, kid. Doesn't look like herpes. Looks like a nasty skin infection. You wash your balls? It's important to wash down there, you know. Lots of folds and pockets. Moisture and whatnot. Dark too. You could grow mushrooms down there if you really tried."

"That's disgusting. Yes, I wash my balls."

"Could be syphilis too, then."

"Syphilis?"

"Yeah, syphilis. Al Capone died of that. People say he had the intelligence of a 10-year-old at the end. Shitting in his pants and drooling like an invalid. It eats away at your brain if you don't get it taken care of. The dumbass was one penicillin shot away but decided to roll the dice instead, I guess. Course, he was having sex with hookers without a condom so maybe the guy didn't have all that much sense to begin with."

"For a doctor, you don't have a much of a filter, do you?"

"I only got so many days left, kid. What're you gonna do, sue me? I'll be dead in five years—I'll just put you in the will, how 'bout that?"

I laughed. I decided I liked this doctor very much.

"So I'm prescribing you a round of antibiotics," he continued, writing something down on a little pad, and handed it to me. "But just to be safe, I'm ordering you a blood and urine test. You're gonna head down the hall and put your name on the list for the lab, and they'll take care of you."

"Thanks."

"And pull up your pants, kid, the exam's over. I'm tired of looking at that thing."

I made my way down the hall, wrote down my name on the list, and sat down next to an old woman covered in liver spots. I studied her as she read an article in *People Magazine*.

Her face was dotted with fat, misshapen moles. Long, black hairs grew from them like blades of grass from a mound of earth. The white curls on her head had begun falling away, revealing the pale blue scalp underneath. Protruding, purple varicose veins snaked up and down her calves like rivers on a map.

One day you may have been beautiful, I thought. One day I may look like you. I wanted to ask how she felt about being old. If the memories of being smooth-skinned and agile brought her joy or if they saddened her that they would never again be experienced. Was she happy to have continued living so long, or does she wish for it to end, unable to have the joy she once had? Does she find joy in the new things, now that the previous list continues to dwindle? Or does she pretend that this is a joyful life, knowing in her heart that it's not, but choosing ignorance is the only way forward? Or is she miserable, accepting these terms of an expiring life that are impossible to reason with? Then, why go on being alive?

I wanted to ask these things. I wanted to ask these things to this old woman but knew that these were naïve questions. Questions only asked by the young who have not seen enough death and life and happiness and sorrow to know what the questions to ask are. To know what to do with the answers even once they are asked.

"Henry Gallagher?"

A young woman in pink scrubs and a short lab coat stood at the lab's doorway with a clipboard. The scrubs shaped to the curves of her hips and down her thighs, filled out and womanly. Tight, golden curls fell over her shoulders. The first thought that invaded my mind was, If I am now a diseased whore, I will never get to fuck another woman like you again. A wave of guilt and sadness washed over me. I felt like crying. The second thought that wrestled in between my eyes was, You are an addict.

This is a woman, not a fix. Act accordingly. The next thought was: But you may still be a diseased whore. Diseased whores, addicted or not, still need love—don't they? No woman will love a diseased whore. These are two traits of an undesirable person. You will die alone.

The woman looked around the waiting room. "Um, Gallagher? Henry Gallagher? Anybody?"

The fourth and final thought provided an amount of solace, however abstract the connection may have been: But, Henry, think of *The Sun Also Rises*. Yes! Jake Barnes' dick got blown off in the war. He and Brett loved each other even though he couldn't fuck. She accepted him.

"Last chance," the technician chimed, "Henry Gallagher, come on up."

But wait, I recalled, Brett chose that Mike motherfucker instead. Shit. Fuck. It ends with Jake dickless and alone. I am Jake Barnes. I will be dickless and alone. Jesus, fuck. This is a doomed scenario.

A sudden slap connected with the back of my head. "Jesus, kid," said my doctor, appearing from the hallway, "are ya deaf? You know your name when ya hear it?"

I shot up out of my seat. "Yes, me, that's me. Sorry."

The doctor shook his head and shuffled off, mumbling under his breath, "Dumb fuckin' kid."

"Well, alright then," she laughed. "Come on back."

The technician directed me into a chair and asked what arm I'd prefer to have blood taken from.

"The right," I answered. "Can't feel it as much." One of the few benefits from having a stroke at birth that affects the entire right side of your body is that your pain tolerance goes up tenfold from the numbness and loss of dexterity. A punch thrown into your right eye becomes more of a nuisance than anything, a dull pressure. Tattoos are less of a chore, more of a vague burning sensation. For this reason, I was more easily able to adorn the right side of my body with expansive and colorful artworks that may otherwise have been a struggle.

The technician grasped my wrist and tapped on the veins on the inside of my elbow before running her fingers down the intricate piece covering my forearm. "That's beautiful," she said.

I forced a smile. "Thank you."

"I've got just the one, wanna see?"

"Sure."

The technician pulled down her scrubs from the collar, revealing the entirety of her cleavage and the lacey, red bra supporting it. Above the left breast was a line that jutted up and down like a mountain range and twisted up into a heart at the end. "You know what that is?"

"An EKG line," I assumed, eyes dutifully unwavering from the subject at hand. "Like a heart monitor."

She nodded. "I got it done when I received my associate's degree to get this job. It's from the EKG machine I have at my house. This line"—she slid her index finger across the tattoo, the rest of her hand gripping the crimson undergarment beneath—"is an actual read I took when I was...excited."

I looked around the empty room. Did this woman just break in and steal a lab coat? Where were the professionals? "I can...I can tell," I stuttered, eyeing the needle she had taken out of a drawer.

"Now...just hold still." She pulled the skin taut until the veins popped out against the surface. "Are you scared of needles, honey?"

"No," I said.

"Good. No need to be scared." With a prick, the needle plunged into my arm and the blood began filing up into the cartridge. "Y'know," she spoke, setting down the full cartridge and replacing it with a new one, "you should come over and try out my EKG machine some time. It's kind of...invigorating, watching your own life appear on a screen right in front of you."

I was beginning to wonder if there was any EKG machine. If not, the euphemism was lost on me. I didn't answer.

When she finished, she wrapped my arm in a red bandage. She walked over to the desk across the room, took a pen and jotted something down on a packet of alcohol wipes. She walked back and handed it to me. On the package was written: **209-678-XXXX Andromeda ;)**

"Give me a call." She smiled. "Come try out that EKG machine. Promise it's worth it."

Andromeda the alleged technician then handed me a
plastic container that I was to piss in to find out if I had a
venereal disease.

All the tests came back negative but things had only
gotten worse. Each time I pissed, it was like knives digging
away at the inside of my urethra. The kind of pain where you
need to make a conscious effort not to have an audible
reaction. Small blisters had begun to form on my tongue until
they covered the whole organ—red, oozing wounds dotting
the pink flesh like gopher holes. The pain was so excruciating
that the act of eating became impossible. I was wasting away.
My temperature hovered around 101, my face constantly pink
and drenched with sweat. I began to wonder if I was dying.

The next stop was Urgent Care. I walked into the lobby
and approached the first woman behind a desk. She wore a
surgical mask, but I could see in her eyes she was uninterested
in my untimely, approaching demise, and I did not like her. She
asked if I was experiencing a fever and/or flu-like symptoms. I
said yes and she handed me a mask to match her own and told
me where to wait for a doctor to come see me.

I sat in the waiting room next to an old woman wearing
a mask like mine, and a sweaty, fat man distracted by his very
loud, very public discussion over the phone.

"I DON'T FUCKING CARE WHAT SHE SAID, MARTHA.
NO, LISTEN TO ME—NO. I WAS WITH JEFF, MARTHA. JEFF.
JEFF FROM FUCKING CHURCH, MARTHA, YOU'VE MET HIM A
HUNDRED TIMES. ASK HIM. HE'LL TELL YOU THE SAME
GODDAMN THING. WELL, SHE'S A LYING BITCH. SHE'S
EXTORTING US, MARTHA, THAT'S WHAT THIS IS. I
WOULDN'T FUCK'ER IF SHE PAID. SHE'D BE SO LUCKY.
MARTHA. MARTHA. MARTHA?"

The woman stared ahead and pretended not to hear
what was going on. She had some kind of nasty chest infection,
hacking up gobs of phlegm and snorting with her head back to
swallow whatever mucous made its way back onto her tongue.
Once the debris was cleared, she would rear back and unleash
a violent, raspy cough that sounded like it was tearing away
the walls of her lungs as it rocketed out of her body like an
exorcism.

After a half-hour of enduring this, I was directed into a white room. A nurse who didn't speak took my blood pressure and temperature before leaving.

The silence that followed stimulated the pain. Fire ants biting away at the inside of my mouth, crawling down through my insides, and clawing their way out of my cock hole, using their pincers like climbers scaling a cliff with ice axes. I meditated on the agony while waiting for the doctor. Christ sweating blood in the Garden of Gethsemane, contemplating the coming crucifixion.

The doctor was a young man with a clean face who didn't look much older than me. I tried not to think about the implications of that fact. He read over the chart and asked me all the questions I'd already been asked a hundred times by technicians, nurses, doctors, priests: "So you'd already been tested for everything?"

"Yeah, that's right. Everything was negative."

He was in the process of observing my crotch, pausing for a moment to ask the next question. "Hm. Well, do you have any idea when you might have contracted something? When was the last time you were sexually active without protection?"

The idea of recalling anything past the last twelve hours was laughable to me, but I did my best to rouse up the memory. It could have been any number of people. It hardly mattered any longer. I wasn't in contact with any of them. "Probably around a month ago," I decided.

"It's possible the tests came back negative because not enough time had passed for the infection to be detectable in your system." He stood and reached into a cabinet on the wall. "I think the best idea is to retest for everything. Make sure we know what we're dealing with for sure this time. I'm also gonna swab you down there to test for herpes."

"So you have no idea?"

He brushed my parts with a few Q-tips. "Not yet, it could be anything. It's quite the mystery right now!"

"I'm glad you're enjoying the novelty of it all," I said. "So it might not even be an STI?"

The doctor slipped the Q-tips into plastic capsules and labeled them. "Oh no, it's definitely sexually transmitted."

"Cool." I stared into the sterile white floor, the breath leaving my lungs like a death rattle. "That's cool."

"And you said something about your mouth?"

"Yeah." I stuck out my tongue, explaining the situation through mush-mouthed vowels as he shined a light on the sores.

The doctor talked into my open jaw: "Yeah. Hm. Well that does help."

"Wha oth?"

"So that's called oral lichen planus." He turned off the light and allowed me to talk like a human again.

"What's that?" I asked.

"It's an autoimmune response. Your immune system is attacking its own cells. Whatever infection you've gotten is causing so much stress on your body that it's gone into overdrive. Basically, your immune system has gone insane. Like a regular guy that has that one really bad day that just makes him...snap and chop up his family. Does that make sense?"

"No," I said.

He frowned. "The point is, once we get you a treatment, that'll go away and your immune system will calm back down."

"Alright. So what now?"

"Well, I'm gonna have you get retested for everything, including from the swabs I've taken, and you'll get a call in three to five days when we get the results."

"Okay."

"But first, I'm gonna have the nurse come in here and give you a shot of penicillin."

"Penicillin?" I asked.

"Yeah. What it most looks like is syphilis. And that bad boy can get taken out with one quick round of doses. It's better to be safe than sorry with these things. Nip it in the bud and take care of it now just in case I'm right. You don't wanna end up like Al—"

"Like Al Capone, I know." I let go of a heavy exhale. "Alright. Yeah, man, fuck it. Bring 'em in."

The doctor left with the samples and the room again became a white vacuum. I sat in silence for ten minutes before there was a knock at the door and a large man in blue scrubs entered with two large syringes in his hands. He was built like a linebacker.

"You the nurse?" I asked.

"Yeah," he laughed. "Not what you pictured, huh? I get that a lot."

I pointed down at the needles, trying to mask my anxiety with an attempt at humor: "So are those going in my ass?"

Without missing a beat, uncapping the tops from the syringes: "Yep. Pull down your pants and lay down on the exam table for me."

I chuckled. I waited. The linebacker nurse looked at me expectantly. "Okay it was funny, now it's not funny." Another awkward pause. Then the epiphanic moment. "Oh. Oh no. Oh. You were serious?"

"'Fraid so, buddy. Faster we get it done, the faster it stops hurting. Well. That's a bit of a lie. It'll take a while to stop hurting."

I pulled my pants back down, laid upon the table and presented my bare ass to the fluorescent ceiling lights.

The nurse stepped forward, looming over me, his massive shadow casting across my body. "I'm gonna do the left cheek first, okay? You're gonna feel a pinch and lot of pressure and some pain."

I held my breath as he counted to three and the needle disappeared into my flesh.

He pushed down on the plunger and the penicillin sunk down inside of me. The pain was unlike anything I'd ever felt, as if some heavy pressure was pulling on the area of entry—all the muscle and fat and tissue—from inside myself like suction from the end of a vacuum cleaner. A dull, burning sensation then spidered out and sat there with the deep pressure, festering together.

The nurse tossed the first syringe into the biological wastebasket. "How'd that feel?"

"*Great*," I said.

"Yeah," he laughed, "when I was in the navy we used to call this the 'fun tax.'"

I shifted the weight off the aching side of my body. "You were in the navy?"

"Four years." He uncapped the second syringe. "When I was stationed at a port in Thailand, we'd have guys going into town, messing around with stuff they shouldn't have and come back needing to get the shots." He stabbed the needle into my right ass cheek. I winced. "It started happening so much that the admiral came up with a rule: Every time some guy came back to base bringing chlamydia or somethin' with him, and he'd get the penicillin shots, that meant that every single sailor on base had to get the shots too."

"Jesus." I smirked, appreciating the distraction from the fire being lit underneath my skin.

"So it got to the point where guys were just letting their STDs get worse and not telling anyone. 'Cause if word got back that you were the guy that made the whole base get stabbed in the ass, well we'd...tune him up pretty good."

The pain in my backside was spreading out like a snake's venom with each pulse.

The nurse tossed the second syringe and bandaged both wounded ass cheeks.

I stood up and pulled my pants back on. "Why didn't anyone just wear a condom?"

The nurse grinned. "Why didn't you?"

I limped down the stairs, down a wide hallway towards the lab. The pain wove itself around me, constricting my thoughts and breathing. All I could do was laugh. People walking the opposite direction gazed at this masked, limping, cackling young man coming upon them, and moved out of the way. I felt like Frankenstein's monster. I almost preferred this kind of attention than anything else. It was a type of fear, an uncomfortable reaction to an unknown, unsure if what they saw was a threat or not. I liked being feared because I was the only one who knew I wasn't frightening. That knowledge was my protectant. A sheep in wolf's clothing.

I sat in the lab's waiting room across from a mother and her infant plopped against her chest like a flimsy toy.

Sitting sent daggers shooting through my lower half but the pain was my punishment so I remained seated, pressing harder against the chair until I had to grit my teeth.

The infant leaned forward and flopped its head over with its rubber neck to stare at me. I stared back. Fuck you, baby. You don't know what's coming. I want to ruin it all for you now. You don't know about the AIDS crisis, the murder rates, what ugly, old men do to pretty, young girls chained to radiators in their basements. You don't know what taxes are, or what it means to be destitute, to be homeless after fighting a pointless war for pointless things, fucked in the ass by Uncle Sam, or car payments, ex-girlfriends who key your car and write **CHEATER** with chicken blood across your garage door for the neighbors to see and judge you. You don't know the Earth is burning us away with her hurricanes and rising oceans and locust famines. You don't know what cancer is or that you'll die or that that mother of yours probably will before you, if you're unlucky. You don't know that life is pain perforated by brief glimpses of joy brought to you by things that shrivel away and die or disappear before your eyes. Why do you get to sit in your ignorance and I have to sit here with all of this? Why can't I give you this knowledge, just for a moment, and I can have the empty room of a mind you possess, just for a few seconds, baby, and I'll take it right back. You don't know how lucky you are.

An older, Hispanic woman appeared from the hallway and called my name. She reminded me of my mother, plump and short and glowing with maternal instinct. She held out her hand and gave me a plastic cup. "Here you go, honey," she said, her thick South American accent coming through like a cat's purr. "The bathroom is over there. Then come back and I'll take your blood."

"Thank you." I smiled. I wanted her to know I didn't think of her how I thought of most people. She deserved all the good things in life. She had lived many lives before this one, and she was good.

I stood over the toilet bowl with the cup aimed where I planned the stream to go. The second it began, the intense burn set in and the fire ants and their ice axes commenced their climb up my urethra. It was almost enough to make me double over. By the time the cup was filled, I felt a warm, sticky liquid trickling down my lip. I reached up and touched it. It was blood. I hadn't realized how hard I was biting down on my lip. The stream continued into the toilet. I aimed at a fly floating on the yellow-tinged surface that I thought to be dead, but once the urine hit the insect, it exploded to life, lifting up, its wings vibrating, and collapsed back against the porcelain wall as it drowned under the piss, crushed with the pressure of a fire hose. "Don't worry," I told the fly.

"There's enough booze in what's filling your lungs to keep you good and drunk while you die. And so there are worse ways to go." I zipped up my pants, sealed the plastic container, and walked out to where the blood drawing stations waited.

I found the Hispanic technician and sat at the chair beside her. She went to work checking for a vein and pulled out a syringe. Needles no longer bothered me. I had been giving blood half my life, since I was diagnosed with epilepsy at 13. The drugs can take a toll on your liver, so the doctors need to check every six months to make sure you're not turning yellow and your liver can still process what it needs to. I also used to give blood in high school. It wasn't for any humanitarian cause, but because we had all heard that if you give blood before smoking weed, it will get you ten times higher. They were right, so I became a regular donor. I hoped the drugs in my system didn't make the blood unusable. I did want to help people. I suppose I did.

As the technician was about to plunge in the syringe, she noticed me trembling and laughing to myself. "Are you scared of needles, honey?" she asked.

I looked at the nametag on her chest. "Gloria," I said, "I just got stabbed twice in the ass. Needles are the last of my worries."

She said nothing. Gloria stuck me with the needle and we watched the dark red blood fill up the cartridges.

When it was done, Gloria tied a pink bandage around my arm and smiled. I stood up. "Thank you, Gloria," I said.

"You are very welcome," she replied. "I'm sorry about your bum-bum."

When I got the news that it wasn't syphilis but herpes, I drove to a bar. I drove to the first bar I saw where no one would recognize me. A row of Harley Davidsons lined the sidewalk in front. I thought of my Uncle Morgan. What would Uncle Morgan do? A mantra I would never act on for any other circumstance. But this time felt right.

All the bikers were sitting together along the bar top. Behind the bar was Angie, who used to bartend at the Twelfth St. Saloon, an old haunt of mine back in the day. I wasn't expecting this but it didn't change my plan. I sat at the end of the bar next to a burly, mustached man still wearing his sunglasses indoors with a **White Power** tattoo stretched across his suntanned left bicep. Angie approached, watching me for a moment before her eyes lit up. "Henry, that you? Hell, it's been a while! How you been?"

"Fine," I said. "Shot of whiskey. Well is fine. Thank you."

"Oh, alright then," she said, put off by my curt answer, but bartenders know how to read moods on people's faces, and know when to leave it alone.

I shot back the drink and looked at the tables behind me. Over in the corner, sat three college-aged men in cutoff T-shirts and backward baseball caps. A blonde in high-waisted shorts and a yellow crop top hovered behind the largest of the three. I waved Angie down and asked for another shot to replace the empty glass. It arrived and I picked it up, twisting around in my barstool to stare at the group.

One of the men met my gaze for a moment then shot his eyes down to his drink, as normal people do when you accidentally make eye contact with a stranger. I sipped at the whiskey, making it as apparent as possible that I had not and was not going to stop looking at these people. After another minute or so, the group became aware of my presence and all three men were looking back towards me. I emptied the rest of my drink.

Finally, it happened, from the largest of the three, which is always how it goes: "You have a problem?"

"No problem," I replied. I held up the shot glass for Angie to fill and turned back towards my new friends.

"Then get your fucking eyes off me, dude."

I drank my shot. The alcohol was working. "Ah, it's not that," I said loud enough that the bikers turned to see what was going on. "It just looks like you're celebrating." One more shot would have helped, but I could go through with it. "So what're you celebrating? The judge drop your rape charges?"

The men stood up and walked towards me. "Ah, I didn't mean nothin' by it," I said, standing up to meet them. I pointed to the blonde hiding from the confrontation. "I'm just saying, if these guys are holding you against your will then blink twice. Unless you're just another one of their cunt bimbo bitches of the week."

The first punch flew over my head as I ducked and made solid connection with the largest guy's chin. Before I could swing again, a fist hit against my temple and I stumbled over. One guy grabbed me with both arms and slammed me onto the floor. Two kicks to the ribs, a hand pulling me up by the shirt collar and a fist slamming into my nose, knocking me back down flat. I looked up through the blur and watched a biker crash into my assailant, then straighten himself and stomp the kid's face into the ground with the unmistakable snap of a breaking bone. The largest guy recovered and turned his focus to another biker who then lifted him off his feet with a sweeping uppercut to the stomach. I tried to laugh and choked on the blood running down my throat. A massive hand lifted me by the back of my shirt like a mother cat grabbing her kitten. I put up my fists beside the biker with the **White Power** tattoo who had helped me, thinking we were on the same team. That's when his knee flew into the center of my chest. I felt the crack and doubled over. Two bikers grabbed me by each arm and I was dragged towards the exit, blood dribbling onto my shirt. They kicked open the door and threw me onto the concrete. I curled up to defend my organs from further assault, but the door closed behind me.

Then it was quiet, and I was alone. Oranges and reds like celestial pastels blended across the sky. It was beautiful.

The door opened again and Angie's voice appeared at my back: "Henry, what the fuck are you doing? I don't see you in four years and this is how you act?"

I did my best to sit up but the pain in my ribs was too great.

"Don't ever come back here, man. You're lucky I'm not calling the cops."

I held up a hand, nodding in submission.

"Get the fuck outta here before those guys come back out to get another piece of you."

I laughed and spit up blood onto the sidewalk. "Yes, ma'am."

"Jesus Christ," she mumbled and walked back into the bar.

I stayed on the sidewalk for a while, watching the sunset. Once the pain subsided enough to stand, I got up and checked my phone. There was an email from my publisher: **Hi, Jack. Hope you're well. Just wanted to check in and remind you that tomorrow *Skipping Record* will officially be available to purchase online and in-store. Get back to me when you can and let's talk book readings. Congratulations again.**

—David West

I stared at the screen. In all the chaos of recent, I'd forgotten. Tomorrow morning *The Skipping Record Waltz* would be on shelves across the country. Henry Gallagher, published author. Look at me now, world. A success.

I limped back towards my car, turned the key, and drove home.

V.
REVELATION

FEBRUARY, 2019

Uncle Morgan died on a Thursday.

I was alerted via text. The bar I worked at was busy and the only indication I would receive that he had even been sick was encrypted into the soul of a lone electronic vibration I was unable to answer. I poured drinks for the packed bar top, took credit cards and bills and loose change and slurred promises of "IOUs," removed the empty glasses, and loaded the glassware into the dishwasher. I thought nothing of what information may be awaiting inside my pocket.

Once the rush lulled, I stepped into the back to see the message. It came from my mother to my sister and me, and the sentence was simple and cold: **Just so you know, your Uncle Morgan died today.**

What? I replied, unable to take in the brief statement. I hadn't seen him in over a decade and was unsure how I was supposed to feel.

How? was all else I could think to type.

Old and broken. my mother responded.

Old and broken. A life 74 years long, a life of stories and memories and feelings and experiences, reduced to a blunt sentence fragment upon reaching its end. My blood, my father's blood, thrown away by three words. A churning unease rose and settled hard at the base of my stomach. It didn't feel right. This was a human life.

Did he get to talk to anyone? Did you talk to him? I texted.

No. my mother answered. **He was not a good person. Disowned by the family. For good reason.**

I didn't disown him, I thought. I never had a choice.

That's not fair. I replied. **He was a person.**

Then came a response from my sister, Carmen: **Did he die alone? At least tell me he didn't die alone.**

Doesn't matter. my mother texted. **He fell into a coma yesterday and didn't wake up. We got the news today. Just figured we'd let you two know.**

Before I could process this or the callous response his sister-in-law offered, a shrill call rang into the backroom: "HENRY, WHERE THE FUCK ARE YOU? WE'RE GETTING SLAMMED, STOP JERKING OFF BACK THERE AND COME HELP."

I put away my phone and ran back to serve more poison.

Uncle Morgan was, by most sources, not a good person. Almost objectively so. He was the only one of six children who did not make something of himself—at least by Gallagher family standards. While his siblings were studying for the bar exam or working through officer ranks in the U.S. Navy, Morgan was selling cocaine and military-grade firearms for a little group of friends who liked to ride motorcycles and avoid bathing or working a day job. They called themselves the Hell's Angels. Because being a member of one of the most feared motorcycle gangs in the country wasn't a valid excuse to avoid the draft, Uncle Morgan became a private in the Marines and was shipped off to Vietnam. He enjoyed the abundance of drugs and cheap hookers available in Saigon while on R&R, but wasn't a fan of every other aspect of military life. He was dishonorably discharged a year later, but not before finding a few connections that helped him smuggle out enough rifles and explosives to start a government takeover. These were brought to the Hell's Angels in exchange for their narcotics plugs who seemed to fuel the entire organization at the time.

Upon returning stateside, Morgan decided to brush up on his knowledge of the law, if only so that when the time inevitably came, he wouldn't have to hire a lawyer in the numerous court cases he would bring upon himself. Some time in the '80s, my uncle earned himself a law degree and became a bona fide criminal defense attorney.

Less than two decades later, Uncle Morgan's law expertise would prove necessary. I'll just read an excerpt from an article dated September of 2002:

A Boston resident and criminal attorney who was booked on suspicion of nine felony drug and weapons charges—representing himself—waived his right to

arraignment Monday afternoon and is scheduled to enter a plea today in Superior Court in Boston.

"We had information which led us to believe Gallagher had drugs and guns in his house…and just followed the trail to Southie," narcotics officer James Bearing said.

Police found more than 15 pounds of packaged marijuana, 171 budding marijuana plants that were hung up to dry and several dozen potted plants in Gallagher's basement and garage. In addition, police said they seized 15 grams of cocaine, 12 grams of hashish, and an arsenal of assault weapons including submachine guns and assault pistols.

"Gallagher had an elevator lift covered with a throw rug in the kitchen which led us to the basement where most of the drugs were found," Bearing said. "After that, he temporarily waived his Miranda rights and showed us where the guns were hidden, stating that he didn't want us to feel 'uncomfortable' or get hurt because they were all loaded."

According to Bearing, this isn't the first time Gallagher has been arrested. He has a prior record and has been arrested for transportation of drugs, possession of drugs, and two convictions for driving under the influence of alcohol.

Gallagher strongly argued his own case in the hopes of getting his bail reduced, stating that he has Lou Gehrig's disease, a disorder that results in muscle deterioration, paralysis, and eventually death, and that Gallagher has a prescription for medical marijuana—valid only in the state of California. It should be noted that Gallagher does not hold residency in California. As for the cocaine and illegal weaponry, Gallagher stated, "One thing at a time here, fellas."

Neighbors on the street where Gallagher has lived for more than 30 years said they were dismayed and horrified when more than 30 drug enforcement agents descended on their neighborhood Friday morning and uncovered the arsenal of weapons and drugs.

Katie Wilson, who runs KinderCare Preschool out of her home two doors down from Gallagher said she always knew he was an offbeat criminal attorney who represented members of Hell's Angels, but was shocked to learn that he had weapons in his house.

"Dear God, what is this world coming to?" she asked.

So that's my uncle. After the dust had settled and Morgan finagled for himself just six months house arrest, three years' probation, and an enormous fine, his financial state was in ruins. He became desperate. His sister Lyla, before landing in a nursing home for the last fifteen years, had amassed a large sum of money, put away for her upcoming cancer treatments. Being the oldest living member of the family, Morgan had been put in charge of the fortune by her lawyer, acting on her behalf. Morgan dipped his hand into the account and promptly emptied it.

This obviously did not go unnoticed by his siblings. My father cut off all contact with Uncle Morgan, barring him from ever talking to his brother again—including his niece and nephew. His niece and nephew who loved him very much. I was nine or ten at the time and had only met my uncle twice, but had talked to him on the phone as often as he was allowed. His odd way of speaking, drifting and lilting through a deep, croaking voice was wonderful to me. Like walking down a twisting and turning gravel path. He listened to everything I had to say—proud when I told him I had aced my spelling test, excited when I said I hit a triple at my Little League baseball game. It was apparent that he wanted to be there as much as he could, but even before the court case my father was wary of his lifestyle and possible influence on his children.

After my father made this decision, Uncle Morgan was enraged. A week later, through his brother Harry, he learned that Morgan had put a hit out on his life via the Hell's Angels. Harry was able to talk Morgan down, eventually getting him to call off the hit, but this act of attempted fratricide was the final blow to the crumbling building that was the Gallagher family. That was the last day that Uncle Morgan ever talked to a blood relative.

But I didn't know any of this.

Once I had rounded up the stragglers and locked the doors behind them, I sat at the bar alone and poured myself a drink. It wasn't until this point that I was really able to pause and soak in what had happened. I barely knew the man, and though he was blood, I didn't feel any particular sense of loss. But there was this uncomfortable feeling itching at me, this sense of remorse and pain for a man who died unloved. I regretted that I wasn't able to talk to him, to regain a relationship with my uncle in my adult years. Did he miss me in his last decade of life? Did he care? Did I?

As I sipped the expensive, pilfered liquor in the dark, I wracked my brain, sifting through the fog of my childhood memories, trying to find the moment I first met him. In the haze and blackness, one memory burned through the thickness like a lighthouse beam.

I couldn't have been older than six. My dad had sat me down and told me that a special person was coming to stay at the house for a few days. When he said "special," he meant special as in strange and not as in a person of worth. He told me this person was Uncle Morgan, and he was very excited to meet me.

It's peculiar which moments choose to stay lodged in the recesses of your mind and which fall away into the ether as time goes on. I don't remember what he said to me, or what he did while staying at our home, or if we ever spent time around each other beyond basic, fleeting interactions in passing. But what I do remember was his entrance.

The door opened to the most amazing sight I'd ever witnessed. As if produced from a puff of smoke, a magician's trick, he appeared. Wearing a red kimono loosely tied around the waist, revealing the gaunt, elderly frame of a man who once was formidable, stood my uncle. His toenails were painted red to match, secured by a pair of cheap sandals. On his arm was a Thai sex worker he'd picked up at a local rub-and-tug, whom he introduced as his girlfriend. Before a dialogue could be introduced, though, she was asked to leave, at which point my uncle pulled out a wad of cash, slid it into her visible G-string, told her he would come back for her, and

that he was in love with her. The door closed behind the
hooker, giving way to the sense of regret emanating from the
two adults staring ahead at the man they were now letting into
their home. I stared up at Morgan as he dropped his bags to
the ground and grinned. This was the most fascinating man I'd
ever met. I wanted to know everything he knew. I loved him
from the first moment I saw him. He was like nothing I'd ever
seen. He was everything my parents weren't. He was an
original.

Once I finished the drink, I called my sister.

"I don't feel right about this," I said.

"Neither do I," Carmen told me.

"Let's get drunk about it."

"It's what Uncle Morgan would've wanted," she said.

"See you in twenty."

We met at an old dive somewhere on the north side of
town where she lived with her longtime partner, Anthony.
Carmen and I sat together at the empty bar top, holding our
drinks in the air.

"Well...I don't know what to say."

"I don't either," I said.

Carmen paused for a moment. "You know he offered to
call up one of his Hell's Angels buddies to come up and take
out my 7th grade algebra teacher?"

"Of course he did," I chuckled.

"The teacher had said some very inappropriate things
to me. I called Morgan and he said he'd have someone inside
his house in 24 hours. He was my favorite relative."

"Bat shit crazy," I added, "but he meant well. And who
isn't bat shit in this family anyway?"

"He was the only family member that seemed to care
about me," Carmen said. "What do you think of when you think
of Aunt Patricia or Uncle Daniel? Have you even ever met
Lyla?"

"No," I said. "Morgan was the only one that bothered
talking to me."

Carmen sniffed at the tequila in her glass, gagged, and
held it away from her face. "The only thing I remember about
Patricia is her telling me I was giving her a migraine."

"When did you last see him?" I asked.

"I must have been 18. I went up to visit him when Mom and Dad wouldn't communicate with me. When I had just gotten out of treatment. He was the only family member who responded to my calls and emails. 2008."

"I responded," I said.

"I know you did, little brother. You know what I mean. You were just a kid. I needed help, I needed family."

"Yeah. I know."

Carmen looked down at the aged wood of the bar top and pivoted before the conversation became too personal. We knew we loved each other, but it was difficult to put that kind of thing into words. We weren't big huggers. "He showed me the elevator down to the grow-op," she said. "That article wasn't exaggerating. The place was enormous. It was like something out of a Bond film."

"Did you see all the guns?"

"I slept in the spare bedroom. Which was the room where he kept all the guns."

"You slept in a room filled with loaded assault weapons?"

"He just told me not to touch anything."

We looked around the empty bar, our glasses still hovering above the counter. "Do you think he missed us?"

"I don't know," said Carmen. "I wish I could have talked to him one last time. Sometimes I wanted to call him and just say, 'Fuck you. Why didn't you wanna know us?'"

"I think he did," I sighed. "Mom and Dad just wouldn't let him. At least I hope that's what it was."

"I think that's what it was too." I could hear the weakened faith in her voice.

"Do you still have the T-shirt?" I asked.

"'Free Morgan Gallagher'? Hell yeah, I still wear it. The Hell's Angels raised all the money themselves to pay for his bail with the proceeds."

Another long pause, our glasses hovering.

"I hate how his death has been handled," Carmen spoke, finally. "Mom and Dad could have talked about me the same way if I had died before being prescribed Lithium. I've spent so much time trying to get to know our family without any success. I don't want the last thing that someone says about me to be that I died old and broken."

A light above the bar flickered and went out. I suddenly realized that I hadn't taken a sip yet. "You wanna know my favorite memory of Uncle Morgan?" I asked.

"What is it?"

"It was when we both went with Dad to stay at his house. You were probably like twelve or thirteen so I must have been eight. It was the last time I saw him in person."

"I remember that trip," said Carmen. "You were obsessed with the—"

"The floating bed!" I shouted, slamming my hand down on the bar. "I was so fucking fascinated with that thing, I couldn't stop looking at it, trying to figure it out. Morgan told me it was held up by magic and promised to teach me the magic one day."

Carmen laughed, "And you were too dumb to notice the wires connecting it to the ceiling."

"Well, I'm glad I didn't," I said. "I'm glad the magic didn't go away. I remember thinking, 'My uncle is a wizard. My uncle is the coolest guy in the world and soon I'll be a wizard too and I'll sleep on a floating bed like him.' It's all I could think about that trip. But then the next day, he took me out and showed me the whole city. Of course Dad wouldn't let him take me by himself, but he seemed so happy. I remember he took me into a toy store and asked Dad if he could buy me something. He didn't know much about me and I think he was just pretty nervous and didn't know what kids liked, so after a second, he comes back and hands me a Gumby doll—you remember those things? I have no fucking clue why he thought I'd want a Gumby doll—I didn't even know what it was—but I loved it because my magic uncle got it just for me. He was really trying. I know he really loved us even when he wasn't talking to us."

At that moment, the light above us flickered once more and came back on. The bar was a little brighter now. We both looked up and laughed.

"I hear you, old man," I said, grinning up at the ceiling. "We hear you. Love you, you old, broken bastard."

Carmen held up her drink. "To a good goddamn uncle."

"To Uncle Morgan," I said.

"To Uncle fucking Morgan."

I lifted my drink towards the light over our heads. "To one last conversation."

The niece and nephew then touched glasses, and had a drink with their uncle.

OCTOBER, 2018–APRIL, 2019

The letter had been sent to the address where I lived five years previous. The current residents of that address happened to be my parents so the letter was forwarded and dropped onto a soggy welcome mat at the foot of my studio apartment.

I didn't realize people still wrote letters.

Ginger. I read the signature before I read the letter. I hadn't thought of that name in a long time. The last time I'd talked to her, I was 21 with a bottle of Wild Turkey creating a wildfire out of my brain, describing to her over the phone my plans to empty my entrails onto the base of an oak tree upon collision via vehicular-assisted, high-speed impact. She told me to go ahead and do it. Lucky for us both, I was all talk and threats those days. She was a good friend.

Dear Henry,
I hope you're still trying to get to the moon. If you are, I hope you've found it.
Ginger

It was a reference to a poem I wrote when I was 20 and burgeoning into a less hopeful person, and when she was barely legal. It was the poem she read online that spurred her to reach out to me for the first time. On the back of the letter she had written her number. A wave of memories flushed through my mind. I missed her. The last thing I knew about her before our falling out and my falling off the map for three years was that she was expecting a child. A child she decided to keep at age 19 after experiencing a revelatory acid trip while it was forming in the womb. A child whose birthday was expected worryingly right around nine months after we'd had sex. She was furious with me when I had floated the idea that these two facts could be connected, and insisted she knew who the father was. They had moved in together, and I had moved closer to my addictions and further away from any semblance of mental stability, and with the disintegration of my sobriety and grasp on reality, so too came the disintegration of our friendship. And that was that. The kid would be four-years-old now.

When I called and that familiar voice reached out through the phone, the first words she said were: "I thought you might be dead."

"I'm not," I told her.

"Good. I'm glad, Henry. I'm happy to hear that."

We arranged to meet downtown that night at the Dead Rabbit for a drink. She said it was close to her work and afterward she could walk from there. I sat at the end of the bar, hunched over a whiskey-soda, my beard trimmed to a presentable five o'clock shadow, my short, curly hair smoothed down like this was a nervous first date. I wanted to appear as though I'd been taking care of myself in the time she'd missed. I wanted her to think I was doing okay. No part of me floated in the hope that we may rekindle whatever romantic connection we'd had. For reasons I didn't quite understand, I wanted her to be proud of me more than anything else. After the state she'd left me in those years ago, I just wanted her to believe I'd turned a new leaf.

When she entered, it took me a second to register that this was the person I was supposed to meet. The freckled, youthful face I remembered was there, but beneath a thick layer of eyeliner and makeup. There was a feline sexuality about her: narrowed eyes and fuller lips, her face more gaunt and adult, having shed the rounded, more childlike shape around the cheekbones. The short, strawberry red hair that I'd remembered was dyed blonde and pulled back into cornrows, the natural reddish brown like worn copper still appearing at the roots. She wore fishnets running into six-inch, black stilettos. Some kind of corset was obscured underneath a bulky winter jacket.

She made eye contact and noticed me right away. I stood up and was hoisted into her chest for a hug. "Hey, man!"

"Hey, hi," I said, scanning the outfit.

We sat down together.

"So...um." I balked, adjusting to the surrealism of the moment. "What're you getting? I'll get your drink."

"Sure, thanks," said Ginger, looking at my face and smiling, assessing. She waved down the bartender and ordered a martini. Then turning back to me: "You look good. You look the same."

"Given my lifestyle since I last saw you, that's one of the best compliments you could've given me." I laughed, then immediately regretted telling her that. Self-deprecation is the go-to when I'm nervous but this was the wrong interaction to talk like that.

She hesitated. I was already worrying her. "Well, I'm just glad you're alive. And you have aged a bit." She tapped her finger on my forehead. "A few wrinkles up there I can see. They call those worry lines. How have you been?"

I took a sip. "I've been okay. Ups and downs, y'know."

"What have you been doing?"

"I write for a few magazines. I started working at a bar."

"Of course. My Henry, right at home."

"And I wrote a book."

"I wouldn't expect any less. When does it come out?"

"Next year. You're in it."

She smirked. "I hope you made me look good."

"It'd be hard not to. You might like it."

"If not, I'll just sue."

"There you go. So it's win-win for you." My leg bounced beneath the bar, shaking my stool. It was a nervous tick I always had. I was uncomfortable keeping the conversation on myself. "But what about you?" I pivoted. "How are you? What's your life been like?"

"Well," she said, stirring around the olive in her martini, "I had the kid. His name is Oliver."

"That's amazing, Ginger."

"And another one."

"Another one?" I looked down at her torso, as slim and shapely as the day I met her. "I wouldn't even be able to tell."

"He just turned a month old. Liam. With Ollie's father."

"Oh," I blurted, grasping at a response. "That's a...fresh baby. So you're still together then? That's good—if you're happy, I mean."

"I am." She grinned, holding up her left hand to show the ring. "We're married."

"Married? Jesus, Ginger, what else have I missed?"

"I think that about covers it." She looked at me with her head cocked, trying to gauge something from my reaction.

"I wish I had been there for all of that," I said finally. "I'm sorry. I've missed you."

"Don't worry about it, Henry. We're here now. I missed you too."

A pause filled the static air where we both knew certain things wanted to be, but weren't going to be addressed, our eyes drifting into our drinks. I closed the gap before the pressure of the lull in conversation forced our past out of us: "Thank you for reaching out, Ginger."

"I needed to know what happened to you. I thought about you a lot. Where you were, what you were doing." She played with her wedding ring, spinning it around on her finger. "I worried a lot. I had dreams you were dead. I try not to look into dreams too much. But I was scared for you."

"I'm doing better now," I said before cracking and letting slip, "And I'm sorry for—"

"We don't need to talk about that. It happened. I said things I wish I didn't. I'm glad you're doing better."

I sensed she was uncomfortable, or that she knew I was lying, so I dropped it. We touched glasses and finished our drinks. "Can I buy you another one?" I asked.

"Can't," she said. "Can't drink too much until I get to work."

"Right, work," I said. "So, what do you do again?"

"I dance at the Aquarius Gentlemen's Club down a couple blocks from here, over on 2nd."

"You're a dancer?" I leaned over in my seat to gauge her outfit once more. "Well, it explains the attire. When did you start doing that?"

She laughed. "Since I turned 18. I was stripping when you met me. I never told you that?"

"No... No, you never did."

"What did you think I did for a living?"

"Well," I thought about it, "didn't you say something about fast food?"

"Yeah, during the day. Not anymore though. You should come visit me some time."

"Yeah," I said. "Sure." I put money down on the bar and Ginger stood up.

"Walk me to work?"

We left the bar and started down the street, stepping around the smokers huddled by the benches and the homeless curled into the covered entrances with sleeping bags and empty boxes of takeout food from the trash.

She lit a cigarette, using the inside of her jacket as a windshield. "You should meet my husband if you want, and my kids. I know they'd love you."

"Yeah, I'd like that."

"Good. You're not going anywhere this time, Henry Gallagher, you got it?"

I managed a weak smile. "Yes, ma'am."

"Alright then."

We arrived in front of the club, a dingy place right next to a male strip club called The Hard Spot. She finished her cigarette and stomped it out under her heel. "You better text me. If not, I will. You're staying in my life."

"I will," I said. "I promise."

She pulled me in for another hug and turned around, waving to the bouncer, and disappeared into the darkness of The Aquarius. This is how Ginger came back into my life.

The next week, Ginger pulled me out of my stupor long enough to join her and the kids at a park in her neighborhood. She said I wasn't fooling anyone and that I needed some exercise and fresh air.

We met up in the parking lot and she waved while unloading the baby stroller from the back of her minivan. She reached into the backseat and pulled out what resembled a lumpy potato in an onesie, plopping it into the cushioned seat. The adjacent door opened and out jumped a small child with long, straight, black hair hanging across his eyes and hiding his ears like vines growing over a window. Ginger took his hand, grasped the stroller in her other, and came closer. She bent over towards the child and talked softly, "Ollie, this is my good friend. Can you say, 'Hi, Henry'?"

Oliver stared up at me with an empty expression.

Trying once more, Ginger leaned in to pet his hair and asked, "Don't you wanna say hi, baby?"

Oliver said nothing, but maintained the blank stare. I looked into his eyes: blue-gray. My eyes were green. His hair was black and straight. My hair was brown and curly. Maybe she was right. One could hope.

She stroked his hair again and shrugged with a smile. "Sometimes he can be shy around new people. And that's okay—isn't it, Ollie?"

A gaggle of geese feeding on the grass by the pond had drawn his attention away from me, and he began to chew on the hand she'd been holding. I couldn't tell if it was out of absentmindedness or anxiety.

Ginger pushed the stroller forward, allowing me to take a look at the gurgling potato.

"And this is Liam."

Liam had brilliant blue eyes, a striking feature in contrast to the otherwise ordinary-looking bald and beige blob. He wriggled around and looked up at me in awe. Not frightened but curious. I crouched to give a small wave, smiling. "Hi, buddy."

"Carl wasn't able to come today, their father. But I'm sure you'll meet him soon. He knows all about you."

"Oh does he?" I laughed. "All about me?"

"Yes, you pervert. Being the husband of a stripper requires a certain amount of self-confidence. He trusts you."

"Good," I said. "He should."

I meant this when I said it. Any kind of urge I'd feel with a woman of her beauty wasn't there, not out of respect for the husband, but because there was something deeper there I couldn't quite articulate. Some kind of maternal love I felt from her, a platonic love one feels from someone they know will keep them safe. I felt secure and taken care of with Ginger. I wasn't on the cusp of an episode or a bar fight or a binge while beside her, because I knew that if I was, she would comfort me before it escalated. That aching fear always lingering and vibrating beneath my skin slowed to a steady hum when with Ginger. I loved her very much. I always had.

I watched her walk ahead of me towards the playground with her children, on the surface a completely different person. Her professional uniform traded for that of a dedicated mother: a denim jumpsuit with a tie-dyed fanny, within it an assortment of items prepared for any temper tantrum or preschool emergency. Her blonde-tinged cornrows taken out and let loose around her shoulders, and high heels swapped for dirty flat-tops.

Oliver skipped over rocks and twigs, eyeing the structure with caution where a group of children had commandeered the slide and monkey bars. Ginger would ask Oliver questions as we walked, asking if he could identify the things around us: "Ollie, can you tell Mommy what that is?" When the child wouldn't answer but continued walking ahead, always close to his mother, Ginger would try again: "Ollie, is that a bird? Do you know what kind of bird that is? What sound does a bird make?" And again he would fail to answer, looking back at his mother as if registering that she was asking him a question, but unable to muster a response.

"He knows what it is," she told me. "He has trouble articulating. We've been taking him to a speech therapist for the last few months and that seems to be helping. He's able to say his name now." She cooed at Oliver, "Baby, can you spell your name? Can you spell 'Oliver' for me?"

Again there was no answer and Oliver instead motioned towards the playground.

"Yeah, go play, baby. Just make sure that Mommy can see you. Henry and I will be right here on this bench, okay?"

He nodded with a finger in his mouth and took off towards the play structure. She and I sat down with Liam in the stroller beside us. I watched Oliver stop far away from the other children and begin combing through the bark dust, looking for sticks on his own. "Is this normal?" I asked.

"No," she said. "We thought at first that he was just a slow learner, but I started to worry and took him to see a child developmental therapist. It's always hard to say this early but it's more than likely that he's autistic. He would be starting preschool but now I'm trying to find a special program for him. I wanna give him as much a chance as I can as early as possible." Ginger watched her son digging in the dirt, his attention trance-like upon the ground and nothing else. "I just don't want him to grow up and be that one weird kid who *Naruto*-runs everywhere he goes."

I thought of the dose of acid that introduced itself to his expecting mother, wondering how much of an effect the drug could have had. Had Ginger caused this? Halted the synaptic connections that would have led to healthy brain development? Or was this inevitable?

A failed roll of the dice during the age-old game of the genetic lottery? A separate outcome dealt by the outside circumstances relating to his birth? The answer wasn't mine to know. All I knew for sure was that this was a subject I could never bring up to her, much like the burning question I'd harbored for four years before looking her child in the eyes. We're all children of circumstance, outside or otherwise. The specifics aren't ours to know. We are given what we are given and from that moment forward it is entirely on us to decide what happens next. I understood that better than most. The past hardly matters when time moves as quickly as it does. In fact, the past doesn't exist at all.

I recognized that logically, but why then did the past control every fiber of my being?

"Where's your husband?" I asked. I wondered if Ginger had ever told him.

"Oh, off on business somewhere," she said. "He's always gone it seems like. Or locked away in the spare room on his computer."

"Does that bother you?"

"No, no. I work nights so I need something to do during the day anyway. And who wouldn't wanna hang out with these little babies?" She gestured up towards Oliver, who had begun some kind of non-verbal communication with another child, pointing to the small pile of sticks he'd accumulated. The younger girl seemed interested and squatted to inspect Oliver's cache. Her eyes drifted from the sticks to Oliver, and she giggled before nudging him with a rubbery toddler hand

and took off around the play structure. He took a moment to register what had been initiated, then cracked a wide, open-mouthed smile and chased after her, weaving around the monkey bars and slides, kicking up bark dust. Ginger lit up. "Oh my God! He found a friend!"

My eyes followed the two children chasing each other, then Ginger, who cupped her hands on either side of her face, the afternoon sunlight illuminating the constellations of freckles dotting her cheeks and the white behind her curled lips. "Does he have trouble making friends?"

"Nobody ever wants to play with him," she said, still beaming, her eyes glued to her child racing through the park. "He never smiles like this around other kids. Doesn't he look so happy?"

"He does," I said.

Ginger began to tear up, her smile wavering and trembling just briefly. "It can be so hard sometimes. I just want him to be happy so bad. I'd give him everything if I could."

"You are," I said. "You're giving him every chance to be. I'm sure he knows how lucky he is to have you for a mother."

Ginger glanced at me before turning her attention back towards her son. "Thank you," she said.

The soft gurgling coming from the stroller erupted into wails, and Ginger's trance broke as she stood to check on her baby. "What's going on now? Did you poop? Are you hungry, baby? Aw yeah, come here, honey, come here." She hoisted the child up and against her chest, swaying back and forth in her flat-tops, humming close to Liam's ear.

I looked up, making sure we still had eyes on Oliver, and found him frozen, staring ahead at nothing with those glazed eyes. The younger girl had stopped running to look back and find her playmate, and upon seeing that he had given up on the game, returned to her own fun, disappearing into the play structure. A dark spot was growing wider and elongating from the crotch of his pants, down into the left leg.

"Ginger?" I tapped her waist. "I think, uh—I think Oliver wet himself."

She craned her neck over, zeroing in on her son. "Oh no. Okay. Henry, can you hold Liam?"

Before I could answer, the baby was thrust into my arms and his bright blue eyes were fixed upon my own. "I'll be right back," she said. "Looks like we might need to cut this short, I'm sorry." She took off towards Oliver, who hadn't moved a muscle or even acknowledged the wet spot that covered so much of his pants its color had changed.

The spit bubble Liam was blowing popped and became a viscous mess dribbling down his chin. He smiled at me. "Hey, buddy," I said. "Okay, hi." He was so light. I understood he was a newborn and couldn't have weighed more than ten pounds but I had never held a baby before. I had nothing to compare him to. Holding Liam instilled an immediate low-level anxiety: This was the most fragile thing in the world. Completely incapable of self-sufficiency. I, for however brief a time, was in charge of maintaining and protecting a human life. I wrapped one hand under his bottom and held him against my chest with my other hand firmly but gently against his little back. Maybe my heartbeat would be calming for him. I patted his back and rocked back and forth like Ginger had been doing. "Okay, buddy. This is nice, huh? Hope so. I don't know what the fuck I'm—oh, sorry. I don't know what the heck I'm doing, so, y'know, bear with me, little guy."

Could I be a father? I thought. Could I harbor this specific anxiety for the rest of my life, as long as the life I created exists on Earth? Would I be able to instill in it good morals and respect for people and a good work ethic? If it were interested in girls, could I teach it how to treat women, like how it would want its mother to be treated? If it were interested in boys, could I teach it how to stay safe from harm? To avoid the creeps and abusers? To learn how to spot them? Could I teach it self-love, self-worth? Could I come to terms with the fact that I had struggled or continue to struggle with all of these things? Could I reconcile how I'd treated women in the past, with what morals I had chosen at one point or another to ignore, but what had nonetheless been instilled in me? Would it make me a hypocrite? Unfit to be a parent, to bring life into the world and teach it values *I* struggled to live by? Or what of my genetics? Could I in good conscience father a child knowing the risks I could be implanting into my child's code? How could I forgive myself if my child drowns in the addictive nature I burdened it with? Or succumbs to the suicidal nature of the mental illnesses I passed down upon it? What if the abuse I suffered as a child at the hands of my father somehow awakens something in me? What if I continue the cycle of abuse? What if I fail as a father?

"Henry." Ginger returned with Oliver loosely hanging onto her fingers. "I gotta take this little munchkin back home and clean him up."

"Oh, that's alright," I said. "Do what you need to."

"Thanks for coming out of your cave for a while to meet my kids." She reached her free hand out and pulled Liam away from my chest. An empty hole opened up where he was and I stabbed back the urge to get drunk. "That's alright, Ginger. Thank you for letting me meet them."

She smiled. "Don't get into too much trouble, okay?"

"I won't," I said.

We walked towards the parking lot.

Ginger loaded Oliver into the backseat of the minivan. "I'll see you soon then?" she asked, wrapping an available arm around my waist with Liam tucked into the crux of the other.

"Yeah," I answered.

Ginger opened the driver's door and tilted Liam over her shoulder before disappearing into the car. "Say bye to Henry, baby. Say bye-bye."

"Bye, Liam," I said. "Bye, buddy."

The door closed, and the car drove away.

The further I fell into my habit of isolation over the coming months, the less I saw of Ginger. She would make sure to call me at least once a week if I was unwilling or unable to trade the comfort of a bar or a dark room for her company. She referred to them as "welfare checks." So when I received a call from Ginger one night almost a half-year since the day we reconnected, I assumed what would follow was the typical "You dead? No? Okay. I love you, be careful." On this night, though, that was not the case.

She sounded drunk, almost irritable. "Henry? Henry! Get the fuck over here! I need someone to get fucked up with and you're the best person I know at doing that." The slurred words fell in and out behind blaring hip-hop music.

"Where is here?" I asked.

"At my work! You and I are gonna go out together once I'm off. But you have to come here now! NOW, Henry!"

Drinking in the company of anyone who knew me on a personal level sounded deeply unpleasant, but the next words out of Ginger's mouth got me into the car: "I'm buyin'."

The Aquarius Gentleman's Club was an 18-and-up strip joint, meaning two things: The clientele was composed of either college kids blowing through their loan money that was meant to get them a degree in a field they'd never end up working in anyway, scuzzy, meth-scabbed high school dropouts forgetting to study for their GED while pumping gas at the station down the street, or dirty old men locked in the eternal struggle of avoiding a statutory rape charge. But more importantly for me, it meant that the establishment couldn't legally sell alcohol. The type of person who can be sober in a strip club without a rush of shame and powerful urge to throw one's head into the soda-bar mirror is an individual I have no business knowing. It's for this reason that I decided to make a stop next-door to construct a thin wall of inebriation between myself and what was to come.

I had never been inside The Hard Spot. It wasn't all that difficult to picture what that might look like though. The bar sat lined up against the right wall while the rest of the club's open space was taken up by three circular stages all connected to the low ceiling by their metal poles. Two men in thongs navigated the space between stage and ceiling, twirling in the air and arching back with the strength of their core allowing them to remain perpendicular to the floor, their arms outstretched and curved, swan-like, then running their hands up and down their bodies, massaging the sinewy muscles in the arms and torso before spinning to the floor, thrusting hips into the air on their backs, the men around the stage raining dollars upon their naked forms. The third man stood in front of the pole completely nude, unabashedly spinning his cock around and around like a psychiatrist's hypnosis tool, his hips gyrating in circles. After witnessing the event, I wished to un-

see it but this was now an image seared into my mind to be
recalled at inopportune times until the memory would at last
fall away to make room for newer, more important or scarring
recollections.

The bartender greeted me as I sat down, a clean-cut
young man with a thin mustache and something not unlike a
speedo with a bedazzled vest over a waxed, bare chest as his
only means of attire. "What'll it be, handsome?"

I surveyed the multi-colored wall of liquor bottles.
"How 'bout a double shot of tequila. No training wheels."

Tequila was generally the type of liquor I avoided, as it
had a tendency to break any connection I once had to civility,
congratulating me at the end of the night with a fistfight and a
broken hand, but it had stimulating effect, and whiskey was
too numbing, too depression-inducing to be drinking in the
company of those expecting you to keep the party going.

I drained a few doubles in quick succession until I was
confident the alcohol had brought me forth into a sunnier
disposition. The strobe lights flashing from every corner of the
ceiling made it difficult to see, and when I closed my eyes, a
kaleidoscope of colors like fireworks popped and erupted over
each other in the darkness until I opened them again, and like
haunting specters, they followed into the world beyond my
eyelids, now glaring, amorphous blotches dancing and
skipping across the bar and over my reflection in the mirror.
Being an epileptic, I paid the bill without a word and left
before I found myself seizing under the vibrating lights with
the cock-spinning stripper applying mouth-to-mouth.

Before the Aquarius' bouncer had the chance to ask me
for the $10 entrance fee, Ginger's voice, loud and slurring,
appeared behind me: "It's fine, Benny, he's with me."

I turned around and there she was, elevated to match
me at eye level by the massive heels clacking against concrete.
The bouncer nodded, avoiding eye contact, and Ginger pulled
me through the door and up the stairs into the club. In the
darkness, it was still evident how much her appearance
differed in her professional attire. There wasn't much left to
the imagination, but I guess that was the point. The form of her
body was on full display, everything sexual about the female

anatomy expertly accentuated to guarantee the highest influx of cash she could hope to accumulate in a single night.

"Do you need anything to drink?" she yelled into my ear over the music.

The club looked to be underpopulated, a few sleazy drug dealers and their addicts talking at the booths along the walls, shaded by the forgiving lighting and the hoods over their eyes. One young woman danced alone at the center stage, twerking and clapping her heels while on her back, putting on a show for no one but herself. The stark white flesh of her naked body appeared bright neon under the passing strobes crisscrossing over the stage.

"I thought this was a dry club?" I yelled back, my hand on her shoulder.

"The club is, but I'm not." She flashed a grin and raised her eyebrows. "C'mon back with me."

Ginger led me by the hand behind a long, black curtain, waving to the security guard standing watch. We sat down at the booth—a stretching, leather couch-like thing along the wall, the surrounding space done away with tables or chairs to facilitate what went on back there—and upon seeing the area was empty, Ginger spread my legs and pressed her ass into my crotch. "If we don't wanna get caught, it's gotta look like I'm earning money back here." She began the lap dance, wriggling and thrusting to the music, and while dipping down to present her ass to my face, furtively reached into her high-heel boot and pulled out a half-finished pint of cheap vodka.

Sliding her body up my chest, the back of her head on my shoulder, she slipped the bottle between my legs and grabbed my cock through the jeans. "We can't let them see us drinking," she whispered into my ear. "We've got a song and a half, tops, before this starts eating into my money." She flipped around to straddle me, her body strategically blocking the bottle if the security decided to take a peek over the curtain to see how things were going. "Keep it low," she said. "Like you're sucking on my tits." Ginger undid her bra and threw her head back.

I unscrewed the top, leaned towards her breasts and suckled at the pint as well and for as long as I could at the

---

awkward angle afforded. "I can just pay you," I said, screwing the top back on and letting it slide into the crux between our bodies.

"Friends don't pay for lap dances," she said. "I invited you and you came. This is my thank you."

"So what's going on?" I said. "You seem…different."

She reached down and opened the bottle against the side of my body, drank with her head resting on my shoulder.

"Oh, you know…this and that. You're hard." She adjusted my erection between her legs.

"That's the point, isn't it? Don't change the subject."

"Okay." She took another nip, employing less discretion. "Well, I'm getting divorced." Another song started, some bouncy, explicit Ludacris joint. Ginger changed her rhythm, grinding faster into my crotch. "Carl fucked up and it's over and I'm done and fuck him and he'll never get to fuck this pussy again. His loss."

"Ginger, what're you talking about? What happened?"

"Well. Ha. Well, he cheated. There's that."

"Did you catch him in bed with someone?"

"Jesus." She threw her head back and laughed. "I wish. It would be less embarrassing. He's been having a relationship over one of his stupid fucking online computer games with some bitch from Iraq. At least now I know what he's been doing in the spare room."

"I don't even know what that means," I said.

"He and some bitch he met through this, like, social online game have been talking and flirting and sexting behind my back for months. The motherfucker told her he loved her. LOVED HER. Some dumb cunt in a desert on the other side of the world who he's never met. He wanted her to meet his kids—MY kids. MY fucking kids. Piece of shit cheater. So yesterday I told him to be outta the house that night and that he'd hear from my goddamn lawyer. And now he's out and I'm going out drinking. We're celebrating my upcoming divorce with that fucking embarrassment. So, cheers." She tipped back the bottle, making no attempt to conceal her drinking, and handed it to me to drain the last of its contents.

The song ended, and Ginger stood and slid the empty bottle back into her boot. "And I don't want your sympathy. Tonight I just wanna drink. Can you do that for me, Henry?"

I breathed out, unsure of what words to come up with: "Whatever you want, Ginger. We can do whatever you want."

"Thank you," she said, and vanished behind the black curtain.

We sat across from each other at some downtown outdoor bar across the street from a homeless camp. The air was thick with cigarette smoke and stale piss. It hadn't rained for the past week so any human byproduct remained and became the only atmosphere recognizable to the senses. Ginger changed into a T-shirt and jeans after getting off work. A line of six empty shot glasses created a fence between us.

Ginger put out her smoldering American Spirit in the ashtray and lit a new one without pause. "So...I read the story about me that you sent over. It was definitely...you."

I'd gotten into the habit of sending her stories from the upcoming book, and chapters I'd been writing for the new book I'd recently started for the exact purpose of garnering these kinds of reactions. Ginger was a blunt person. It didn't matter how close we were, she never sugarcoated things. I needed someone to be honest with my work.

She took a drag and flicked the ash, missing the tray. "You sure can be romantic, Henry."

"I appreciate the sarcasm," I said. "I'd like to think I'm better at what I do now. I'll make it up to you in the next one."

"Oh God," she laughed. "I'm not saying it's bad, it's just...did you have to describe my tattoo in exact fucking detail? I gotta keep up some level of anonymity too, you know."

"I wouldn't worry about it." I took one of her cigarettes from off the table and lit it, the smoke curling out through my nose as I spoke. "The thing will sell ten copies and you and I will both maintain our precious private lives."

"Oh I don't know. I hope it does well."

"We'll see," I grumbled.

"Because how else am I gonna get any money out of you when I sue?"

"I feel like that's started to become less of a joke and more a threat."

She smiled and winked. "Get us another round of drinks. Then I'll tell you some more stories for your book."

Since I'd known her, I couldn't recall ever seeing her drink alcohol. Our outings always consisted of something healthy, something productive. I imagine it was in an effort to provide my life with some balance, some brief respite from my lifestyle, the severity of which she began to fully understand. That before tonight she had failed to show this side of her was for my benefit. It wasn't until tonight that the two could no longer be held separate.

"*Sláinte*," I toasted, and the sixth shot of tequila burned its way down our throats.

Ginger coughed and shivered like a ghost had passed through her. "What is that, German?"

"Klingon," I said. "So what's first?"

"What do you wanna hear?"

"Something I'm not supposed to hear."

"Well, Mr. Bartley came in tonight."

"What is he, a senator or something?"

"No," she laughed, "it means I made a thousand bucks in one night."

I lifted another drink and we tipped them back in unison. The glasses came down with a sharp clack against the table. "Jesus, a grand? I'm in the wrong line of fuckin' work."

Lighting two cigarettes in her mouth before handing me one: "If you're willing to put on stilettos and step on a 50-year-old man's balls for twenty minutes, sure."

I absorbed the information given to me, weighing my options and tolerance for the perverse. "You sure he's not a senator? And you don't even pay the medical bill?"

"He loves it."

"Hey, whatever does it for ya. What else you got?"

Ginger dragged her cigarette, tried to blow an O. "Well, Mr. Schaeffer, he comes in every Thursday night. It's when he can get away while his wife is at her book club."

"He tells you this?"

"They tell me everything. When a man is in such a vulnerable position that he's on his knees, drinking the breast milk squirting out of your tits, you'd be surprised what kind of deep-seated shit comes outta these guys' mouths. When they're not filled with breast milk, I mean."

"Excuse me?"

Ginger eyed me with penetrating sincerity. "What, is that a shock to you? Haven't you ever wanted to drink breast milk?"

"Yes. When I was a baby, Ginger. I'm sure I met the quota back then that nixed the urge to find any more in my later years. And even if I did, I imagine it would be frowned upon for a 25-year-old man to attempt procuring breast milk." I paused and stared at the table before abruptly sitting back up and returning to my point. "Now that I mention it, even thinking of where to get breast milk already feels like I'm committing a crime."

Ginger raised another drink and we finished the liquor waiting for us within. A solid wall of stacked up shot glasses accumulated upon the table. "You could try mine."

"Your what?"

"My breast milk," she said.

I tilted my head in wonder, staring at Ginger's tits. "You can just...turn 'em on like a—like a faucet?"

"Pretty much. You get a good few months of it after having a baby."

"The human body is a fascinating thing," I marveled.

"So you wanna try?"

I looked around. "What, like here? Like now?"

"Yeah."

"You're just gonna whip out a tit?"

"Yeah, it's easy."

"Well. Alright," I said. "For free? I don't have to pay for the product or...labor or anything?"

Ginger ignored me. "Open your mouth."

I did as I was told, and Ginger pulled down her collar and pulled out one of her breasts, pinched the pink nipple between her index finger and thumb.

"Ready?"

"Uh-huh."

The warm, pinpointed stream launched out from her nipple, hitting the back of my tongue. Instinctively, my mouth snapped shut and I gulped back the milk. It was a mild kind of sweet unlike something sugary, unlike anything I could put my finger on. Natural. Warm and sweet. The last of the stream that failed to make it inside my mouth dripped down my chin. I wiped it with the back of my hand and looked at the watery, white liquid before rubbing it off onto my pants.

Ginger stuffed her breast back inside her shirt. "What did you think?"

"I think I could taste the booze," I said.

"But not bad, right?"

"There are worse liquids to have squirted into your mouth."

"That was worth a good hundred bucks to Mr. Schaeffer," she said. "So you're welcome."

The table was devoid of more liquor to consume. It bothered me that I wasn't drunk enough. Even though my company seemed to have provided Ginger some escapism, there remained the itching responsibility I felt I had to dig past the surface of why we were here in the first place. Hesitating, I asked, "Ginger, do you wanna...talk about it?"

"My breast milk? No, I think we covered it."

I grimaced. "No...y'know."

Any semblance of ignorant satisfaction she'd built up over the night shrank and evaporated behind the darkness that emerged in her eyes. "Are you gonna be my friend or not? I didn't ask you out for a fucking therapy session. You're a drinker. We're drinking. That's it."

"Alright," I said and held up my hands in surrender. "Heard. Well, if you wanna drink"—looking at the time on my phone—"the bar is about to close."

"Fine." Ginger shot up and grabbed her bag without looking at me, turning towards the door. "Then we'll go to my place."

"Your place?"

"Yeah," she snapped. "Is that a problem?"

"No, no. Uh, where are the kids?"

"They're at a friend's for the night. I'm not a shitty mother, Henry."

I backed off. "I never said that. You know I don't think that."

Ginger responded over her shoulder as she spilled out into the city street: "Are you coming or not?"

I stuffed my cigarette into the ashtray, mumbling as I jogged to catch up with her. "Yes, ma'am."

Ginger's apartment was a messy two-bedroom in a suburb where gentrification hadn't dismantled the Hispanic and lower-class communities. The living room floor was decorated with an unsettling dichotomy of children's toys and the aftermath of a violent argument. Strewn between blankets and *I Spy* books were a shattered plate and coffee mug swept into the adjoining kitchen corner, and Ginger's framed wedding photo, unceremoniously leaning at an angle against the back wall, had glass fractured from what I could only surmise was blunt force trauma.

She stepped around all of this and opened up the fridge, pulling out a large box of white wine, holding it up and shrugging to ask if I'd like any.

I nodded.

"It's some awful, cheap shit," she said, pouring it into two plastic cups. "So it should make you feel right at home." She handed me the drink and sat next to me on the couch. "One day, once you're rich and famous, you can upgrade to some booze that won't burn a hole through your stomach lining."

"Yeah," I laughed, taking a long swig. "When I'm rich and famous."

She stretched out and rested her legs over my lap. "Do you ever want more than this?"

I looked around the room and down at my cup. "What do you mean? More than what?"

"This." Her eyebrows furrowed and a frown bloomed out of the inebriation apparent across her face. "You're dying, Henry. You can see that, can't you? I've been around you for less than a year since we had our falling out and I can already see you aren't going to live past 30."

Caught off guard and unsure how to respond, I shot back with the aggression I may have held back if it weren't for the alcohol saturating my blood: "Why don't you mind your business? Your marriage just failed and you're talking to me like you know better? Don't start with that condescending shit, Ginger."

"Henry, that's not—"

I sat up and shifted to shake Ginger's legs off me. "No, you know what it is? You're in a shit place so you felt the need to bring me around and feel better about yourself. This isn't new to me, man. I'm fine. Look at me." My fingers pulled up on the edges of my mouth and I bared my teeth to produce a grotesque caricature of a grin. "All smiles."

Before she could respond, I continued, the words falling out as if they'd been waiting inside my lungs for the moment they could escape without my permission: "You're acting like I don't know any of this. Of course, I know what I'm doing. I know what's gonna happen. Half of me wants to die and the half that doesn't, doesn't know how to fucking stop. I can't sleep at night unless I drink until I know I won't dream. I can't deal with the fucking nightmares. I can't deal with the fear of being out in public, who might find me. At this point, the addiction matters more than its outcome. It's the only thing that makes me not care anymore. So let it be."

The wine went past my tongue in three long gulps and I stood to refill the cup.

Ginger got up and followed me into the kitchen. She reached her arm around my waist from behind and pressed her body against me. "What happened to you, Henry?" she whispered into my back. "What happened? Why did you disappear for so long all those years ago?"

The wine went up and up until it sat balancing at the edge, shimmering yellow under the single kitchen light. I lifted the cup, spilling some of the precious antidote on the linoleum tiles, tilted my head back and swallowed it all as if it were water from an oasis in the desert.

When she could tell I was going to ignore the question, she pushed further: "Do you know what I did almost every goddamn day after we stopped talking? For years, you know what I did? Henry, look at me." Ginger grasped my shirt and twisted me around to face her. There were tears welling in her eyes. Dark brown pools reflecting the pain, glittering like dirtied ponds beneath the night sky. "I typed your name into local obituaries. Almost every fucking day I'd look for you in the obituaries, waiting and dreading the moment I'd see you in there. When you got back in contact with me, I can't, I can't explain...the relief that washed over me. I knew—I...thought I'd lost you."

She took the empty cup out of my hand and placed her palm on my cheek, stroking my face, looking up at me like a grief-stricken lover. Her voice lowered again to a whisper, her breath warm on my skin. "Yes, Henry, I lost my husband. Yes, my life is not in a good place right now. But that is why I refuse to lose you too. I'm not trying to nag or judge you, Henry. I just can't...lose you too. Please."

Ginger's lips pressed against mine. A sensation I hadn't felt in five years but had remained unchanged. She pulled away slowly, her eyes opening, focused. "You have something real. Something that can take you out of this endless circle you've gotten yourself into. Get the hell out of here before it consumes you. The universe saw your talent and it's giving you a shot. This book, your words, it's a way out. You can be someone else, the person I know you can be—who you are. Someone who makes a difference with the ability you have. But it won't happen until you leave."

My hand went for the cup, unable to confront the gravity of what I was being told.

"Stop it." Ginger grabbed my wrist and held it away from the wine. "Is this how you want to be seen? Is this how you want me to see you? An addict, reaching for the booze any time shit gets hard? God forbid you died, is that the legacy you'd want to leave? Really though, Henry, answer me. Would that be enough for you?"

I stepped away from her. I thought of all the things I could say, all the answers in the world I could give. I thought of the hurricane of events that brought me here, of who I was, who I'd become. Of whether I was even able to change course or if my addiction's grip was too tight, my mental strength too diminished, engrained so deep these facts had become a part of my makeup. Of whether people would understand and forgive that trajectory, the swirling alignment of random events and my reactions that may have informed my fate, of whether that would matter or elicit comprehension. Of whether I wanted this, the chaos, or if it was what I thought I deserved.

Ginger let go of my wrist as I reached for the cup and poured more wine.

"Do you wanna know what happened to me?" I asked. "Why I disappeared?"

"Yes," she said. "I wanna know."

I sipped at the cheap drink, letting its bittersweet taste rest on my tongue before making its way to rot through my stomach. "It's because **[REDACTED]**"

Crooked Smile

JULY, 2019

The room is quiet and full. How I was able to fill even a small bookstore with enough people willing to listen to me talk is a mystery. I sit at a table facing the people and they sit in rows and rows of chairs, facing me. A woman introduces me and says the name of my book. Henry Gallagher. *Skipping Record Waltz.* The people clap. Strangers and those I recognize. Ginger, Joseph, Rita, Rebecca, Marcus, Lauren, Colin, McEwen. Nadia, Emily, Chris, Miles, Anna. My sister Carmen sits in the front row, weaving in her seat, battling with too many shots of tequila in her system. People from my past, present, and future. People I will never see again.

I wrote this book alone in a small room for three years, letting spill any dark, violent, depressing, frightening words I deemed necessary, never believing the words would ever come across anyone's eyes but mine. Simple and pure catharsis. Stark truths and revelations because it was only those words and me, and I could let go of anything I needed and wanted to for self-preservation and nothing else. It was my way of finding purpose in the seemingly meaningless suffering I had imposed upon myself.

Something good needed to come from this era of pain I'd slogged through. I wouldn't let it be for nothing.

Now that time has passed, and I sit in front of a quiet and full room of people, my book standing at the table beside me, on its cover that man with his face buried into the bar, his hand still grasping the bottle, never letting go. The halo glowing above his head because, despite his guilt and sadness, somewhere deep within him, he believes he is still good. He believes he is still good because he has to. Or he will never sit at this table at the front of a quiet and full room.

I wrote a book. And this is my reading.

I arrive at the Guilty Sparrow an hour before I am to go on. The bookstore is close by and I will get as drunk as my nerves ask of me before walking over. I place the cardboard box full of copies that I am to sell on the barstool next to me, and Anna slides a whiskey-soda into my hand.

"Are you excited?" she asks.

"I'm sober," I answer. I pull out a copy from the box and give it to her. "This is for putting up with me all these years."

She smirks and sets the book on the counter behind the bar. "Nervousness and excitement come from the same area of the brain. Just depends on how you choose to see it. Try to be excited."

I hold up the glass and nod before letting the drink down my throat. "I'm not nervous," I say. "Just sober."

Anna grabs a Jell-O shot from the fridge and ducks beneath the eye of the camera before tapping it against my glass and sucking it out of its plastic cup. "Sign my book at the reading. I get off at 8, so I'll be there."

"Sure, Anna. Just gotta see if I remember how to write in cursive."

Carmen walks in and sits down beside me. I asked her to join me. I don't want anyone else around to see me get drunk beforehand. "Alright, little brother," she says.

I nod. "Alright then."

She reaches into the cardboard box and holds up a copy. "So this is it, huh?"

"Yep," I say. "That's it."

"Have Mom and Dad read it?"

I laugh and order her drink, hand it to her. "What do you think?"

The question is rhetorical, and so she changes the subject to what I know will be brought up and needs to be brought up, but what I don't want to talk about. "Did Mom tell you what happened?"

"Yes," I say. "I'm sorry you had to deal with that. He'll get better soon. He'll say sorry."

"I don't care what he'll say," Carmen answers, and shoots down the tequila, coughing into her sleeve.

"Dad's been having a hard time. With the meds and everything. You of all people should understand that."

Carmen glares at me and pushes the shot glass forward, nudging me to ask Anna to get her another drink. She has trouble talking to strangers. "That's not an excuse for what he said to me," she snaps.

"I'm not saying it is," I answer, staring forward at our reflections in the bar mirror instead of making eye contact. "I'm sorry it happened is all—for everybody. It shouldn't have gone down like that."

I drain my whiskey and stack the shot glass inside of my own. Anna sees the empty drinks and goes to refill them. When she returns with our second round, I decide to introduce her to Carmen to divert from our conversation. "Anna, this is my sister."

Anna waves. "I thought she was your girlfriend or something. You two look nothing alike."

Carmen is disgusted by this assumption and scoffs uncomfortably, boring her eyes into the center of her new shot glass. She has decided she does not like Anna.

"Yeah, well, with any luck I'm adopted," I say.

"We can hope," my sister mumbles.

Anna floats away and Carmen and I wordlessly drink.

A week ago, my sister got a call from the police. My dad had been taking a very strong anti-psychotic medication for the better part of a year, another attempt among many to find the correct cocktail that would curb the worst symptoms of his mental illness. These pills did their job but had, in effect, rendered him a mindless zombie. My dad is one of the most interesting, most intelligent people I've ever met. But seeing him as he was under the influence of that medication would give zero indication that these things were ever true. Any time I'd visit, he was lying on the couch, silent, staring ahead at whatever was playing on the television. Any questions you would ask would be left unanswered, his eyes glazed over, his mind a blank. It was painful seeing him this way.

He obviously felt the same way, because almost as soon as the drug's effects took hold, he began tapering off of it. The viciousness of this drug's effect on the human body was so much so that it required six months of steady tapering every few weeks, or else the side effects would risk his life. And a week ago, the drug level in his system was low enough that it no longer protected him from his own mind, while still attacking him with the unavoidable side effects of withdrawal, no matter how slowly the process had been going. My dad's brain was at war with itself, from both sides—the drug and his illness.

He began speaking often and at length of his desire to kill himself, sharing these thoughts at his weekly AA meetings. After one meeting, someone called the police, asking to do a welfare check on my dad. By some shitty mistake, his emergency contact the police department found was not my mom, but my sister. So the police called Carmen, telling her that her dad was threatening to kill himself.

Carmen called my dad, to which he didn't answer, in the throes of a severe manic attack. She called my mom, who didn't answer, so she did the only thing she could, which was to text him how loved he was and how badly she needed him to live, to see her get married and grow older. To stay in her life. My dad's short-circuiting mind took this as an attack, or an insult, or...we can't be sure. I can't imagine my dad knew either. He responded by cussing her out, telling Carmen he hated her and to leave him alone and that he couldn't handle what she was saying and that she didn't love him and if he wanted to die, he was going to die and to never talk to him again. His manic state disowned his daughter.

My mom soon got in contact with Carmen, and then my dad, so he was rounded up and taken into psychiatric care. He was sedated, put back on his medication, and a better plan was implemented to get him off the anti-psychotic and on a less severe mood-stabilizer. He would get better. But my sister was shaken and had not yet forgiven my dad. They wouldn't speak again for months.

Weeks after my sister and I sit together in the Guilty Sparrow, I will be in the car with my dad. My computer will have died, and after finding out how much I am making in royalties from my book, he will insist that he buy me a new computer so I can continue with my career and my dream. And so we will be driving to the store to get a new computer, and we will be listening to Jimi Hendrix's *Blues*, an album he first showed me when I was a small child in the car with him. He will tell me about the day it happened, and the medication, and about his bipolar, and his depression, and his PTSD, and it will not be told in a way to elicit sympathy, but in a way to relate to his son, who struggles with many of the same things. He will tell me how much he hates how difficult it has to be, but that it is something he has to do because he wants to feel better, and all he has ever wanted to be is a good father. He will tell me that he knows the things he struggles with have made it difficult to be a good father, and that he is sorry. I will tell him that I love him and I will tell him about my struggles with mental illness and medications and I will open up to him more than I ever have. I will tell him that he is a good father, no matter what has happened, and that he is the greatest man I have ever known. And we will smile and go silent, and my dad will turn up the volume and we will listen to Jimi Hendrix play the guitar, like we did twenty years ago. And I will think about how much I love my dad. The strongest man I know.

This is something I've written not to push forward the narrative or fill in gaps in a story, but as something to leave for the person it's written for, something that will not burn away as time does memory. This is something that may be permanent and read by the man I am unable to speak these truths to in person. This part is not for the reader. It is not for you. It is for the person who may never read this anyway, but this is the best way I can say what has never been said. And if it is not read, then it will be a reminder of the words that could have been shared in person but never were. And if you die before me being able to share these truths, then let this be the unsaid that we both wished to be made real. Because it was all I ever wished to say to you.

"If I'm going to show you anyone," he said, "it's gonna be this guy right here." My dad slid in the CD, and the car became alive. The guitar screamed and wailed and soared across the speakers. "This is someone who knew the blues. Some people make music, and some people make sounds that paint pictures. Can you see it, Henry?"

I leaned into the notes, wanting to make sense of what my dad had said. "I see it," I answered.

My dad grinned, glancing at his son. "Let's turn it up then, so you can see it even better. You want me to turn it up?"

"Yeah," I said. "I wanna hear the colors."

Carmen finishes her drink, the wobbly sway knocking over the shot glass. "You're supposed to go on in fifteen minutes," she says. "We should go up?"

I set the glass upright. "Yeah, go ahead. I'll catch up."

Seeing this as a way of getting out of paying, Carmen stands, steadies herself on the bar, and blinks hard in the way drunk people do as if it will realign their blurred focus. "Alright then, little brother. I'll see you there."

I glance at her and chuckle. "You good? You know better than to keep up with me. You're a hundred pounds soaking wet."

"I'm fine, I'm fine," she mumbles, and staggers out.

"You know where you're going?" I yell after her.

She tries to form her mouth around the word "yes" and instead arrives at: "Yeeauuahp."

The door closes, and the outside smell of pollen dissolves back into the suffocating, sour aroma of stale beer and urine. I hold my hand above my hunched shoulder to get Anna's attention. "One more for the road, huh? How much do I owe you?"

Anna comes over, fills the glass high and places it over the ring of liquid left by the previous six. "No charge, Henry.

I'm getting off and heading over now. Don't take too long, alright? You're the man of the hour."

"Man of the year," I say. "Man of the century. Yeah, yeah."

She shakes her head and walks away, and I am left alone with the man in the mirror. We stare at each other for a long time, the drinks in our hands hovering over the bar, trembling, causing the ice to crackle against our glasses like wind chimes.

"You're an ugly motherfucker, you know that?" he says.

"Yeah, you're not so great yourself," I answer.

"Do you feel happy?"

"No," I say. "Do you?"

"No," he replies.

"Are we supposed to?" I ask him.

"I'm not sure," he says.

Together, we take a sip of our whiskey, and think.

"I think it's overrated anyway," he says.

"Yeah, maybe."

"Maybe we're too hung up on how we're supposed to feel. Maybe we're not supposed to feel anything. Maybe that's our problem."

"That's very astute of you," I tell him.

Again, our glasses go up to our lips. The whiskey goes down into our body and we feel warmer than we did before.

"It's just one more high in a series of events," he decides.

"If this didn't, and the last didn't," I say, "then I'm gonna go out on a limb and say none of these highs are gonna be the answer. Are they?"

"No," he replies. "No, I don't think so."

We look down at our glasses. In the shimmering ice and whiskey, we can see a mutated reflection of each other, almost as clear as in the mirror. "Then we've been looking in the wrong places haven't we?"

"Yeah," he tells me. "But we knew that this whole time."

"Yeah," I say. "Yeah, we did."

We hold up our drinks, nod, throw our heads back, and the whiskey disappears.

"So. You ready?"

"Yeah," I say. I stand up, pick up my cardboard box, and walk out of the Guilty Sparrow for the last time.

The summer evening air cools my skin. It's a nice night for a walk.

I don't remember how the reading went. The drinks kicked in once I got inside the bookstore, aided by the nerves that stunted my appetite. By the accounts of those who congratulated me afterward, it seemed to have gone fine. And that's just fine. The cardboard box I carry with me is empty, but there is over $400 unceremoniously stuffed into my wallet, so I must have sold them all. That's just fine.

People had come up to me, people I didn't recognize, and said things and gave me business cards and their numbers and I don't know who, if any, did this in hopes of fucking me or if it was for purely professional reasons. Some people wanted to head back to the bar and buy me drinks, but I declined because it was so nice out, it was a nice night for a walk.

And at this exact moment, as I wander down a silent and yellow-lit residential street, I decide that I am going to stop drinking, and that tonight will be my final, glorious bender. Whether it will be my final because it is the last time I will choose to drink or because this bender will kill me is inconsequential. Tonight is such a nice night for a walk and it will be the last time I drink. These are the facts I know.

Seeing as this may or may not be my last night on earth, there seems to be no reason to hold on to the wad of money in my pocket. As the night progresses, I have no doubt that the true purpose for having this money will reveal itself, but in the meantime, the first and most obvious course of action is to pick up liquor.

I walk to the nearest store, pick up a fifth of Old Crow for $10, and continue on, taking swigs out of the bag as I go towards a destination that I have never been more sure will reveal itself to me. My phone buzzes but this is the furthest thing from my mind, and in fact, it is so much so that I take the phone out of my pocket, drop it on the sidewalk, and step on it until it crushes under my shoe. This is now one less aspect of reality that needs to be accounted for. Tonight I will shed everything I do not want or need, and this phone is the first to go.

Feeling lighter in head and body, I allow the flow of red traffic lights and blinking walk signals to guide me forward, keeping me in a constant state of motion. The whiskey drips down my chin as I drink, and soon the smell of cheap liquor overtakes the miasma of car exhaust and excrement the dirty city streets produce. Though the stars are sparse, hidden behind the orange glow of light pollution, my eyes stay fixed on the crescent moon hanging over the city skyline in the distance. It's such a nice night for a walk.

A small bridge appears before me, below it the four-lane highway heading south. I stop at the center to watch the cars pass beneath me, my whiskey bottle dangling over the railing. On the other side, across the street, something is alive. A building. Its stained-glass windows burn through the dark with reds and blues and yellows and greens. The windows speak with humming voices, quiet behind the colors, just whispers, but now it is all I can hear. Nothing has ever made more sense than this urge to approach the building.

I reach the steps to the front doors of the church—heavy and wooden, ancient doors. Above them is the largest window, the centerpiece, its radiant artwork so much brighter this close up that it forces me to squint. It's an image of the Virgin Mary. Blue tears like diamonds fall down her face, her arms outstretched and head bowed. The halo fixed upon her head such a brilliant yellow that it dims the colors around it. I try the door handle and find it unlocked. The door opens with a shrill creak that echoes into the building, and I walk inside.

All sound behind me swallows up into silence. The lighting within the church is dim, a soft orange that leaves shadows across the walls and tapestries. It smells like my childhood. The scent of a church is a specific one, like wood and bark dust left for centuries to go sour. It's not unpleasant but it is such a unique scent that I can't separate it from memories I would rather not revisit.

I drink from the bottle and stumble forward, the rows of pews stretching out on either side, reaching their end at the edge of the pulpit. As a child, I'd been told that within the pulpit of every Catholic church lays a single bone from the saint whom it bears its name. There are 206 bones in the human body, if that human is lucky, so this would mean each saint could only have so many churches named after them. This is something I never bothered to check up on. The idea that each school-mandated mass I attended was presided over by a man of God with a box harboring evidence of a dead body was more interesting to me than a rapist with an empty box.

Above the pulpit hangs a massive crucifix. I'm reminded of the time when, during a school-wide mass, an earthquake struck and our church's giant, metal crucifix began to swing, unmoved for so long that the hinges moaned, and the church full of grade-schoolers erupted into screams of panic, believing the Second Coming had arrived. This is what happens when you are taught of hellfire and eternal damnation before the scientific method.

Suddenly, out of the silence, comes a man's voice: "Ay! Who are you?"

I look around among the pews, hoping to find a living man. I am unprepared to talk to God. "Yo! Who are you?" I call out into the church.

From somewhere closer to the pulpit comes, "It's me!"

I spot the top of someone's head. I begin to yell but stop and lower my volume, as my voice carries as if shouting into a canyon. "Hey, sorry. I didn't mean to barge in. I'm just—"

"He's not gonna answer," the man interrupts, his head facing the pulpit. "If that's what you came here for."

The bottle goes up to my lips on instinct. "No, I was just..." Realizing I'm unsure why I came here in the first place, the sentence trails off. "Can I sit with you?"

The man doesn't answer.

Taking his silence as an invitation, I walk towards the unturned head. He sits at the center of the pew, a man wearing a beanie and a tattered, brown coat. White, untrimmed whiskers grow in patches across his face. His nose is bulbous and bright red like a Christmas ornament. Even as I stand at the end of his pew, he fails to turn and see whom this new person is.

194 | *Crooked Smile*

I slide into the pew, taking another slug from the bottle. The stench of body odor and urine wafts off his body. "Hi," I say. "I won't bother you if you don't want. We can just sit here if you'd like."

After five minutes of silence, the man finally turns to me. His eyes are a burning blue-gray like layers of ice under a flashlight. "I have an exclamation point on my head," he says. He takes off his beanie and pulls back the long strands of matted, white hair over his left temple. "See?" Over his temple is a line of black stitches. The wound beneath looks infected, weeping yellow pus that's crusted over.

"Pretty cool," I tell him and hold out the whiskey bottle. "You want any?"

He takes the bottle out of my hand and drinks, then hands it back. "My name is Merlin," he says. "I'm 700-years-old."

"Nice to meet you, Merlin." I hold up the bottle and nod before taking a drink. "My name's Henry." We sit together for a while in the quiet of the church, watching the crucifix over the pulpit. The bottle gets lighter in my hand. "What's it like being seven hundred years old?"

Without taking his eyes off the crucifix, he tells me, "The great thing about being born ugly is that you never have to look back at pictures and miss what you used to look like. You're blessed. You never get uglier. You just get older. You never have to look to your past and wish for it back. You never had it." He takes the bottle out of my hand and drinks before handing it back. His blue-gray eyes begin to glaze over. "So all you have left is the only thing that really matters: experience. And you know another word for that? A lot of people won't tell you because they don't know it. They could have had it but they lost it for one reason or another: wisdom."

I sit with those words. I drink until it feels like I'm holding an empty bottle, and I gain the courage to ask, "What if I've lost it?"

Merlin shrugs. "Then you'll never know you had it in the first place. It won't matter. It's hard to lose this game, Henry. People don't seem to get that. But if it makes you feel better, I didn't even figure it out until I was about 400. That's the point though. Not much changed after I knew. Still the same game."

"But what if I want out?" The whiskey isn't blunting my emotions. It never really did though, it occurs to me. "What if I don't wanna play the game anymore?"

Merlin turns to me, his face a bright red supernova, and laughs so loud that it shakes the crucifix on the church wall. "Now, why the hell would you want that? This is the greatest game anyone's ever come up with! If you're not enjoying it, go do something else. That's the beauty of it. Go do whatever the hell you think will make you enjoy it again. And if it doesn't end up working, try another thing. You never have to stop if you don't want to. There are more possible chess moves than there are atoms in the universe. And that's on one dinky, little board! Imagine what you can do on this one!"

"Well, where do you even start then? What do you do when you don't enjoy it anymore?"

Merlin picks the bottle off the church floor and shakes it around before licking at the last drops at the bottom. "What did I tell you, Henry? I'm not God. He isn't gonna answer if that's what you came looking for."

"I'm not asking Him," I say. "I'm asking you."

Merlin looks back up at the crucifix, still vibrating. "Well. Well, when I was younger I always used to go back to Camelot. And things just made sense again."

"Camelot?" I ask. Nothing has ever made more sense than the revelation this 700-year-old homeless man has just bestowed upon me. "Where is it?"

"Hm," Merlin thinks for a moment. "It's been a long time since I felt like I needed to go back. Can't quite remember where it is now. But I imagine anywhere that's not here has gotta be closer rather than farther away. Right?"

"Yeah," I say. "I suppose you're right."

"I think we just figured it out then, didn't we?"

"Figured what out?"

Merlin grins at me, his teeth a mess of jagged, brown rot. "Your next move on the board, Henry! Keep up!"

I laugh into my knees, the floor beginning to spin. Everything makes sense now. I can see the whole game. Every possible move. "Camelot," I say. "I'm going to Camelot."

"There you go," says Merlin, and leans back in the pew. "Maybe you didn't lose it after all."

Knowing now what I need to do—in truth, something that I've known for years—I stand up, step out of the pew and start walking towards the church doors.

Looking over me from above is the Virgin Mary. Her illumination is no longer present from the inside. As my hand touches the handle, Merlin calls out, "Hey, you left something!"

I turn around and see him standing, holding up my wallet full of cash. "Keep it," I call back.

I open the church doors, stride down the ancient steps, and head towards Camelot.

I do not worry about what direction or how far. It's such a nice night for a walk.

VI.
RETURN

JUNE, 2020

The property is miles away from the city, an open oasis in a green ocean of trees. This is my first time back since leaving all those months ago, what feels like a lifetime. Far away below us, amongst the concrete and riots, the city is on fire. The protests rage and each night the explosions of Molotov cocktails and police munitions echo out like thunder claps. The virus climbs and climbs its way up the unending list of infected and dead. The world is ending, but today we are far away from the world. Today, for a few precious hours, the world has fizzled away into a compartmentalized memory. Today, we are here to celebrate a good thing. Today, my sister gets married.

My partner Rosie and I have made the journey from out of town, along with a select few family members to my brother-in-law-to-be's family tree farm, where the dozen or so of us have donned custom masks ordered by my mother for the occasion. We are handed specially made bottles of hand sanitizer at the door, and on these masks and bottles of hand sanitizer reads, **Carmen & Anthony 06.27.20: Better Together.**

Both of the to-be-wed's immediate families line up for a picture on the lawn, and with our masks over our mouths and noses it is not lost on a single one of us that people will see these photos a hundred years from now and wonder at the extremity and ludicrousness of the world.

My sister wears an earth-toned, old and simple dress, and Anthony wears jeans and his father's sports jacket that he wore at his own wedding decades before. His family's pack of Bluetick Coonhounds and Rottweilers and golden retrievers chase each other around the tables, and the birds sing as the wine is poured and appetizers are brought out. My father chats with Anthony's father about the Grateful Dead, and he is the happiest I have seen him in years. I sit at an end table with Rosie, my sister, and Anthony, and his mother comes around to fill our glasses with an expensive blended red. "No, thank you," I say when she stops at me. "I don't drink."

The journey towards sobriety has been a long and difficult one. I have slipped and relapsed and have tried again, and each day is a battle to ignore the overwhelming urges and irritability that comes with missing the drink. It is a state of constant discomfort, and the remedy to this is never more than a five-minute drive away, but by taking that antidote, I only guarantee further dependence on something that will never cure the root of my discomfort, and thus it would never go away. I have recognized that there will never be a day that passes that will not require a concerted effort to abstain from what I have loved so much for so long. It does not get easier not to drink, but it does get easier to enjoy not drinking.

My life has become what I never thought it could be, but what I have always wanted: Simple. Domesticated. I am in love with a beautiful woman who loves me, supports me, and our relationship, for the first time in my life, is strong and lovely. With help from DBT therapy and competent doctors, I've found the proper medication for my illnesses, and have learned better how to cope with what I fully understand will be one more lifelong battle, yet one I have no choice but to win. It's not a fix by any means but it's progress. The nightmares haven't gone away, but they don't frighten me like they used to. The incessant voices screaming over one another as I suffer through the anxiety that often comes can no longer be quickly silenced with the contents of a brown bottle, but through the clearer lens of continued sobriety. They tell me their fears and they ask desperately for comfort, and I can hear them all, and I can begin to help.

My book is selling well enough, my second book that you now have in your hands is at this time almost complete, and I no longer compile the experiences that may become material for a third. I don't miss the chaos. I don't miss it at all. Every day is difficult. But it's worth it. The benefits are far too great to be given up again.

It's not lost on me that just as I've gained peace, the world around me has fallen into disarray. It's as if the world and I made an unspoken agreement that it would take on all the chaos within my mind, and I would be granted calm as it burned and withered by the same force that lived inside me. You almost begin to gain a survivor's guilt before stepping back and seeing the ridiculousness of that sentiment. But still it lingers. And I know, at any moment, the world may decide it's had enough, and return the burden of that chaos back into me, and then again it will be my turn to hold up its weight.

As if Atlas and I were taking shifts.

Carmen and Anthony asked me to officiate their wedding, and this is something I simply could not turn down. After a drunken blackout over a year ago, I woke up to an email stating that I'd become ordained by the Church of the Latter-Day Dude, and yes, this is an entirely legitimate ordainment, regardless of its tenets rooted in the stoned, pseudo-Taoist ramblings of *The Big Lebowski*.

Really, look it up.

I'm available for weddings, baptisms, and bar mitzvahs.

So as our families stand on the wide, grassy front lawn of the tree farm, and the dogs run to and fro between the legs of those watching, and the city miles away burns to the ground, and protestors are beaten into submission by the ends of batons and rubber bullets, and cop cars are toppled, and innocent black men are murdered in the streets, and the pandemic claims 500,000 lives around the globe, I pronounce my sister and brother-in-law man and wife, by the power vested in me by a website based off a Cohen Brothers Film.

After the ceremony, everybody shuffles back to the makeshift reception in the backyard, and more food is brought out and more wine poured. Carmen sneaks away from her new husband and taps me on the shoulder as I sit alone at a table, watching Rosie talk to my parents, watching all the happy people in their masks. It's always in the eyes. It's always been in the eyes. You can't see their mouths smile, but you can see it in their eyes.

Everybody is smiling.

"Hey, little brother," she says and produces a large joint from behind her ear. "Wanna go get high?"

"Hell, it's your wedding," I say. "Is nobody gonna miss the bride though?"

She shrugs. "Weddings are as much for the other people as they are for the bride and groom. They're all wrapped up having fun, they won't notice. C'mon."

We walk to the edge of the property overlooking the sea of trees, and sit together on a large rock. Carmen lights the end of the joint, turning it around between her lips to get an even burn, and the white smoke fades away into the cloudless, blue sky. She inhales and then passes it to me, and watches a bluebird perched on a nearby branch, the new ring on her finger glinting in the afternoon sunlight. "Did you ever think we'd make it this far?" she asks me.

I stare at the joint in my hand before bringing it to my lips and taking a hit. "No," I answer. "After everything that's happened, everything we've been through—no, I didn't think we would."

"The Gallaghers are a tenacious bunch though." She smirks.

"Yeah," I chuckle, passing it back. "Among other things. Tenacious is definitely one of 'em."

Carmen talks through the smoke as it leaves her lungs: "Ten years ago, I could never have imagined that I'd get to this place. Y'know, happy. Either of us."

I look out at the forest, the city skyline nowhere to be seen, and I grin. "Me neither. But here we are. Let's not overthink it."

My sister glances at me, her eyes focusing there for a moment, and points to my face. "It's gotten better."

"What has?" I say.

"Your smile. The right side, it doesn't droop like it did."

Before I can answer, Anthony's voice appears behind us: "There you two are, we've been looking all over for you!"

I turn around and see him and Rosie standing with glasses in their hands. "It's time for the toast," says Rosie. "Everybody's waiting on you guys. C'mon!"

Carmen stands and puts out the joint on the rock. "Yeah, yeah, we're comin'."

I walk up to Rosie and she puts her arm around mine, smiling. "Ready, baby?"

"Yeah," I say. "I'm ready."

As the four of us begin heading back, I turn to see the view one last time and there on the branch sits the bluebird. The two of us watch each other for a few seconds, the space between us growing larger, before the bird looks up, jumps off the branch, and flies farther and farther away until it's nothing but a spot in the sky. And then it's gone.

I don't know why, but it's the most beautiful thing I've ever seen in my life.

Thanks for reading! Find more transgressive fiction (poems, novels, anthologies) at: Outcast-Press.com

Twitter & Instagram: @OutcastPress

Facebook.com/ThePoliticiansDaughter

GoFund.Me/074605e9 (Outcast-Press: Short Story Collection)

Amazon, Kindle, Target, Barnes & Nobel

Email proof of your review to OutcastPressSubmissions@gmail.com & we'll mail you a free bookmark!

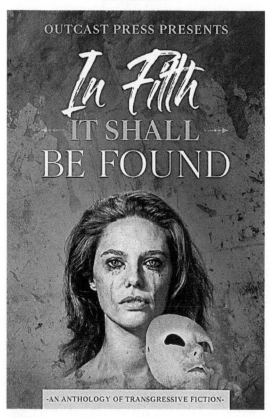

20 dark short stories by debut and veteran subversive writers like Craig Clevenger, Greg Levin, Lauren Sapala, Stephen J. Golds, G.C. McKay, and more! Everything from serial killers and speculative cannibals to strippers and smack addicts.

MORE FROM OUTCAST PRESS

International travels and ayahuasca, oh my! A novel about friendship dragged through the Amazon jungle and spit out through the stars with the aid of decades, DMT, and well-meaning debauchery.

ABOUT THE AUTHOR

Twitter: @Jack_Is_Moody

Jack Moody is a novelist, poet, and short story writer from wherever he happens to be at the time. He is the author of the short stories collection, *Dancing to Broken Records*, released through Beacon Publishing Group. Moody is also a staff writer for the literary magazine and podcast *Brick Moon Fiction*. His work has appeared in *Expat Press, Horror Sleaze Trash, A Thin Slice of Anxiety,* and *The Saturday Evening Post*.

CPSIA information can be obtained
at www.ICGtesting.com
Printed in the USA
LVHW030025110322
712917LV00010B/951